WHEN YOUR WORST NIGHTMARE COMES TRUE . . .

At four-thirty the phone rang. Graham glanced at his watch and then reached for the receiver, thinking it must be Jackie. Maybe something had come up.

"Hello."

"Peck?" the male voice said. "Graham Peck?"

"Yes?"

"This is the Peck who lives on Crown Point in Arlington Heights?"

"Sure. There's a problem?"

"Yes. I'm Detective Bevins with the police department. Your secretary said to call before I came in. Are you sitting down?"

"Sitting down?" Graham grimaced. "Of course, I'm working."

"Stay there. I'm outside with your secretary. I'll be right in."

"What's going on?" Graham protested. "What's happened?"

"I'll explain to you in a moment when I come in your office," Bevins said. "We need you to come home at once."

WIRED

ROBERT L. WISE

THE
TRIBULATION
SURVIVAL
SERIES

WARNER
Faith

New York   Boston   Nashville

Copyright © 2004 by Robert L. Wise
All rights reserved.

Warner Faith

Time Warner Book Group
1271 Avenue of the Americas, New York, NY 10020
Visit our Web site at www.twbookmark.com.

The Warner Faith name and logo are registered trademarks of Warner Books.

Printed in the United States of America
First Printing: March 2004
10   9   8   7   6   5   4   3   2   1

Library of Congress Cataloging-in-Publication Data

Wise, Robert L.
    Wired / Robert L. Wise.
        p. cm. — (The tribulation survival series)
        ISBN 0-446-69163-1
    1. Rapture (Christian eschatology)—Fiction.   2. Electronic surveillance—Fiction.   3. End of the world—Fiction.   I. Title.
    PS3573.I79W57   2004
    813'.54—dc22   2003015779

Cover design by UDG Designworks
Book design by Ralph Fowler

To Sophia Amneh Saphorah Wise
Number Thirteen

ACKNOWLEDGMENTS

Thanks so much to Dr. Fred Pike and David Howlett for assistance with research and framing the issues of the final struggle. In addition, the editorial assistance of Stephen Wilburn and Rolf Zettersten is deeply appreciated, as is the work of my agent, Greg Johnson. Good friends make all the difference!

WIRED

CHAPTER 1

November 1, 2022

THE EERIE RUMBLING of a small boat engine echoed across the murky waters of the Long Beach Naval Shipyard harbor at three o'clock in the morning. Clouds hanging low in the sky covered the moon and killed all light. The craft followed the same route that the passenger ferry took returning from Catalina Island. Cruising in unnoticed through the San Pedro Bay breakwater, the ebony craft aimed toward the rapidly approaching sandy shore. The pitch-black night sealed off the stars and painted the entire harbor in the ominous smudges of darkness.

Hunching over the dashboard, the driver pointed toward the shoreline. "See that string of lights along the edge of the harbor?"

"Yeah," the man sitting next to him growled.

"Underneath every one of them is a surveillance camera. We want to miss getting caught in their glare. Understand?"

The burly man in the thick dark coat nodded. "Don't worry. I don't want Big Brother down here at Long Beach dock to get a shot of my mug."

The motorboat turned to the left and started easing parallel to the shoreline. "We got to watch for naval surveillance as well," the driver said. "You can bet that none of these ships are floating out here unguarded."

"You're the man. Whatever you say."

"Don't forget it," the driver snapped. "This operation has to be precise. Remember, if anyone asks your name, you tell 'em it's Abel, Abel Rabi."

"Abel, huh?" the man laughed under his breath. "Strange name for a boy from San Francisco. You want to know my real name?"

"No," the driver said. "Rabi is Arabic. Leave it at that."

He shut off the boat's engine and the craft drifted toward the shoreline with the incoming tide pushing them toward the beach. For several minutes the small boat floated silently toward a large naval tanker anchored in the harbor. Searchlights shot their huge swords of illumination out over the ocean, but none were aimed low enough to spot the black boat easing toward the tanker a few hundred yards away.

"I don't even know your name," the man in the dark coat said to the driver. "You call me Abel, but I don't have any idea who you are."

"That's correct," the driver said. "And it stays that way."

"How come you people paid me such a wad of money to do this job hauling stuff?"

"'Cause you're big and strong," the driver said. "That's it. Stop asking me questions."

The man now called Abel grumbled under his breath, but he didn't say anything more.

Staying on the backside of the enormous tanker, the driver steered his craft parallel to the large steel hull. The menacing towering side of the tanker loomed over them, completely hiding them in the threatening blackness.

"This tanker won't move," the driver said. "Watch for a rope ladder. It should be hanging around here somewhere."

The motorboat drifted on top of the gentle waves spreading out from the side of the tanker. The driver in a dark coat pushed them away from side of the tanker with a long wooden paddle. Off in the distance another wave of shore lights swept over the ocean. From the backside of the tanker, the outline of a rope ladder dangled just ahead of them.

"There it is," the driver said. "We're right on target. The ladder is hooked on the deck."

"Good. Get closer."

"We have to drift," the driver said. "Get that bundle on your back and carry it up the ladder. Hurry up. We're going to be there in a moment."

The man called Abel bounced over the seat. Sitting behind him was a large package tied to a backpack harness. He slipped his arms through the harness straps and pulled the entire apparatus toward him. "This thing is really heavy," he mumbled.

"That's why we hired you and you're so well paid." The driver pointed at the rope about to float over the bow of their boat. "Get it on, and be ready to climb."

Abel exhaled and took another deep breath. "Man, this thing is really, really heavy."

"There's the rope—grab it and get up there!"

With a quick step, the large man stepped onto the rope ladder and started crawling up the steps. Each movement was labored, but he kept moving. The motorboat floated on.

"It's a long way up," Abel shouted over his shoulder.

"Shut up," the driver whispered. "Just get up there!"

Pulling small earphones out of his pocket, the driver pushed them into his ears and turned on the amplifier in his pocket so he could hear everything happening on the rope ladder and on the deck. The boat kept drifting silently away.

Abel maintained his steady progress, climbing on up to the top. As he neared the deck, a head appeared over the edge. "Who is it?" a sailor demanded.

"Abel," the man puffed. "Abel Rabi."

"Make it quick," the sailor barked. "We don't have much time."

The driver of the motorboat listened carefully, realizing everything seemed to be on schedule. He could hear the man called Abel talking to the guard on the deck and felt confident about the drift of the conversation.

"Where we going?" Abel asked the guard.

"I've been told to take you down to the hold of the ship. We've got to move carefully. Can you carry that bag on your back down several flights of stairs?"

Abel cursed. "Easier than I carried it up that shaggy rope ladder."

"Let's go," the sailor said.

The driver of the motorboat waited a couple of minutes and then hit the starter switch. The engine sputtered for a moment and then settled into a low purr. Turning the wheel sharply to the left, he guided the boat back toward the breakwater and the passenger ferry route out of the harbor toward Catalina Island. Once he cleared the ship's perimeter by a hundred yards, he pushed the throttle to full speed, roaring away from the inner harbor area.

Reaching down beside the seat, the driver pushed a red

button on a switch next to the seat. Suddenly a ball of fire exploded from the deck of the tanker, spewing fire and debris straight up in the air. For a moment the black night appeared like noon as human figures shot through the air with pieces of the smokestack. The 20,000-ton tanker shook like a child's toy and a huge wave ripped across the channel. With vibrant red and orange flames sparkling in the night air, the tanker started to sink.

The instant the motorboat's driver saw the explosion, he pointed the boat out to sea so that the oncoming wave would lift him and carry the motorboat forward. Within seconds a torrent of water picked up the boat and slung it onward. He jerked the speed control forward and the craft lunged forward out of the harbor.

"Goodbye, Abel, or whoever you are," he said to himself. "We appreciate you delivering the bomb." He chuckled. "And yourself to the bottom of the ocean."

CHAPTER 2

November 1, 2022

THE MORNING NEWSPAPER crashed into the front door an hour before the bedside alarm was set to go off. Graham Peck usually didn't hear such predictable sounds, but the noise ricocheted through the house like a burglar intruding and forced his eyes open. For a minute he lay in the dark waiting for the next crash to follow, but nothing happened. The family had lived through another night without incident or assault, as he had expected. No reason not to go back to sleep, but he couldn't.

Graham kept looking up into the darkness and at the strange shapes the outside trees cast, slinging their shadows across the ceiling. Another day had started much earlier than he usually expected. There would be the rigorous ride downtown on the Metro Express train that would hurl him like a guided missile across Chicago at one hundred and fifty miles an hour. He would exit at the stop nearest the Sears Tower and walk on to the mayor's offices where Frank Bridges and the rest of Bridges's staff assembled. The office noise would be as subtle as the Metro Urban train clamoring over loose tracks. Party bosses, secretaries, and political analysts would be everywhere. Media personnel always hummed along behind the scenes, waiting for some big break they could turn into a headline story featuring the mayor on the evening television newscasts. Graham would be in the center of the chaos like a spinning gear in a transmission box. The job as special political assistant to the mayor of Chicago might have pushed anyone to their limits, but Graham took his responsibilities with a personal sense of obligation. The thought of the grind left him tired, and he hadn't even got out of bed yet.

"Graham . . ." Jackie reached over and ran her hand down the side of his back. "What was that noise?"

"A ghost."

"*What?*" Jackie leaned up on her elbows. "What did you say?"

"The newspaper."

"Newspaper? I thought you said . . ."

"You were asleep."

"Oh?" Jackie fell back in bed and closed her eyes. "It's too early."

"No," Graham said resolutely. "It's too late." He turned the covers back. "Extra time in the hot shower might make me feel better."

"Sure," Jackie said, keeping her eyes closed. "Sure . . ." She sounded like she had drifted off to sleep again.

Graham got up and stumbled into their private bathroom off of the bedroom, shutting the door behind him. He could keep the sound low and stand in the hot water for fifteen, maybe twenty minutes, letting the sound of classical music soothe him. He always felt empty in the morning and something about a quiet symphony seemed to position his feet more firmly on the earth, assuring him he could keep on moving . . . regardless.

For a moment Graham stared in the mirror. His brown hair hung down into his eyes, but he had a pleasant round face and striking dark eyes for a forty-year-old. At six feet tall, Graham always had a handsome look even after just dragging himself out of bed. A second glance only confirmed the fact that a shower ought to do him a great deal of good.

He reached inside the shower door and hit the digital button to start the music at a low, quiet level. He touched the next electronic switch that instantly produced hot water exactly at the temperature that Graham previously set the regulator.

Haunting sounds of Beethoven's *Moonlight Sonata* drifted across the bathroom, giving Graham Peck the closest thing to a spiritual lift that he had ever received. He needed to start the day with something, anything, a lift.

Maria Peck was already scurrying about the kitchen when Graham came downstairs. The spacious room had a chopping block in the center. In front of lace drapes purchased from Europe, a long deacon's table sat along the back window with an expansive view of the backyard. The large gray floor tile added a majestic appearance to the room.

Although Graham's mother was a small woman in her early seventies, Maria always arose earlier than everyone else. She seemed to get a particular pleasure out of setting up the table for the children to sit down and eat breakfast, but they seldom spent more than a couple of minutes gobbling down whatever they were consuming for the day before rushing off to school.

Maria's childhood had been spent in Millinocket, Maine, near Baxter State Park and the Penobscot River with a cluster of lakes nearby. Her father emigrated from England as a common laborer and Maria grew up with the simplicity of a backwoods child. Life had always been basic, but she had absorbed fearlessness as well as a decided common sense from the forests. The endless buzz of the rampant busyness of her son's family left her somewhat befuddled by the hubbub of everyone rushing off each morning.

"Good morning, Mother." Graham kissed Maria on the cheek. "You look happy this morning." He picked up a glass of orange juice.

Maria beamed. "I'm happy every morning when I wake up in this home, my dear. It's wonderful to be here." She hugged Graham. "You're up rather early this morning."

"The newspaper hitting the house woke me up, but I need to get to work early today. Lots to do."

Maria nodded. "You work so hard, Graham. I worry about you."

Graham smiled for the first time that morning. "You always did fret over me."

"Everything is upside down," Maria said as she popped a slice of bread in the toaster. "Yes, I know. All them people disappearing has made everyone extremely nervous. The election is so important and all these strange events have happened lately."

"Yes," Graham said matter-of-factly.

"Shootings and robberies are everywhere these days and it's dangerous to walk out at night," Maria rambled on. "The weather has turned crazy and the world is upside down. I saw how eerie the moon looked last night. Our mayor has to worry about running the city under such demanding conditions, don't ya know."

"Hi, Grammy!" Mary sailed into the kitchen. "I've got to leave early this morning." She stopped. "Oh, hello, Dad. You up chasing last night's monsters at the crack of dawn."

"Ha, ha." Graham's voice was flat and sounded cynical.

"I thought maybe the vampires or werewolves would attack last night," Mary teased. "Can't ever tell about what could happen on Halloween Eve."

"I wouldn't laugh about such," Maria said, shaking her finger in her granddaughter's face. "I know you young'uns don't believe in much anymore, but I grew up knowing that evil is really out there."

"Come on," Mary taunted. "How could you believe in all that nonsense?"

"I know, I know, twenty, thirty years ago lots of people lost their interest in religious things, but I didn't," Maria insisted. "The Church almost faded away, but then again, your parents didn't go anyway." She abruptly shook her finger in her granddaughter's face. "I'm here to tell you, Mary Peck, that the dark side didn't disappear. It's real and you ought to be careful of what you say about these things."

Mary laughed. "Come on, Granny. You're starting to sound like one of those Wicca freaks at my school. The truth is I don't believe in any of it."

"Your grandmother is trying to tell you something for your own good," Graham said. "Pay attention to her."

"*Whatever.*" Mary rolled her eyes.

"If nothing else, there's too many creeps walking up and down the streets these days. A few people have a lot of money and a lot of people have nothing. Makes for a bad mix. You have to watch out for thugs sulking around the city."

"Sure," Mary said indifferently. "Sleazeballs, plug-uglies, gorillas, hatchet boys, whatever. I know they're out there. Don't worry, I'll stay out of their way."

"Make sure you do!" Maria shook her finger in her granddaughter's face. "We don't want any disasters in this household."

Mary smiled at her grandmother. "I promise I'll be a good girl. Honest. I'll stay out of their way." She grabbed a

Pop-Up Bread from the plate. "I don't need to toast this. I'll eat it on the way to school." She started walking toward the door. "See you this evening. I've got a pom-pom squad practice after school so I'll be home later tonight." She opened the back door. "Bye." In a whisk Mary was gone.

Graham stood there staring. His daughter had come and gone like a whiff of smoke. One minute she was there. Then, boom! She was gone. For a fourteen-year-old, Mary moved through the house like she owned the place. Graham wasn't sure whether he liked her presumption or not.

"She's gone," Maria said and threw up her hands. "By the time they are thirteen, children act like they own the world. I swear, Graham! Your daughter acts like she's going on twenty-five."

"She's a good girl, Mother. That's what gives me some peace of mind. Mary is popular at school—she has lots of good friends. I trust her to do the right thing. She'll be fine."

"I don't know." Maria kept shaking her head. "She can be dad-gummed belligerent, hard headed sometimes. I simply don't know."

"We named her after you. How could she be any other way?" Graham smiled impishly.

Maria kept muttering to herself, arranging and rearranging the dishes lined up on the cabinet. "I wonder how Matthew is doing this morning off at that big university. You know Northwestern is terribly large for such a young boy as he is—and a freshman at that."

"Our son is fine," Graham said. "Matt's always been a good boy."

"I know, I know," Maria said more to herself. "I simply wish they had more religion in 'em."

"What are you going to do today, Mother?"

Maria swished her cheek to one side and scratched her chin. "Well, I told Jackie I would straighten up your garage. I'm actually thinking about painting the walls out there in that no man's land. Heaven knows the place needs a real workin' over. George told me he'd help."

"That's good. George needs to put in more time around the house doing something worthwhile."

"He's only eight years old, Graham, but he'll be a real help."

"Sure. And not having that five-year-old brother hanging around will help."

Maria shook her finger at him. "Jeff is a very bright boy. He may only be five, but he's got the brains of a child twice his age. Don't ever count him out."

"Certainly." Graham slipped his suit coat on. "Jackie won't be down for a while. I'll drive my two-seater to the Metro Urban Express station. I filled it up with hydrogen night before last. She can use the gasoline car."

"Now you be careful, son. Remember all those things you told Mary."

Graham laughed. "Keep worrying about me, Mom. It helps." He kissed her on the cheek and closed the door behind him.

CHAPTER 3

THE RIDE from Arlington Heights to downtown Chicago had changed since the installation of the Metro Urban Express lines. Of course, transportation in all of the big cities had altered radically in the last fifteen years since petroleum supplies had become even tighter. The train's comfortable seat and speed through the suburbs fit Graham's style. The train's breakneck speed fit him like a tailored suit. He had always been a quick moving, decisive person who could make any office hop. The employees straightened up when he came into the office. One of the reasons Graham had risen to the lofty position of assistant to the mayor had been his ability to make instant decisions that turned out to be correct.

The Metro Urban train cruised at such a high rate of speed that travel time was minimized. The inner city had turned into a place of startling contrasts. Plush stores remained as exotic as ever; but the tenement areas were frightening places to visit, much less live in. Poverty had produced children who lived like animals. Anyone could be attacked on the streets by young punks and never know what hit them.

Graham didn't worry much about those possibilities. He carried in his pocket a personal alarm button that the city provided for all their top-level employees. One punch of the button and the nearest police officers would be alerted to come with their guns drawn. At most, he would be exposed to attack for only a matter of a minute or so. Graham stuck his hand in his pants pocket to make sure the quarter-sized button was there.

Like every other city in America, Chicago had grown enormously in the last twenty years, stretching its housing areas toward Peoria and Urbana as well as Freeport and Rock Falls. If anyone wanted to avoid the urban beasts that roamed the streets at night in search of drugs, it was necessary to keep moving toward those outlying areas. Unfortunately, all of the farming land had been devoured by housing developments.

Peck leaned back against the seat and closed his eyes for a moment, trying to tune out the noise of the packed car. No matter where he and Jackie turned, multitudes of people milled around. Even the poor restaurants had long queues. Periodically Graham got tired of feeling like a piece of sand on an endless beach. There almost wasn't any place left where countless numbers of citizens didn't flow back and forth like creatures bobbing around meaninglessly in the surf.

And then he thought about all those people who had simply disappeared. Graham didn't know any of them except for a minor employee in his office, and he virtually didn't know that man. In an instant, millions had simply disappeared. Poof! Gone! And no one knew where.

The unknown was what bothered him the most. Graham's style dictated grabbing a problem by the back of the neck and shaking it until change followed. Not on this one! Researchers had not been able to turn up anyone who seemed to have any idea about what had become of that multitude. Graham had worked with millions of Chicago- ans who came and went every day. The idea such a huge number could disappear without a trace simply left him speechless. The best he could do right now was to dismiss the entire idea.

Graham patted his neck and made sure his sweater was in place. No one wore a tie anymore and Graham liked the change. Sweaters were infinitely more comfortable. Of course, comfort was the word these days. Everyone dressed for ease. Even the mayor appeared on television occasion- ally wearing blue jeans that made him look even younger. Graham didn't like Bridges's extremely casual appearance in those television shots, but the voters did and that was all that counted.

The train slowed and Graham reached for the small computer case he carried with him wherever he went. In a matter of seconds he could turn on the machine, flash a holograph keyboard on any surface and type out what he wanted to remember or send to someone. The pocket com- puter made his job with the mayor easier to handle. He needed the help.

The campaign to reelect Frank Bridges had flip-flopped the city's regular offices from "Administrative Staff" painted on the door to "Election Campaign." Graham kept a foot in both worlds, both working for the mayor and being a major player in the hoopla to win reelection. The task was de- manding.

Within minutes of leaving Arlington Heights, the train pulled into his station and Graham joined the multitudes pouring out for work in the downtown area. He pushed his way through the turnstiles and hurried up the street. When he reached the office, the scene was exactly as he had anticipated. As he worked his way through the hubbub of secretaries and assistants, silence fell over the employees. At the back he found his usually quiet office.

"Good morning, Sarah," Graham said briskly to the secretary in front of his office.

"Oh, good morning, Graham," Mrs. Cates answered. "You're looking sharp this morning."

"Bad lighting," he quipped.

"You're always funny."

"Comes with the trade."

Graham shut the door behind him and sat down at his desk. Momentary solitude surrounded him with the luxury of quietness that few enjoyed. He took a deep breath and looked out the tenth-floor office window across the city toward Lake Michigan. The changing of the trees' colors always imparted a sense of well-being. Like the lake, the scenery flashed beauty in every direction. He had to put the picture behind him. It was time to get tough. The mayor expected him to crack the whip and Graham knew how. He took a deep breath, and mentally put his armor on.

The phone rang.

"Peck here."

"Graham, this is Frank Bridges. Can you get down to my office in one minute."

"Certainly. It will take me less than sixty seconds."

"Good. We've got a big problem. It needs your touch." Bridges hung up.

Graham stood up. Maybe more people had disappeared. The daily riot had started again.

CHAPTER 4

A S USUAL, Graham Peck had already been hard at work at his office for an hour before the family awoke. George Peck opened his eyes slowly and stared at the white ceiling far above him. A now forgotten dream had left him frightened and unsettled. He stirred uncomfortably in his bed. The noises downstairs told him that the rest of the family had already started their day. As always, his father had left for work more than an hour ago and his sister Mary was probably gone before his father left the house. Only his five-year-old brother Jeff would still be asleep across the room from George's bed. He turned the thick blanket back, but didn't get out of bed. His heart kept pounding. George lay there, thinking about how strange everything in his world had become.

His parents had warned him and Jeff about going outside alone. No longer could he wander the neighborhood like he had done for all of his eight years. Everyone was tense, frightened, weird, and George didn't like it, but he was too young to do anything about the problem except gripe. He simply had to accept what he was told to do or find himself in deeper trouble.

Things were like that at school, too. The teachers kept huddling together outside their classrooms, whispering all the time, and watching with raised eyebrows as if at any moment someone was about to do something spooky. Even the principal Mrs. Hammond acted defensive. She stood around the halls with her arms crossed over her chest as if she were running a state prison. Guards were posted on the playground during recess, and they sniffed around like police dogs, making the children run from them. Everyone felt tense, and nervous; although they wouldn't say so out loud, they were scared.

Even last night had been difficult. A red cast overshadowed the moon, leaving it shimmering in a strange crimson glow that sent a disconcerting facade over the entire city. Earlier in the day fierce winds blew a pounding hailstorm across Chicago, hiding the sun and battering roofs and cars. Weather forecasters warned the children to stay inside in case the pounding started again. George had never seen anything like the sight of huge hailstones pounding on the roof, and it only added to his apprehension.

"George?" a small voice said from across the room. "Are you awake?"

"Yeah."

"You getting up?" Jeff asked.

"In a minute."

"Okay." Jeff rolled over and closed his eyes again. "I'll sleep a while longer." He turned back over. "Is it still hailing?"

"No. Go back to sleep."

Living at the end of Crown Point Street in the Chicago suburbs of Arlington Heights, George and Jeff Peck knew the local neighborhood like the backs of their hands. They always thought there was nothing to be afraid of out there. Even with their older brother Matt off to college, the two youngest boys in the family weren't to be restrained from their usual jaunts up the street and around the block. But last night elongated shadows from the tall poplars lined the streets with strange interlacing shapes, looking like long pointed spears or jagged swords, and changed the peaceful neighborhood's appearance into a web of intrigue. Few door lights were turned on. The affluent neighborhood felt more like a city jungle.

The strange sights deeply bothered George. Everything had changed when all of those people disappeared. No one had ever fully explained to him what had occurred and the entire event left him unnerved. The night before, Mary had tried to explain it to them, but the conversation hadn't gone very well. Of course, part of the reason was that Mary always treated him and Jeff like they were nuisances. She had caught them in the street a half-block away.

"You think you're big time," George had challenged his sister. "'Cause you're fourteen doesn't make you better than us."

"Better than *you*?" Mary had sneered. "Always and forever." She always managed the best put-downs any young teenager could muster.

"We're scared!" Jeff had blurted out, interrupting the argument.

"No, we're not," George had said. "Don't listen to short stuff. He doesn't know anything."

"It scares me that all those people are gone," Jeff had said and shivered. "Boom! Up in smoke. Disappeared!"

"I understand." The condescending tone in Mary's voice disappeared and she shook her head. "You boys be careful," she said more thoughtfully. "Nobody knows what's going on anymore and it's not a good time to be out here in the street running around alone even if it is Halloween eve."

"What do you think *did* happen to all those people?" George had asked his sister in a more respectful manner.

"I don't know," Mary said. "A girl at school said they all migrated to some South American country to live on a big farm. Other people think it has something to do with religion. I don't know."

"South America?" George protested. "Listen. Millions of people disappeared in an instant. South America wouldn't hold 'em all. You know that church down at the end of the housing area? Near Monroe School?"

Mary shook her head.

"That old building with a steeple is still locked tighter than a bank. Maybe there's something religious behind all of this?"

"Nope," Mary said soberly. "I don't know what to say. I don't know anyone who does. The whole thing is too gosh awful scary."

"Yeah," Jeff said in that little boy voice of his that could sound so vulnerable.

"Look. Mom sent me out here to tell you boys to come home. She doesn't want you roaming the streets by yourself. You can't tell what will happen next."

"Yeah," Jeff had said again in a compliant tone that always irritated George.

"Don't be telling us what to do!" George protested.

"Listen. You little squeak, don't throw lip at me." Mary marched toward him like she would slap him.

George took off running for the house to get out of her way. At the least, she wouldn't get a crack at him, but that also ended the conversation.

Now George regretted that he had been so aggressive. He should have listened better. Mary might have told him more about the disappearance of all of those people, but she always tried to push him around and that created fights. Still he should have simply listened and not been so belligerent. That's what Mother always told him. Be quiet and listen. Well, he should have listened better.

Jeff sat up in bed and threw the covers back. "I'm going to get up now," he said. "I've got to go to school today."

George started to correct him and say "preschool," but he didn't. Jeff was a very bright boy and Mom and Dad had placed him in a special school that allowed Jeff to work at his own level. He was already reading books far ahead of regular first graders. George didn't feel any competition with Jeff. He simply recognized that his little brother was gifted.

George's problem was he couldn't stop thinking about all of those people who had vanished. Two boys in his class at school had disappeared just as if they simply had walked out for a vacation. Their entire families were gone, leaving behind their houses and everything in them. Although he'd never been in any of those homes, people said even the dishes had been left on the table like they were eating supper and simply got up and left. One of the neighbors reported it looked like they would come back any minute and finish eating . . . but they never did. Some people said there was an explanation in the Bible but he had never seen it.

"You boys get down here right now," Grandmother Maria called up from the kitchen. "You need to eat your breakfast. Hurry up. Get a wiggle on."

"Okay, okay."George got out of bed and reached for the bathrobe lying across the end of his bed. "I'm coming." The truth was he needed to hurry, but he still felt apprehensive about all those people who disappeared.

CHAPTER 5

TEN MINUTES LATER Jackie Peck stood in the doorway opening into the kitchen and watched her boys eating. For a moment she observed the breakfast scene without saying anything. George's ruffled, toast-colored hair nearly hung down into his brown eyes. George's face looked a great deal like hers, oblong and angular. Little Jeff's face was much rounder with puffy fat in his cheeks. His hair was lighter than George's and he had blue eyes. George and Jeff looked like two innocent little children without a care in the world. But their mother knew that was anything but true.

Jackie caught a glimpse of herself in the hall mirror. For a thirty-nine-year-old mother of four children, she had kept her figure well, but she did look tired. Well, who wouldn't? Worrying about her son off at college and these two hellions would exhaust anyone, not to mention trying to keep her fourteen-year-old daughter walking a straight line. Jackie looked again. Her brunette hair still had a luster people admired and there weren't many wrinkles under her brown eyes. Maybe she was looking better than she felt.

George and Jeff were bright children, but Jeff was exceptionally intelligent. Sometimes he sounded almost like an adult and he had a phenomenal memory. They were capable of making up their own minds about almost everything and that worried Jackie. You had to keep a sharp eye on such talented boys.

"Hey, Mom! You had breakfast yet?"

Jackie walked in. "No, I haven't. Maria—thank you for getting everything going this morning. I was so tired that I overslept. I guess I'm trying to catch up on lost sleep."

"Oh, I'm always glad to help," Maria said. "Graham and Mary have already left. I'm sure he's at his office by now."

"Sure." Jackie sat down at the table. "What are you boys talking about this morning?"

"All those people who disappeared," Jeff said.

Jackie stiffened. "I see." She looked away and changed the subject. "I guess you're going to have a busy day today, Maria."

"I think so," Maria answered. "I plan to work on that junk in the garage. Needs more than a touch out there, don't you know."

"Good," Jackie said. "Well, I've got to go downtown to a library meeting, and . . ."

"Why don't you ever want to talk about those people disappearing?" Jeff said.

Jackie gritted her teeth. "It's not my favorite subject."

"You know what one of the kids up the street said?" George asked. "He said the whole business is about religion."

"I wouldn't know," Jackie answered abruptly. "Please pass me the toast."

"You wouldn't know about religion or you wouldn't know about the disappearance? Which one?" George pressed.

"Any of it," Jackie said firmly, forcing a smile.

"We never went to church, did we?" Jeff asked.

"No, dear. Attending a church wasn't one of the things you father and I ever tried." Jackie kept her smile in place, but she knew she looked pressed. "It wasn't part of our, well . . . ah . . . our values."

"I don't believe in any of that stuff," little Jeff said. "I never did believe in Jesus or the Bible."

"Now listen to me," Maria interrupted the conversation. "You boys shouldn't say you don't believe in something you don't understand. I wasn't much of a church person either, but I was brought up to respect those ideas that other people feel are important. I believed in what the Bible said. Sure. I should have read it more, but I didn't doubt anything on those pages." She shook her finger in their faces. "You should do the same."

"Maybe," George said, "but I don't believe in that Christian stuff really. I mean . . . I don't understand much about it."

"See!" Maria shook her finger in Jackie's face. "I always told Graham he should take these children to a church every now and then. You should have read them Bible stories."

"Please, Maria," Jackie said resolutely. "Let's not get off on a wild goose chase this morning. Look, boys. I don't have any idea what happened to all of those people, but I'm sure it didn't have anything to do with religion. Eventually, some scientists or psychiatrists will come up with an answer. Let's not get the day started worrying about a problem we can't solve."

Maria thumped on the top of the stove. "Well, you know what I think about . . ."

"Please, Maria," Jackie said again. "These are only little boys! They don't need to get worried and upset about nonsense. Let's just drop the entire matter. Okay?"

Maria rolled her eyes and threw up her hands. She went back to cleaning the top of the stove.

"I want you boys to hurry up and get your regular clothes on," Jackie said. "I'll take you by your schools this morning. I have a number of errands to run so let's get on with it."

George looked at Jeff and nodded. Jeff didn't say anything.

"Ready to move?" Jackie kept smiling. "I'm going to be in the car and gone in fifteen minutes. You're going to have to start moving fast."

The boys murmured their compliance, got up, and took their dishes to the sink. Jackie kept eating, and watched her silent sons. Far from ending any more conversations, she had merely put a plug in the dike. The truth was she didn't even want to think about the whole complex problem. Everything about millions of people vanishing in an instant left her horrified.

CHAPTER 6

S TORM CLOUDS RUMBLED over the Mediterranean Sea, covering the entire city of Nicosia,
Cyprus, with the possibility of thunder and lightning hanging in the air. While the seven-story building located downtown was not a hotel, the edifice maintained the posh
ambiance that only the most expensive resorts carried. Tables and chairs covered with hand-tooled leather stood on
elegant carpets. Crystal chandeliers hung from the ceil-
ings.

Sitting on a veranda looking out toward Lebanon, powerful men had gathered with their bodyguards standing in
the shadows. A servant walked among the six international
leaders, placing drinks on the small tables at each man's
elbow. Once the task had been completed, the waiter
quickly disappeared.

"My friends," Hassan Jawhar Rashid began, "I appreciate your coming to this island today. Each of us has major
responsibilities that would naturally keep us in our countries. The president of Egypt, Ali Mallawi, certainly always
has such pressing matters, and Abd al Bari carries the weight
of the business affairs of Syria on his shoulders. Each of you
functions at the same intense level."

Both men nodded appreciatively; the others smiled.

"Your call is our summons," a gray-haired man at the
end of the table answered. "Anytime Hassan Rashid wishes

to speak with the head of any Arab state, we are instantly available."

"Thank you, Ali." Rashid gestured around the room. "Such a pleasurable palace seemed a more convenient and secretive meeting place than one of your capitols. I trust you found your accommodations to be acceptable."

"Hear! Hear!" the men cheered and clapped. "Definitely."

"Excellent! Wonderful." The entire group applauded the arrangements.

Rashid smiled and turned the large diamond ring he wore on his pinky finger, but his smile quickly faded. "Unexpected events are going to happen in the immediate future. I want each of you to be prepared to respond quickly."

"What do you foresee ahead of us?" the gray-haired man asked. "Please share specifically with us."

"If we do not allow anyone or any cause to create separations between any of us," Rashid said, "we are poised to control the United States."

Silence fell over the room.

"*You are serious?*" the president of Egypt gasped.

"Quite." Hassan Rashid's eye's narrowed. "I believe the American democratic process is the jugular vein to be attacked for their downfall. While it might not seem so at this moment, I find Americans to be quite vulnerable."

"But they have the most powerful weapons in the world!" the prime minister of Saudi Arabia protested. "We know they have enormous military capacity as well as the nuclear deterrents to stop any nation."

Rashid shook his finger. "No, no." His sober stare didn't

change. "The key word is *control*. We are not planning to engage their military; my plans are to manipulate the plebiscite. Americans like to think their voters are intelligent, analytical thinkers." Rashid leaned over to speak in nearly a whisper. "In fact, they are overindulged, reactionary children who vote *with their emotions*."

"But how can you change the feeling of a huge population of Yankees?" Ammar Aswad of Iran protested. "Such a thing is not achievable!"

"Oh?" Hassan Rashid's eyes twinkled and a slight smile broke across his face. "Is this what each of you thinks?"

The national leaders looked at each other, nodding their agreement.

"*Fear!*" Rashid yelled at them. "The Americans and their reactionary journalists as well as fast-talking television reporters have the emotional core of a six-year-old child. Gentlemen, *fear is the way* that I will shake these fat boys when they enter their voting machines."

"But . . . but . . ." Abd al Bari rubbed his chin nervously. "Making an entire nation afraid is . . . is . . . not possible."

Hassan Rashid sat back in his chair. "If I can create such a result, are you and your countries prepared to stand with me?" He thrust his finger in the face of each man. "Will you follow me faithfully as I resolutely climb the hill to world conquest?"

Silence settled over the group.

"You see," Rashid continued, "I am more than capable of sending a wave of fear across that country like none they have ever known. I already have the ability to do so. My men are poised and ready to strike. But what follows after I have created chaos?" The gentle smile abruptly returned. "I need your assistance. Will you follow me?"

The white-haired president of Egypt slowly stood, clicking his heels and coming to extreme military attention. "If you can humble America, I am with you to the death!" He saluted Hassan. "I will follow."

For a moment no one spoke and then the entire group exploded with their affirmations of loyalty.

For several moments Hassan Jawhar Rashid only listened, waiting for the group to settle again. "Thank you," he finally said. "The Americans will soon be in my hands, and I will drown them in their own fear."

CHAPTER 7

A N OBLONG conference table ran down the center of Mayor Frank Bridges's office. Five men were already seated around this mahogany altar to the gods of progress when Graham Peck walked in. Maintaining distance, Peck kept his usual steel look in his eye and only nodded to the other leaders.

Jake Pemrose and Al Meacham were old acquaintances of his, but Graham usually maintained a distance from the more cold and aloof Jack Stratton and Bill Marks. Although the city had in decades past outlawed smoking in public buildings, three of the men were already smoking cigars. Wearing a subdued pair of maroon suspenders, Bridges sat at the head of the table in a business suit. Since he usually dressed more casually, Peck knew something significant was afloat.

"Graham," Mayor Bridges said, "thanks for coming right down. We need your input."

"Sure," Peck answered.

"Gentlemen, we have a big problem this morning," Bridges continued. "At around four o'clock west coast time, an oil tanker was bombed in the Long Beach Naval Yard. You heard the story on the morning news?"

Peck abruptly realized he hadn't tuned in a television station anywhere. He generally started the day with a television report or at the least an e-mail briefing on his computer, but he hadn't done so today.

"The explosion was enormous," Bridges began. "Get ready. People all over the Chicago metroplex will scream."

"How did it happen?" Jake Pemrose asked.

Graham knew Pemrose well. The councilman had been a political force on the southside for years and Bridges listened to him. Pemrose usually asked the first question.

Bridges shook his head. "How do these monsters always get in? Some collaborator sneaked them or their bomb on to the tanker. I don't know, Jake. The important thing is that this attack provides a new opportunity for our campaign. We've got to address this problem immediately."

"We can hit the noon news if we come out of this meeting with a statement," Graham interjected. "Let's do it."

Bridges stood up with a laser pen in his hand. His suspenders did little to hide his protruding stomach. Bridges lived through his earlier years as a man with great political promise. While his "great hope" had not yet turned into a presidency, at fifty-five he had developed a broad and powerful constituency in Illinois. The years had proved significant, but his body slid downhill. He couldn't do much about the belly, but Bridges was desperately looking for a new, broader power base.

Graham looked around the room once more. Nothing had changed in how these men looked, acted, or thought since the night multitudes of people disappeared. Life went on like any other day, but the truth was they were terrified to look at the subject in anything more than a passing way. Keeping the upper lip stiff was the style of people like Pemrose and Bridges.

"I've already given this problem some thought while coming down here this morning." Bridges started transmitting an electronic message to the board with his laser pen.

"Terrorist attacks aren't new," Graham said. "Are you sure an explosion on the Pacific coast will affect Chicagoans?"

"We may not be a big time port city, but Lake Michigan has plenty of shipping," Bridges answered. "Our city is also a major rail and transportation hub."

Graham nodded. "But I keep thinking about the poverty problems floating around this very building."

"Don't stop with that thought, Graham. We're simply making hay out of today's big explosion in California. It's momentary, but an opportunity."

Graham smiled. He wasn't going to make any points on his favorite issues. Drop it.

"Here's my plan! Open a twenty-four-hour center in downtown Chicago to receive reports on possible terrorist activity. Tie the telephone into the 911 lines and it wouldn't cost the city an additional cent, but it would give people a point of contact. The entire metroplex will be wired. People would think they're getting something, but it's really nothing. Slick, huh?"

The men around the table gave their approval.

"We've had surveillance for a long time, but I'd propose to increase the number of cameras. Sort of like sticking 'The Eye' in everything from the kitchen to the garage. At the least, people would think we had them covered."

"This will at least create the illusion of espionage control," Jack Stratton said. "Who knows? Someone might call in a tip that could make a difference."

"We're still going to need some federal funding," Graham argued.

"Good point." Bridges kept flashing the laser pen images on the board without turning around. "Makes my point number three. We need to request federal funding for the acquisition of new protective gear."

Graham leaned back in his chair. Bridges was the master of reaction, like a fox watching a hen house and then attacking after the last chicken waddled out into the barnyard. Many of his ideas didn't amount to much, but they sounded good in the newspapers. He was a man who created images, and what people voted for these days was illusions, not substance.

Bridges bounced his pen up and down in his hand. "I've got one final point. People need assurances that we won't allow a runaway epidemic to sweep the city." The mayor looked straight at Graham. "What do you think, Peck?"

"I thought our health agencies already provided such services." Graham's voice was flat and without enthusiasm.

"You got it!" Bridges almost laughed. "We'll give them something they already have."

The men around the table broke into applause. Graham watched, but didn't move. Were many of the citizens really this dumb? Yeah. They were.

"Graham's already figured this one out," Bridges said. "We're blowing a lot of smoke. The point is we don't have to spend a dime, and we sound like we're saving civilization." Bridges winked. "That's called good politics."

"Good politics, indeed!" Al Meacham said. "I don't think we ought to underestimate our opponent. The other side is working hard to provide an alternative. They'll respond to us and might get more than a tad ugly about some of these items."

"Which means we're the ones keeping the initiative going," Bridges said. "Initiative, boys. That's how the game is won."

Graham believed in Bridges's campaign and definitely thought he was the better qualified of the two candidates. However, he didn't like these back-room planning sessions. They always sounded like the legendary "smoke-filled rooms" that once made politics pop. Bridges was aiming at the media, not the issues.

The lack of ethical concern also bothered Graham. He wasn't sure why, but somewhere along the way he had picked up a sensitivity to these issues. His mother had made him go to church as a boy. Not much of it stuck, but he remembered the discussions about doing the right things—

that part of their message stayed with him. Graham's mother had always been big on moral issues. She encouraged him to think about what was lasting and true. His father taught him to work hard and instilled an enduring drive in the boy. Graham knew politicians ought to pay attention to these things, but that wasn't where Bridges and his inner circle lived.

"We're with you, Frank, but I want to know what you now consider to be the real issues. What are we truly fighting for?" Graham crossed his arms over his chest and didn't blink.

Bridges pursed his lips and ran his hands through his hair. "Nothing has changed, Graham. Same game as always." He pulled at his chin, thinking about the question. "I don't know what these terrorists are trying to prove or where they came from, but the basic issue is still the same. We need more oil than we can currently obtain. The whole world is locked into this question and people in a city as large as Chicago can't forget it. This country's war in the middle of those Muslim oil fields affected supply. The world's oil supply has slowed down ever since and the prices keep going up. Sure. Many cars run on batteries or hydrogen, but they still need petroleum to produce energy. Everyone remains afraid of nuclear power plants. I need to get a large percentage of the vote to enable me to make the long-range negotiations we need for this city." He stopped for a moment and then looked straight at Graham. "I don't want to talk about this problem in public, but I believe that Borden Camber Carson may be our only hope. We need more production from his Royal Arab Petroleum empire coming our way. Do you disagree?"

Graham knew the mayor enjoyed putting his attackers on the defensive. He didn't want to say so in this meeting, but Graham wasn't a big fan of Carson and his far-flung oil empire. Who knew what this egomaniac was actually about? No one had ever actually seen the recluse. The only clear evidence was that he was good at bringing oil production under his control.

"Do you disagree?" Bridges asked again.

"I don't disagree that energy is our big problem."

"There you have it, boys." Frank Bridges tossed his hands up in the air. "We're all on the same page."

"However," Graham continued, "my contention is that most citizens are terrified of criminal elements in our society and they can't do anything about it. Low income is killing the average Chicagoan right now."

The room broke into an uproar and Bridges lost control of the conversation. Graham watched the verbal melee, knowing he was right; the feverish exchanges guaranteed it.

"Gentlemen! Gentlemen!" The mayor held up his hand. "You're getting off the track. I can't fix the fact we've got many low-income people living in our town. Sorry. I don't control the medical system either or fight the thieves down there on the street. We've got to focus on what I can do. Okay?"

The roar subsided. "We understand," Graham said. "Let's work out what you've proposed." He smiled, recognizing he still had the capacity to turn these conferences in his own direction.

"Let's go back out there and figure how to get this story on television by noon today and then in the headlines tonight." The mayor shrugged in relief. "Thank you, Graham. Thank you, gentlemen."

Graham watched the company disband and disappear. He pushed his notes together and stood up. Bridges walked toward him.

"What'd you think of the meeting?" the mayor said.

"I think we've framed new issues for you to chew on," Graham said. "Ought to make good copy."

"But not the copy you'd like to write?"

Graham smiled wryly. "I like to write what you want me to say."

"What a master politician you are, Graham. Great answer, but the truth is that you'd rather push poverty issues."

"I think they're the bread and butter issues, Frank."

The mayor reached out and put his hand on Graham's shoulder. "I couldn't run this thing without you, Peck. You're my key man. You're the brains in this group. You know that, don't you?"

Graham grinned. "I'm the best you've got?"

"Absolutely."

"*And you* don't ever quit being the politician. Right?"

Bridges shrugged. "What can I say?" Bridges walked away and Graham left the room.

What bothered Peck was Bridges's fascination with this Carson character and his oil fiefdom. Royal Arab Petroleum Company could backfire on the whole campaign. He wanted the mayor to stay away from these people.

"Your wife is on the phone," his secretary said when he walked by. "Want me to send the call into your office?"

"Please. Thank you, Sarah."

Graham kept his relationship with the women in the office on a fairly formal basis. The distance kept him on safe turf and prevented misunderstanding. He picked up the phone.

"Jackie! Is everything okay?"

"Of course."

"Well, I thought maybe something had happened."

"No. No. I realized I'm going to be at a library study club meeting this afternoon, not far from your office. I thought maybe we could have a little romantic supper together."

Graham laughed. "Oh, you still like me?"

"The question is do *you love* me?" Jackie had a coy sound in her voice.

"No question about it. Sure. We can have a great time this evening. The only problem could be if I run into an unexpected issue and run late."

"Call me on my cell phone if you get into a quagmire."

Graham smiled. "What about the children?"

"You are about to discover another value of your mother. Nothing like having a built-in baby sitter in the guest room."

"Looks like everything is set. How about Zio's Italian a couple of blocks from here?"

"One of my favorites. If six o'clock works, I'll be there."

"Good. Love you."

"Love you, Graham."

Peck hung up the telephone and looked out the window. Nothing like a delightful surprise to give one a new boost on a demanding day. Jackie was good at coming up with these wonderful little escapades. They would have a great evening.

For the next hour Graham developed several ways Bridges's idea might be presented. On the noon news, the mayor made a dramatic statement, presenting to the city of Chicago an alternative as well as challenging the entire country to respond in a new way to terrorist attacks.

Graham sat in the conference room with the rest of the staff, evaluating the television appearance.

"What do you think?" Jake Pemrose turned around to Graham. "Did we make it?"

"What do *you* think?" Peck answered.

"Looked good to me." Pemrose tapped his cigar in a wastepaper basket. "I'd say Frank's show was as good as the president's earlier statement. Ought to buy more than a few votes."

Peck's cellular phone rang. "Hello."

"Graham, how did I sound?" the mayor asked in a matter-of-fact tone.

"Good, Frank. Excellent."

"Okay. Glad to hear it. Graham, can you take my statement and expand what I said on the health care issues? That's really your turf anyway."

"Sure, but it will take a good chunk of the afternoon."

"Put the other issues aside and work only on that one. I believe we may need it by the six o'clock news."

"Six o'clock news? Frank, you're really moving on."

"Got to." Bridges said. "My opposition is going to be out there chasing me." He hung up.

Graham looked at his watch. He'd have to move fast to

get this assignment done by five o'clock. Excusing himself, he returned to his office to pound out the words that would come bouncing out of the mayor's mouth later in the day.

At four-thirty the phone rang. Graham glanced at his watch and then reached for the receiver, thinking it must be Jackie. Maybe something had come up.

"Hello."

"Peck?" the male voice said. "Graham Peck?"

"Yes?" Graham said.

"This is the Peck who lives on Crown Point in Arlington Heights?"

"Sure. There's a problem?"

"Yes. I'm Detective Bevins with the police department. Your secretary said to call before I came in. Are you sitting down?"

"Sitting down?" Graham grimaced. "Of course. I'm working."

"Stay there. I'm outside with your secretary. I'll be right in."

"What's going on?" Graham protested. "What's happened?"

"I'll explain to you in a moment when I come in your office," Bevins said. "We need you to come home at once . . . and please stay seated."

CHAPTER 8

THE DIRECTOR of the University of Illinois Microfabrication Research Laboratories finished studying the proposal for the funding of the facilities. Hidden underground, the nanotechnology projects remained secret and far out of the public eye. A tall man, the gray-haired scientist had been a pioneering researcher for more than five decades. He was a natural to both run an extensive program and struggle with the politicians to get the money at the same time.

"Paul Gillette!" Dr. Allan Newton said as the older man walked in to the lab. "Extremely good to see you, sir. I trust you are well."

"Quite fine." Paul shook hands. "How's the research going?"

"More than interesting," Newton answered. "I'm turning up new possibilities all the time."

"Good. Good." Dr. Gillette paused and stroked his goatee. "This is totally off the subject, but you're such an extensive research man, Allan." Gillette forced a smile. "And my area certainly isn't astronomy, but I noticed again last night that the moon had . . . a, well, how should I say it? A strange look."

"A most distracting color!" Dr. Newton grinned. "Sure does. Never saw a crimson moon in my life."

"Do you know why?" Gillette pushed.

"I'm sorry, Paul. My work is at the other end of the scale. What worries me is that it seems like Mother Nature had an unexpected nervous breakdown. Reports say that the tides aren't coming in on schedule, as they should. That's more than a little disconcerting. Unfortunately, I can't make any sense out of these bizarre changes. My work frightens me enough as it is. Your guess is as good as mine."

"It's all certainly strange!" Dr. Gillette adjusted his glasses. "Well, let's get back to the subject at hand. I need you to update me on how nanotechnology is progressing. I'm working on the budget today."

Newton pointed to his electron microscope. "Sit down, Paul." Allan scooted closer to instrument. "Take a look for yourself. Down there in that solution are some of my latest creations. Tell me what you think."

Dr. Gillette stared into the dual lens. It took him a moment to realize what he was seeing. The microscopic world appeared predictably filled with amorphous microzoan creatures. Strange irregular shapes floated by. Suddenly an unexpectedly rigid form shot past and disappeared. Gillette adjusted the machine and looked again. Objects smaller than a speck of dust zoomed by as if traveling on prescribed missions. Abruptly one of the gizmos stopped, turned around, and appeared to be surveying the area. At the tip of the cylindrical tube-shaped objects a singular eye seemed to study the microbic scene. The circulatory eye moved upward and seemed to be looking straight at Gillette. He felt a cold, frightening dread surge through his body.

"Grotesque," Dr. Gillette said. "Allan, I hate to say it,

but these gadgets of yours operate almost as if they have a mind of their own. Scary little devils indeed!"

"Yes, Paul, they can put one on edge."

Gillette looked back in the microscope. New shapes worked their way into view. The tiny computers had long extension legs with hooks poised for an attack. Other machines looked like guided missiles or robots with wheels and gun turrets prepared to assault any blood platelets floating by. The nanoid devices moved with a precision edginess that resembled a rattlesnake preparing to strike.

"I . . . I . . . I can see their potential. Frightening. I had no idea your research was moving so rapidly."

"You have no idea," Dr. Newton said softly.

"These nanorobots act like they have a brain. Surely something must direct them."

"We have been able to equip the nanorobots with on-board computers. Of course, that's what the world of computational nanotechnology is about. We work on an atomic and subatomic level. Actually some of the relays and internal guidance systems in those machines are the width of several hydrogen atoms."

"Those nanorobots are absolutely monstrous!" Gillette gasped. "They move at frightening speed. You've certainly done an extraordinary job in creating those gadgets."

"Though microscopic, notice how detailed they are, Paul." Gillette looked again. Nanorobots with wheels looked like moon landing craft with fully functional bodies the size of rockets. Other nanorobots appeared to be bombs with highly developed shafts and tail pieces. The edges were pointed and sharp like creatures crawling out of a crypt.

"Astonishing!" Gillette said.

"I've been giving some attention to swarm intelligence. We have other people doing research with both micro-motives and macrobehaviors. The work is progressing on schedule."

"Good. Glad to hear it. As you're aware, the government has been pumping around six hundred million dollars a year into our research and the funding will be coming up before Congress soon." Dr. Gillette smiled. "Of course, it's always hidden in the budget so no one could ferret out what we are doing."

"Certainly." Newton pointed to a small container. "I've got enough of these computerized machines in that flask to affect a thousand people. They are small but mighty."

"In my office I was studying pictures of your dental nanorobots. Seem to be guided missiles with a torture chamber attacked at the base on each side. Frightening appearance, old man!"

"Yes. Some of the robots look like ballistic missiles; others appear to be fully armed landing craft from outer space. Quite startling."

Gillette adjusted the lens for greater amplification. To his consternation some of the robots had turned around and assembled into what looked to be an attack formation. Moving through the liquid like a line of army tanks preparing to descend on a target, the surfaces of these circular machines were dotted with strange objects, almost like tiny missiles hooked to the infinitesimal slaughter machines.

"Those devices function like a cross between machines and deadly locusts," Gillette said. "I can see appendages like multiple legs thrashing around at incredible speeds." Gillette caught his breath. "Hey! Here comes a long missile-like nanorobot with a mouth filled with serrated teeth!" He felt his stomach knot. "It's chomping away like a butchering machine!"

"You can see what could be done with these gizmos. Right now I'm trying to reproduce devices to be used only for security purpose, but nanorobots obviously could chew their way through anything in the world."

Gillette watched a dental nanorobot zoom up to a particle of food. It paused and appeared to assess the substance before tearing into it. "Your nanorobots function almost as if they are savages taken out of some jungle."

Dr. Allan Newton nodded soberly. "Well put. When you realize some of these gadgets are a thousand times smaller than the diameter of a human hair, it takes your breath away when you observe them operating as if they had a brain."

"A brain *but no conscience!*" Gillette shivered. "They're actually miniature computers, aren't they?" Dr. Gillette asked. "I mean, if I spoke of the nanorobots in that manner to the president of the United States would I be correct?"

"Close enough," Dr. Newton said. "That term tells most lay people what these gizmos are capable of. They can crawl through arteries and make your teeth self-repairing . . . or destroy them. Watch this."

Dr. Newton picked up a pipette with liquid in the stem and slowly lowered it over the nanorobots Gillette had been observing. "I'm going to release an extremely small amount of serum holding amoebas in suspension. Observe what follows when I place these amoeboid protozoan in with the nanorobots." He lifted his thumb off the pipette.

Paul Gillette watched silently for several moments. Suddenly the robots marshaled together in an attack formation. Almost as if a signal had been sounded, they hit the amoebas, slicing through their membrane exteriors and hacking away at the nuclei.

"Good gracious!" Paul exploded. "The nanorobots struck the protozoans like army tanks fighting a battle. They tore them up like cannons blowing holes in the side of a building!"

"You can see the potential of these gadgets."

"Are you certain the first models are ready for release and usage?"

Dr. Newton thought for a moment. "Well," he said slowly. "Y-e-s. They are functional, but not entirely predictable."

"What on earth do you mean?"

"They work well on simple tasks, but more complicated procedures tend to develop glitches. We are still studying why variations occur."

Dr. Gillette leaned back in his chair and stroked his thin gray goatee. "These issues are highly sensitive, Allan. We won't be able to maintain our funding if we don't have a product the government can use immediately." He rubbed his head thoughtfully. "Of course, we don't want to unleash a microscopic device that could kill someone. We cannot afford a problem or a scandal that would discredit the program."

Dr. Newton took a deep breath. "As of this moment, I cannot guarantee these devices won't attack."

"*Attack?*" Gillette's eye's widened. "You mean like . . . say . . . human tissue?"

"Yes." Allan Newton raised an eyebrow.

Paul Gillette felt his heart skip a beat.

"If one of the advanced models were in the blood-stream, an erratic out-of-control nanorobot might just disintegrate *your brain.*"

CHAPTER 9

M ARIA PECK walked out into the garage with some hesitancy in her step. The task was formidable. Boxes were stacked along the side of the wall and a pile of junk had settled into a far too familiar lodging. Along the back wall a tool bench stood littered with assorted tools and pieces of unfinished projects. The walls of the three-car garage had taken on a dingy, stained cast. The entire area needed paint after the mess was straightened up. Maria glanced at her watch and realized it was already 3:30. That meant George ought to be strolling in the front door at any moment. Jeff had already gone over to his friend Max's house for the rest of the afternoon. The time was perfect to get some serious work done. She pushed the button on the wall near the back door and the garage door opened instantaneously. New cry-o-lite plastic allowed manufacturers to build a door weighing only twenty pounds that a runaway truck couldn't knock down and the door was even bulletproof. She switched off the house's security system.

Bright sunlight threw a golden glow over the fading grass. The first freeze had already sent the summer stand of flowers into full fall retreat. Most of the ones planted last May were wilted and nearly dried. The front lawn had an inviting look, but the green would soon disappear.

Maria noticed a man standing across the street watching her. Partially hidden behind the massive oak in the neighbor's yard, the man's disheveled appearance made a sharp contrast with the wealthy neighborhood. Wearing a dirty shirt and worn sweatpants, his hair was unusually long; the bum needed a good scrubbing. Maria stared and he withdrew behind the trunk of the tree.

Trying to avoid the appearance of scrutinizing the stranger, Maria turned back to her work in the garage. She moved several boxes of old Fourth of July decorations toward the back door. Maria wanted to throw them out without asking, but Jackie might have some objection.

She gave a quick glance out of the corner of her eye to catch what the bum was doing. She looked a second time. The man wasn't there. He might be hiding behind the oak, and that would truly be suspicious. A couple of steps out in the driveway ought to clarify the situation. She strolled out and looked again, but it appeared the man had walked on.

Maria felt relieved and started back to work. She didn't like weird characters showing up around their house. Years ago types like that would never have shown up around her home. My, but how everything had changed! Life was so secure thirty or forty years ago, but that era was gone now.

Maria stared out the back door, remembering the past. She hadn't been one to go to church much, but she believed those things were important. Of course, she'd sent Graham. Every child needed a good dose of religion. It made them into better people. Maria had enjoyed those times when she did attend a church. She had met friends there and liked the warmth of the people. At that moment she saw George walking down the sidewalk.

"Georgie!" Maria hollered. "Hurry on home!"

George waved back and picked up his pace. "I'm coming." He started running.

Maria put her hands on her hips and watched the little guy hurry up the street. She had always loved George and he was easy to work with. Mary wasn't. Maria always found her granddaughter to be on the belligerent and difficult side. She'd argue and try to act like she didn't hear when Maria asked her to do something. Well, George wasn't that way and she liked working with him. He made being a grandparent fun.

"Hi, Grammy. Looks like you're already hard at work."

"Not really, George. I've been sort of rearranging some of the mess out here." She bent over and whispered. "I was actually waiting for you to come home."

"Great!"

"We've got lots to do."

"I'll put my books and stuff in the house. Gimme a minute."

"You do that. I'll get a few other items in order."

George disappeared through the garage door into the house. Maria watched him hustle off to his room like a good boy. Maybe she shouldn't have favorites, but George came close to being her number one grandchild. Of course, Matt

off at Northwestern University still remained a top con-
tender for the number one spot. Matt was such a thoughtful
boy.

"What do you want me to do?" George bounded out of
the back door.

"I see you changed your pants in about half a second.
That'll keep your mother happy."

"Got to make Mom smile."

Maria smiled at his thoughtfulness. "What'd you learn
at school today?"

"We learned about biology."

"In elementary school?" Maria shook her head. "My,
my. Isn't that something. How everything has changed. To
an old woman like me, it's almost unbelievable you learn
such."

George smiled. "But we do!"

"Sure." Maria pointed to the workbench. "Now you
start by helping me clear the trash off the top. Most of that
stuff is nothing but leftover trailings of *your* projects."

George grinned. "Maybe Jeff did it."

Maria raised an eyebrow. "Jeff's too small to do much at
that workbench, young man. Takes somebody *your* size."

"Can't ever tell," George teased.

"George." Maria stopped and looked through the open
garage door. "You didn't see anybody standing outside when
you came walking up? A man maybe?"

"What d'you mean?"

"A bum was standing out there." Maria pointed across
the street. "Did you see a such a feller?"

George shook his head. "Nope. Why?"

"I saw a man across the street. We use to call 'em pan-handlers. And . . . well . . . him standing over there bothered me."

"Maybe he was looking for a girlfriend." George grinned.

"Now, don't you get smart with me." Maria shook her finger in her grandson's face.

George kept grinning. "Come on, Grammy. Be honest."

Maria hugged her grandson. "Okay. Okay. Maybe I'm overreacting."

"Yeah, I think you are. I didn't see anybody. Maybe the guy was nothing but somebody hanging around from last night in a Halloween suit."

Maria snickered. "George, I swear to goodness! You've got the biggest imagination I ever saw."

"No! *You've* got the imagination, Grammy. Don't kid me."

"My, my, what a household I live in. Okay, George. Let's see how much we can get done. Time is flying."

"Grammy," George said more thoughtfully. "I overheard you talking about evil last night. You really believe in it?"

"Why would you ask me such a strange question?"

"Nobody in my school believes in such stuff. I think the devil is just a big joke."

Maria frowned and looked perplexed. "Don't believe? I'm sorry, George. I still live in a world where evil really means something."

George shrugged. "Well, it was just a thought."

"You're a good boy." Maria patted him on the shoulder and turned away. She didn't feel comfortable saying much on this subject and Maria didn't want to upset her grandchild. Better leave it alone.

The back door suddenly swung open and hit the wall with a bang. "Don't move!" a man demanded.

Maria stared. The same person she had seen standing across the street stood there in his unwashed look. Only then did Maria realize he was holding a 9mm pistol.

"Make a noise and I'll kill you," the man growled.

Maria stiffened and grabbed George, pulling him close to her.

"Who are you?" Maria demanded.

"Shut up, you old fool. I'm hungry and I want your money."

"Get out of here!" Maria demanded.

"I ain't goin' nowhere." The man motioned with his gun toward the house. "Keep your voice down. I don't like loudmouthed women."

Maria pushed George behind her. "Listen, you punk. I'm not afraid of you. Don't think you can scare us."

The man raised the pistol to shoulder level. "Don't mess with me, grandma freak. You get me riled up and I'll kill you." His hand started to shake.

Maria watched his eyes. The man looked terrified and high on something. But for some odd reason, she didn't feel particularly afraid of him. The bum seemed more intent on frightening her than anything else.

"You better get out of here," Maria threatened. "Our

house is filled with people who could walk out here at any second."

"I don't think so," the man said. "Ain't nobody in there."

"You don't know about the upstairs!"

The intruder blinked his eyes nervously. "I didn't need to know about the upstairs. Ain't nobody up there either."

"Yes there is!" Maria insisted.

"Then, I'll take their money too." The man gestured with his gun toward the house. "Go on in or I'll kill all of you out here."

"Listen!" Maria shook her finger in his face. "I'm not afraid of you. You're trying to scare us. Well, get this straight. I'm not giving you a dime."

"You want to die?" He cocked the pistol.

"Watch out!" George warned his grandmother. "He's crazy."

"You give me that gun." Maria took a step forward. "I'm not going to put up with this nonsense any longer." She abruptly thrust her hand straight toward him.

The bum's eyes widened and suddenly he fired. The booming explosion echoed through the garage with a deafening roar. The large pistol jerked straight up and the burglar stepped backward and fired again.

Maria felt pain rip through her abdomen. For an instant it felt like a knife had struck her stomach and gone on through her back. In the next second, she knew her abdomen was filling with blood. Never in her life had she felt such sensations, but she knew life was running out of her. In a matter of seconds Maria felt a horrible lightheadedness. The garage filled with a blinding whiteness that quickly turned into blackness like someone had turned off all of the lights in the world. Maria felt her knees buckle. Her reeling fall was the last thing she experienced. The crunch of her knees smashing against the cement floor never registered in her mind and neither did any pain when she fell face forward into the cement.

George couldn't move. Every muscle in his body froze and his feet melted into the cement floor. The intruder took a couple of steps backward. He didn't say anything, but turned and ran out the back door. George could hear him rushing across the backyard and hitting the back fence. A crashing, crunching noise erupted off in the distance and then silence.

"Grammy?" George reached out, but was afraid to touch her. Two crimson stains spread across the back of her blouse. He reached out again to touch her, but drew his hand back.

"Grammy?" George said louder. She didn't move.

George opened his mouth but nothing would come out. The last thing he remembered clearly was his feet breaking loose from the floor and running out of the garage toward a house, any house. Somewhere halfway out in the street his voice returned and he couldn't stop screaming. He didn't remember anything else until long after the police arrived. Mary was holding him then. They both kept crying, but that's all he could remember except that strange men in blue uniforms kept going in and out of their house.

CHAPTER 10

WHEN GRAHAM and Jackie Peck pulled up in front of their house on Crown Point Street, police cars were everywhere. The front lawn around the entry to the house was sealed off, but the garage door was still open and parked police cars blocked the driveway. From his car he could see a crumpled form lying on the garage floor under a sheet. Graham opened the car door slowly and walked halfway up the driveway. He stared at the figure under the shroud.

A policeman stepped in front of him and grabbed his arms. "Please, sir. You can't go in there."

Graham nodded, but didn't move. He muttered, "She's my mother."

"Of course," the policeman said. "We've identified the body. This is a sight you certainly don't want to see. She's been shot a couple of times and the situation is difficult. Please come inside and talk to your children."

"We understand." Jackie clutched Graham's arm. "We're deeply concerned about our kids."

For a moment Graham's head spun and a flash of blinding light obscured everything around him. Slowly the whiteness dissipated and his breath returned. "Yes," he resolutely agreed.

"The coroner's officials will be here shortly and they'll take your mother away," the policeman said. "That's standard procedure. You'll need to tell us the name of a funeral home where they can take her after their work is done." He started pulling Graham toward the front door. "Let's go inside."

Graham's feet kept moving, but his legs seemed like pillars of wood inching forward, plodding toward the front door. The distance felt like miles and miles.

"Please go on in," the policeman said, pushing the front door open.

Cops were everywhere. Police kept walking back and forth, in and out of the room. In one corner Mary was sitting in an overstuffed chair, holding George in her lap. Jeff was huddled up in a ball at her feet.

"Oh my children!" Jackie gasped and rushed across the room. "My babies!" Jackie knelt beside them, hugging, clutching, weeping.

Graham sank down on his knees beside Jackie and pulled all of them toward him. They cried with a passion beyond anything that any of them had ever known before. All sense of time had disappeared.

"She's gone," Mary finally said. "Grammy's gone."

"I know," Graham said. "I know. I can't believe it."

"A man shot her," Mary said. "For no reason except to rob us. He killed Grandmother."

Graham reached out for George. "You were there?"

George didn't look up or answer. He kept shivering and holding his arms together.

"You were with your grandmother?" Graham asked again.

George squinted his eyes together with fierce intensity

as if he were trying to squeeze the memory out of his mind or erase what he couldn't stop seeing. He only nodded his head slightly.

"George . . . George . . . can you talk?" Graham said.

George didn't answer. Tears ran down his cheeks again and he appeared to be frozen to Mary's side.

"Son, we're going to get through this," Graham said. "We can make it together."

"Mr. Peck," a plainclothes detective said from behind them. "May I speak to you for a moment."

Graham pushed himself up from his family and turned. "Yes sir."

"Let's walk back here to the kitchen." The detective gestured for Graham to follow him into the large kitchen area. "My name is Smith. Mac Smith, and I'm a homicide detective."

Graham stumbled and sank into one of the chairs around the deacon's table. "Yes sir," he barely mumbled.

"Your older son was in the garage when the shooting occurred," the detective said. "We haven't been able to get him to say anything, but we know he saw the shooter. Your boy doesn't seem to be able to talk right now."

"I understand," Graham said.

"We need him to help us identify the killer."

Graham nodded.

"I want to give you my card. I need you to call me the moment you think the boy is ready to identify pictures. Our computerized system will allow us to move through thousands of pictures quickly, but we need his help."

"Of course."

"Kids today see so much killing on television and at the movies that many of them seem to absorb violence better than your boy has done, but . . ."

"We don't watch violence on television," Graham interrupted him. "George is in no way prepared for what happened today. I'm sure he's going to have a difficult time. You see . . ." Graham bit his lip and stopped talking for a moment.

"I understand," the detective said. "Well, he's severely traumatized right now." He rubbed his jaw thoughtfully. "It may take a while before . . . well . . . before he's ready to talk with us."

"Probably," Graham said.

The detective stopped and looked out the window. "The ambulance is here now. They will remove your mother and then we'll probably be on our way. We checked the grounds thoroughly before you arrived. We don't have much left to do."

A policeman walked up. "Detective, we're sure the man went over the back fence and ran down the other side of the street. We've got a couple of eyewitnesses over there."

"Good!" Smith nodded his head enthusiastically. "We need to make sure we've got police chasing anyone running down that side of the street."

"Already got it covered, sir."

"Excellent! Good!" Smith said. "I'll be out there in a few minutes to join the chase." He turned back to Peck. "Anything you want to ask me?"

Graham shook his head.

"We know who you are, Mr. Peck. You're an important

person downtown. Don't worry. We pay attention to the people working with Mayor Bridges."

Graham blinked several times. The detective's words startled him. "Don't you take care of everybody?" he snapped.

"Sure," Smith said. "But there's so much crime these days we can't keep up with it all. Since those millions of people disappeared the world's gone crazy. Frankly, some of these cases slip between the cracks. Don't worry. We won't let that happen in this situation."

Graham thought the police were on top of everything in Chicago, but this man had told him quite the opposite. The admission was staggering. It was wrong, but this wasn't the time or place to take up that problem.

The detective walked away and Graham took a long, deep breath and walked back into the living room where the police were starting to thin out. Jackie still lay huddled over the children.

Graham sat down on the floor to be on eye level with George. "Son? Can you talk to me?" He looked straight into George's eyes.

George didn't answer. His eyes looked empty and he didn't move his head.

Graham stared. His son was acting more like a patient coming out of a post-trauma stress crisis. The boy seemed to be completely detached. George couldn't speak and looked like a person in a dissociative state.

"Son . . ." Graham reached out for him, but George didn't move. Graham took his son in his arms and hugged him close. The boy didn't resist, but neither did he respond.

George's body felt like it was hanging in suspended animation, limp like a worn-out inner tube. "Oh, George," Graham whispered in his ear, "I'm so, so sorry."

George could faintly hear his father's voice, but it sounded like it was coming from the other end of a long tunnel. George felt locked in a soundproof room where a straightjacket bound him tight and secure. Voices buzzed around his head like gnats circling in the summertime. He tried to understand even though nothing made any sense.

A terrible, roaring noise returned over and over again. Like two blasts from a car backfiring, the sounds came in rapid succession. The explosion would occur and then die down sometimes for as long as a minute. After the blasts had almost faded away, suddenly the cracking and popping would happen again. Two short staccato bangs repeated in the same time sequence. Over and over, over and over, the sounds ricocheted around in his mind.

Everything happening around George moved in slow motion as if all the clocks in the world had geared down to a slow ticking where every second lasted a minute. People walked in long extended strides like giants taking slow steps. George watched the men in blue uniforms who came and went through his house but he didn't know who they were. Most of the time he didn't understand anything they said. Their voices slurred together in a long blur of sound.

And then there was *something* out there in the garage . . . he couldn't . . . grasp. Some strange . . . event had unfolded out there, but George couldn't . . . quite . . .

remember what it was at that moment. He let his mind wander in that direction, but he could only go so far . . . and then a horrible noise exploded in his ears again. The sound turned into a ringing roar that drowned out every other intonation. The crashing blurred into a frightening racket that made it impossible for him to think.

George knew that he needed to see what was out there in the garage, what was lying on the floor, and as if struggling through a moss-filled swamp, he tried to get closer, but the explosion erupted again. Blackness fell over everything and a deafening silence settled around him as if a thick blanket had been wrapped around his entire body and over his head. Then fear suddenly gripped him like a vise, squeezing his life out.

And then the world swirled out of control and George felt like he was falling, and falling, and falling into oblivion. The emptiness drank him in like a catfish swallowing a minnow. Once the hollowness devoured him, George knew his voice was completely gone. He couldn't talk or think. All that was possible in the silence was to stare into the blankness that held him captive.

CHAPTER 11

SEVERAL HOURS PASSED before anyone ran Matt down, but he turned up studying in the university's library. Matt jumped in his small hydro-coupe automobile and drove like a maniac to Arlington Heights.

The traffic was fierce and it took him longer than he antic-ipated. Attempting to avoid the crowded freeways, Matt took several back roads that proved to be even worse. Bewil-dered, frightened, confounded, angry, nothing seemed to be fitting together right and it only increased his bitterness. The only message the student gave him in the library was a handwritten note saying, "Your grandmother's been shot. You need to get home as quickly as you can. She's gone."

Gone.

The word rattled around in Matt's head like a runaway cartoon figure in a video game. *Gone.* The word wounded and stung. His grandmother Maria had always been there. She loved him, cared for him, remembered him on his birthdays. And now she was dismissed with a simple one-syllable word. *Gone.*

Matt beat on the dashboard while he whizzed down the narrow side roads. He had always loved Maria and never questioned the fact that she loved him. How could anyone have shot and killed his grandmother? She was the most wonderful person in the world.

Cars shot past him like little meteors, flashing through a dark sky. Overhead the moon had an extremely strange cast, giving it a crimson glow in a totally black sky. Matt didn't want to think about why the night had taken on such a macabre look. He tried to concentrate on driving, but he kept thinking about his grandmother and the good times they had shared back before George and Jeff were born. He remembered that Mary had only been a small child when they went to see Maria in Peoria.

"Why, here's my little bundle of joy," Maria said and

picked up little Matt. She had tickled him under the chin. "Have you come to Grandmother's for a big turkey dinner?"

"It's Thanksgiving!" eight-year-old Matt said. "Yes and I'm hungry."

"Well, it is indeed." Maria carried him into the kitchen. "Unfortunately, we don't start the feast until this evening." Maria sat him down on the edge of the cabinet top. "But I think we need to make sure that the desserts are ready." She stuck a fork in one of the pies sitting a couple of feet from Matt, and cut off a fat piece filled with cherries. "Would you like a small bite?"

"Oh, yes!" Little Matt grinned ear to ear.

"Open your mouth wide." Maria put the pie into his mouth. "Now how does that taste?"

Matt chewed for a moment. "Oh, Grammy! That was wonderful."

"Good!" Maria winked at him. "I would have had to throw the whole pie out if you didn't like it."

"Really?"

"Of course!"

Matt remembered how Maria always made him feel special, exceptional, the king of the house. Of course, she wouldn't have thrown the pie out, but Matt didn't know it when he was eight years old. She made Matt think everything he said was law.

He abruptly laughed at himself. Maybe the back roads journey home was worth the extra distance because he had more time to remember the incidents that meant so much to him as a child and that seemed to comfort him.

Maria didn't let him get away with much and neither

did his parents. Matt was raised with more discipline than most of his friends. Maria's hand was unseen, but evident in how his parents reared Matthew. He didn't like the raps on the knuckles, but the extra attention made a difference at school. He was soon known as an outstanding student and that made it possible for him to enter an exceptional university like Northwestern. Probably the added attention was one of the reasons he stayed with mathematics as his major at the university.

And now Maria was *gone*.

Tears rolled down Matt's cheeks. The idea that Maria had disappeared was gut wrenching and intolerable. The pitch-black interior of his car sealed him off from the rest of the world. No one could see him now. Matt sobbed while the car raced through the night.

He resisted being known as a sensitive person, but in truth, Matt was extremely sensitive. Maria never quite understood that side of his personality, but she respected the fact that little things could make tears swell up in his eyes. A slight, someone's personal pain, recognizing when people were lonely, issues that were small to someone else, all this affected him deeply.

And Matt's heart was touched when Grandfather Peck, Maria's husband, died. Matt was barely nine years old when Albert died of a heat attack. Matthew didn't know him nearly as well as he knew his grandmother. People tended to call the white-haired old man simply Al, and Matt knew his father respected Albert, even though there was some distance between them.

Matt went down to the funeral home in Peoria with his

father. The house looked huge, towering over him like a medieval haunted house where bats flew in and out of iron-barred windows. The interior of this terrifying Bastille was filled with dark shadows hovering across hallways that looked endlessly long. He and his father went to one of the back rooms where the long, brown box with brass handles lay on a metal gurney.

Matt's face reached only slightly above the edge of the casket, and when he peered over the side, his nose was only inches from his grandfather's ear. He remembered how Al's eyes seemed to be sealed shut with glue. Grandpa Albert's cheeks were puffy, and looked hard like a piece of sagging clay. His face had turned into a lifeless mannequin. Everything about the scene was grotesque for a little boy. Matthew remembered shrinking back and wanting to run, but his father caught him by the arm.

"It's okay," Graham said. "You don't need to be afraid." He kept a firm hand on Matt's arm. "Grandfather's fine."

But Matt was afraid, and even to this day he dreaded a funeral. He didn't want to see his grandmother stretched out like Albert had been and hoped the family would come up with something better than another trip to one of those awful funeral homes, but they probably wouldn't.

Matt knew it was a problem. Since all of those people disappeared in a flash, almost every church was closed. Of course, the Peck family never attended a church anyway, but they didn't have many alternatives to a service in a place like where they had kept Grandfather Albert. Matt didn't like those alternatives in any way, shape, or form.

Paying no attention to the television/radar speed monitors, he drove through town far too fast. Still, Matt pulled into the outskirts of Arlington Heights later than he wished. His grandmother's death scrambled and changed everything in the world of the Peck family. Matthew knew big adjustments lay ahead for all of them.

Matt turned off his car and started to walk slowly toward the house. After only a few steps, he broke into a run. He grabbed the front door and burst into the living room.

His mother sat on the couch with her eyes closed, holding George in her lap. He hadn't seen them in at least five weeks and expected some sort of special welcome, but George didn't move. He didn't even blink his eyes. His mother slowly opened her eyes and looked at him remorsefully.

"Mom?" said Matt, quietly.

"Come in Matt," Jackie said. "Sit down."

George still made no movement. He looked disconnected and mute.

Matt walked slowly across the room. "I heard . . ." He stopped. "I heard what happened," he said more definitely.

"Yes. Your grandmother is gone."

The word came back again to Matthew with the same hollow depressing sound he had felt earlier in the day. He couldn't answer.

All he could say was an affirmation. *"Gone."*

Matt sat down across from her and looked at George, who seemed to be gone as well.

CHAPTER 12

THE ROOF GROANED and cracked under the force of a cold wind blowing over it, dead in the middle of the night. An eerie glow from the moon cast long shadows across every bedroom in the Pecks' house. A red reflection bounced off the window. The night was long and difficult. Matthew stayed in his old bedroom across the hall from Mary while Jeff curled up in a pallet at the end of Mary's bed. George slept between his mother and father. No one really fell asleep until well past midnight.

At 7:30 the next morning, Graham's bedside telephone rang. After the second ring, he stuck his arm out from under the blanket and picked up the receiver from the nightstand. "Hello." His voice sounded groggy.

"Graham? Is that you?" the deep, resonant voice asked.

"Frank?"

"Graham, a few moments ago I heard what happened to your mother. Graham, this tragedy breaks my heart."

Graham pushed himself up in the bed. "Frank, I'm sorry to sound so blurry. We didn't get much sleep last night and I'm afraid I'm not up to my usual self."

"Graham, don't give it a thought. I wanted you to know that all of the resources of the city of Chicago are at your family's disposal. I'll tell the police commissioner to pull out the stops on this case. I'm demanding they find the lowlife scum who has done this reprehensible act."

"Thank you, mayor. Our entire family appreciates your concern."

"What can we do for you personally, Graham?"

"I won't be at the office today. I hope that's not a problem."

"Well," the mayor said hesitantly, "we have a hard time making everything work right when you aren't here, but everyone certainly understands. Take as much time as you need."

"Thank you, sir."

"Graham, what about your security system? You know we have your electronic devices hooked up with our central network for ultra-security. I would have expected an alarm to have gone off down here where our police network operates."

"Mom had the garage door open and that would have shut the system down. As best we could tell, the system was turned off in the morning and never flipped back on. We simply weren't operational."

"I see," the mayor said. "One simply can't be too careful."

"How sadly true," Graham said. "The times are tough and dangerous. We're paying the price."

"Yes," Bridges agreed. "Crime is everywhere. Well, remember our best thoughts are with you and call me if I can be of any help. Share my condolences with Jackie."

"I will, Frank." Graham hung up the phone and turned to his wife. Jackie's eyes were open, staring at the ceiling. "That was the mayor, expressing his condolences."

"Yes. I heard."

Graham didn't say anything more for five minutes. He lay quietly with his eyes closed. George stirred next to him. The child felt small and still.

"I think we need to get up." Jackie finally broke the silence. "The rest of the children will be downstairs."

"Yes," Graham eventually said and turned the blanket back, letting his feet drop on the floor. "Last night was terrible. Beyond terrible."

"The sky looked so strange," Jackie said. "Bizarre . . . the red glow. I simply don't know how to describe it."

Graham stood up. "I'm not sure if I can go on today, Jackie."

"We have to." Jackie looked out the window. "We have to," she repeated.

Graham didn't answer, but walked into the bathroom and turned on the shower. The water splattered against the door. Graham leaned against the glass, pressing his head against the pane and listening to the pounding of the water. The shower sounded certain and predictable. If there was anything he needed, it was something certain and predictable.

When Graham came downstairs, Matthew was sitting at the kitchen table with George next to him. George had on his bathrobe and silently stared at the tabletop. He had slipped into the chair at the end of the long table.

"Good morning, boys," Graham said.

"Good morning, Dad," Matt answered.

Graham leaned forward and put his hand on little George's shoulder. "Good morning, son."

George looked up. His eyes weren't as blank as they had been last night, but he still looked disengaged. For a moment he stared at his father as if waiting for the right words to come out by themselves. "Yes," he finally said.

Graham sighed. "Good. Good. Can you talk to me, George?"

George frowned and his eyes teared up. "I . . . I . . . think so."

"Fine." Graham patted him on the hand. "I'm glad to hear it."

"Dad," Matt said. "What are we going to do?"

Graham ran his hand through his hair. "We have to take it one step at a time today, son. We have to be tough."

Mary came in leading Jeff by the hand. She sat down and put Jeff next to her. Mary had on an old sweatshirt and Jeff was still wearing his pajamas. Jackie followed them with her wet hair wrapped in a towel. She looked plain, drawn, and worn.

"Grammy always fixed breakfast," Mary said and sniffed. "Now we have to do it for ourselves."

Nobody said anything.

Finally Matthew asked, "All the churches I know about are empty and closed. How can we have a service for Grammy?"

Graham looked at Jackie. "That's the last problem I've thought about, but Matthew has a point. Apparently most churches are locked up."

Jackie didn't answer. Her eyes looked almost as empty as George's did.

"I mean," Matt muttered, "I don't know . . . after all . . ." He stopped.

"Son, the funeral homes have rooms, auditoriums,"

Graham said. "I'm sure we can work out something with them."

The family sat at the table, staring into space with each person thinking about their own special set of memories. No one said anything for several minutes.

"I never thought about death." Matthew finally broke the silence. "In fact, other than Grandfather Albert's service, I've never even been to a funeral. Of course, I was young then. I didn't even know what to think about someone dying."

Jackie nodded. "My parents died before you children were born. They were killed in a car wreck." She shook her head and covered her eyes. "It was a terrible, terrible experience. I guess we avoided talking about death after the accident." Jackie looked at Matthew. "We never talked about the subject with you children."

"It's been like a topic that didn't exist," Matthew said. "Always unmentioned. I don't know anybody at college who ever brought up the issue. Death simply hasn't been in any of our discussions." He cleared his throat. "But I need to know what it means when someone dies."

Silence settled over the kitchen again.

"George," Graham said, "maybe you would like to go in the other room?"

George looked up slowly. He shook his head.

"You want to stay with us?" Jackie asked.

George nodded very slightly.

"Matthew, I don't know how to respond," Graham said. "No one ever sat down and gave me any input on this subject and maybe I avoided thinking about it." He gestured aimlessly. "I guess that I assumed people's lives just stopped. Ended. You know . . . they were gone."

"Grammy's *gone?*" Matthew protested. *"Only gone?* I can't accept that idea. My precious grandmother can't simply have disappeared like a dinosaur vanishing. I simply can't handle that."

"Matthew, we don't have to decide this issue this morning," Jackie pleaded. "We're trying to keep from going over the edge ourselves, son. It's way too early to think about a philosophical problem."

Matthew shook his head. "I don't buy it! I know we have a lot of problems to deal with and I'm sure you and Dad have to make hard decisions, but I've got to know what's happened to my grandmother. She was good to the core and she loved us. Grammy did everything she could to teach us how to be decent, respectful people. I can't accept the idea that her life stopped like a car running out of gas." He pointed his finger in rapid staccato motions. "I need a better explanation."

Graham nodded. "I understand, Matt. The problem is that I don't have anything better to tell you at this moment. I'm sorry. Our family didn't pay any attention to religious matters. Maybe we should have, but your mother and I simply aren't prepared to answer your questions. That's the best we can say."

Matthew pushed back from the table and scowled.

"Son, your father is not trying to be difficult. He's telling you the truth."

"Okay." Matthew rubbed his chin and crossed his arms over his chest. "I'll accept what you're saying for right now, but I want you to know that I'm not going to let this matter die. I intend to find out what happens when a person's heart quits beating. I'm sure somebody at the university, at the funeral home, someone out there somewhere has some insight and I'm going to find it."

"Sure, Matthew," Graham said. "I want you to find out, but right now I can't say much of anything. I'm drained. That's the best I can do."

Jackie reached over and took George's hand. "The police will probably come back this morning. I know they will want to talk with you, son. Do you think you'll be able to talk to the officers?"

Tears started to roll down George's cheeks. He looked blankly at this mother.

"That's okay, son," Graham insisted. "No one's going to make any of us do more than we can."

"We must all get dressed," Jackie said. "We will have to go to the funeral home first thing today." She looked around the table at each of the forlorn children. "Of course, no one has to go. If you want to stay here, you can."

George slowly lowered his head and looked at the floor. He made a slow shaking motion.

"You don't want to go?" Jackie asked.

"No, he doesn't," Mary said.

George kept looking at the floor, saying nothing.

"Okay," Graham said, "we'll leave the three younger children at home."

Mary looked relieved.

CHAPTER 13

M ATTHEW OPENED THE DOOR for Graham and Jackie to walk into Cassoday's Funeral Home. The foyer was orderly, clean to the point of smelling sterile, and extremely quiet.

"You think it was okay to leave the children at home with Mary?" Jackie asked.

"It's all we could do," Graham answered, "but I know she'll take care of them properly. She'll certainly keep the doors locked and the security alarm on."

"Sure," Matt added. "George and Jeff didn't need to be down here with us; besides, they're too stressed to give her any trouble."

A woman who looked to be in her sixties stepped out of an office at the far end of the foyer. Wearing a dark blue suit, she looked like a person who officiated at funerals. With quick, certain steps she walked toward the family.

"You must be the Pecks." She flashed an ingratiating smile.

"Yes. I'm Graham Peck and this is my wife Jackie and our son Matt."

"Welcome to Cassoday's." The woman extended her hand in a slightly affected way. "I'm Mrs. Hutchinson." She pointed toward her office. "Please come back and sit down. Mr. Cassoday and our Services Counselor will be with you shortly."

Mrs. Hutchinson led the Pecks into a large office situated behind hers. Original oil paints hung on the walls and the furniture looked expensive, but Cassoday's office had the same sterile smell as the foyer.

"I'll close the door while you wait," Mrs. Hutchinson said. Her professional smile never flickered or shifted.

Graham sat down in a large leather-covered chair and picked up a newspaper. "She's about as warm as yesterday's toast." He glanced at the headlines and quickly scanned the side columns. "This isn't a good time to talk about the subject, but the morning paper says that Borden Carson and his Royal Arab Petroleum Company are contemplating hitting the USA with an increase in the cost of oil. Just what I suspected!"

"What do you mean, Dad?"

"I don't trust Carson and his company. They're trying to control the world through the price of oil."

"Yeah, but the Russians have all the oil we can buy," Matt answered. "In one of my economics classes I read about production at the arctic oil terminal in Varandey where one of Russia's biggest oil companies sent 200,000 barrels of crude oil to Houston in one month. Conoco Oil Company has a big production outlet at the Ardalin Oil Fields as well."

"Yes," Graham said. "But Carson's maneuvers are driving the prices up for everyone and who knows what he's trying to work out with the Russians behind closed doors."

"I thought Mayor Bridges was an ally of Carson? At least that's what I picked up at the University."

"Bridges and I disagree on that call, son. The mayor trusts him far more than I do."

Matthew rubbed his chin. "I know this isn't the right time to discuss an issue like international petroleum, but how did Carson get to the position where he controlled so much oil?"

"The problem started several decades ago, Matt. You've probably read about several Middle Eastern wars in Iraq and Iran not long after the turn of the century. Of course, Saudi Arabia got blasted in the backlash of a couple of those nuclear exchanges and their oil fields were seriously disrupted. I've never had anyone tell me exactly where Borden Camber Carson came from, but he started out in business restoring damaged oil wells."

"You know anything about his nationality?" Matthew said.

Graham shook his head. "His background is something of a mystery. I don't know why the press is sitting on the story, but no one seems to have printed any of the inside details yet."

"Interesting," Matt continued, "Carson's position seems to be getting stronger every day."

"Yeah. He had an uncanny ability to unite oil companies and come out on top in each of those mergers. Before long Royal Arab Petroleum had the capacity to buy out other producers. One thing led to another and Carson emerged as the top dog. He knew how to play his cards."

"I guess he did," Matthew said. "Sounds like he's still trying to put his pincers into the Midwest."

"That's my fear," Carson said, "and I think that . . ."

The office door opened and a large heavyset man walked in with a small thin man behind him. The pudgy neck of the first man rolled over his white collar and his puffy cheeks had an unusually bright red tint. "Thank you for coming so promptly, folks." He flashed a smile that slightly resembled Mrs. Hutchinson's grin. "I'm Joseph Cassoday and I'm pleased to assist you. This is our service counselor, Eric Jackson. We won't have your mother ready until this afternoon, but we are moving right along." He dropped down in the large desk chair behind his long mahogany desk and pulled out a price list from the right-hand drawer. "Do you have any questions before we start?"

"I do," Matthew said.

"Certainly!" Cassoday beamed.

"Aren't almost all of the churches closed? I mean, where do people have services?"

"Right here!" Cassoday's voice had an enthusiastic sound. "We can take care of any needs that arise here in our building."

"Oh!" Matthew slumped back in his chair. "I guess I assumed people had funerals in churches. Mr. Jackson handles these issues?"

"Well!" Cassoday kept smiling. "Years and years ago they did use church buildings some, but times have changed. We can get you in and out much faster in our facilities and, if you wish, we have a curtained area you can sit behind where no one will see the family."

"*Not see* the family?" Matthew frowned.

"Often folks appreciate the seclusion, the privacy. Of course, that's entirely up to you and the family."

"Yes," Matthew said thoughtfully. "Mr. Cassoday, I'd

like to ask you a personal question. What happens to people when they die?"

Cassoday's eyes widened in surprise. "Where do they go?" He took a deep breath. "Son, I'm just a funeral director. You'd have to ask a clergyman a question like that. Of course, Mr. Jackson handles the issues of fear or grief."

"I don't know any clergy," Matt said, "and I hear that most of them disappeared when all of those people vanished."

Cassoday pursed his lips and rolled his eyes. "Those matters are far beyond me. Sorry, I can't give you much of an answer to that question. I'd suggest we get back to planning the funeral services."

"I'm available to talk later," Jackson said.

"You know anything about what happens after people die?"

Jackson looked embarrassed, and shook his head.

Jackie looked sternly at Matt. "Mr. Cassoday is here to help us with the planning. Let's stay on that subject, you can set a time to talk to Mr. Jackson if you wish."

Matt raised an eyebrow, but didn't say anything.

Graham smiled at his son and winked. "I'm sure you've had a number of difficult questions to answer since those people vanished, Mr. Cassoday."

Cassoday shook his head. "Please call me Joe. Certainly been a tough problem explaining those disappearances, but I'm afraid I don't have any more insight than anyone else. One day they are here and then, boom! Friends and neighbors disappeared." He leaned across the desk. "Maybe there really are aliens." He lowered his voice. "Abduction by space creatures makes more sense than anything I've heard to date." Cassoday straightened up and took another pad out of the desk. "Well, let's get down to business."

An hour later the Pecks returned home. Once again the family gathered around the kitchen table. Everyone sat down without saying much. Graham quickly outlined what had occurred at the funeral home.

"I don't like the place," Matthew said, pushing back from the table and crossing his arms over his chest. "Gives me the creeps, particularly that counselor character."

"I think you're overreacting to the staff," Jackie answered. "It's a business after all. They were only doing their job and trying to be friendly."

"Maybe so, but I don't like anybody being *friendly* about Grandmother's death." Matthew looked out the window defiantly.

Graham patted his son on the arm. "Cassoday certainly sidestepped your questions, Matt. Frankly, I don't like holding her services in their place either." Graham rubbed his chin thoughtfully. "It's not so cold outside right now. I think Mother would prefer a graveside service."

"Great idea, Dad!" Matt sounded positive for the first time.

"Hmm." Jackie sounded thoughtful. "That might be the right approach."

Mary and the children listened, saying nothing.

"We could have an outdoor service where we share our

thoughts and feelings," Matthew continued. "The atmosphere would be more personal, meaningful."

Jackie nodded. "I like that idea much better than having a fake preacher come in and read some words out of a book."

"What do you mean?" Mary asked. "A *fake preacher?*"

"Your mother's saying that there don't seem to be any professional ministers left. At least, Cassoday at the funeral home didn't seem to know any. They bring in some local person to lead the service. The Cassoday Funeral home still uses some of the Prayer Books and Service Manuals left over from former days, but regularly ordained clergy are apparently rare."

"Gee!" Mary grimaced. "It does sound *weird.*"

"Yes," Graham agreed. "I don't like some functionary who comes in only to mark time. That's not my style. Let's call Cassoday's and tell them we'll take care of the graveside ourselves."

"Sure you don't want to sleep on that decision?" Jackie asked.

"No," Graham said. "Matthew, you feel strongly about this issue, don't you?"

Matt nodded his head resolutely. "Absolutely."

"Jackie, why don't you call that lady? I believe her name was Hutchinson. Tell her about our decision?"

"Okay." Jackie stood up. "At least, we have settled one thing. Graham, you'll have to be in charge of what's said. Not me! You understand?"

Graham took a deep breath. "Heavy decision. Maybe Matthew and I can work out what we actually say and do."

"I'll help you, Dad." Matt grinned. "I know we can do it."

"I think we'll go back in the other room and watch television," Mary said. "This is *your* show."

"*Show* isn't the right word," Matt objected.

"As far as I'm concerned this is some kind of production to say goodbye to Grammy," Mary pushed. "Yes, I'm as brokenhearted as any of you, but I don't like all this religious stuff. No one in my school ever thinks about or talks about religious junk. We consider the subject to be weird. Just leave me out of any religious stuff."

"Mary," her mother said sternly, "that'll be enough of that kind of talk."

"I guess so!" Matthew sounded offended.

"Whatever!" Mary raised an eyebrow and left with the boys following her. Jackie walked toward Graham's home office to use his telephone.

"Thanks, Dad," Matthew said. "I know this won't be easy, but it's sure better than having one of Cassoday's cronies doing the service only to make a few bucks."

Graham shrugged. "Yeah." He ran his hands nervously through his hair. "Son, I'm sorry that I couldn't answer your questions better." He stopped and blinked several times. "But the truth is that your concerns about death touched a place in me that has raised some old questions I need to answer for myself."

"What do you mean?"

Graham pushed back from the table. "Your questions make me wonder the same thing. I want to know where your grandmother went, too."

Matthew looked his father straight in the eye. "Somebody has to know, Dad. There has to be someone who can give us some information we can hang on to."

"Find them, Matt." Graham squeezed his arm. "Find them and tell me what you learn."

CHAPTER 14

SNOW DRIFTED while the cars streamed bumper-to-bumper in a seemingly unending line into the Arlington Heights Public Cemetery. Even a few limousines were interspersed among Fords and Chevrolets that rolled into the cold cemetery. The early November weather had abruptly taken a strange and unpredictable turn, dumping tons of snow across Illinois. The staff from the funeral home kept running up and down the narrow lanes, trying to direct the cars where to park to avoid getting stuck. Few of the mourners actually knew Maria Peck, but as friends of Graham and Jackie or the children, the crowd had come to fulfill their obligations.

"We keep getting these bizarre changes in the weather." Matt turned up the collar on his overcoat. "First there's this weird business with the moon, and then it's hot before we turn into the North Pole."

"Yeah," Graham answered. "Never seen it snow so deep at this time of the year."

"Can you believe the number of people?" Graham asked Jackie.

"Your mother has been in Arlington Heights such a short time I didn't really expect many people." Jackie shook her head. "Astonishing."

"When you're a politician, anything is possible." Mary's cryptic comment carried a cynical twist.

"I'm not a politician," Graham corrected her. "I'm an advisor, an assistant."

"Ha!" Mary laughed. "All depends on your definition of things."

"Stop it!" Jackie demanded. "This is no time for you to get smart, young lady."

Mary arched an eyebrow, but didn't apologize.

During the night, the manicured terrain disappeared beneath a sea of white. Stone markers in solemn, precise rows stood like silent sentinels watching over the large graveyard. Flowers from earlier funeral services had long ago dried and now hung in strange patterns from their wire hangers. Snow covered the arrangements with accents of white, giving a touch of purity to the faded brown plants. The wind picked up, scattering the dried leaves down the narrow paths between the rows of graves.

Graham knew it would be difficult for so many people to hear anything above the moan of the wind. He gave Matt a little hug to lend a touch of warmth.

"Certainly are a lot of people," Matt said.

"Yeah." Graham shook his head.

Peck looked at the gray tent over the gravesite, standing erect like a three-sided fortress against the biting weather. The sides of the canvas were flapping, but it broke the wind. Flying snow bounced off the sides of the tent and drifted in small piles along the ropes securing the pavilion.

Wearing a scarf tied around his neck, Joseph Cassoday hustled up to Graham. "Certainly is a nasty day. Most unexpected." As he huffed and puffed trying to catch his breath, white steam rolled out of Cassoday's mouth. "I expected quite a few people, but nothing like this crowd! We did bring a speaker system. I'll have one of my employees set it up right now."

"Good," Graham said. "Additional sound will help the people near the back."

"We can start as soon as everyone gets parked." Cassoday pointed toward the head of the casket. "I presume that's where you'll stand?"

"Sure." Graham said. "We'll stand at the top of Mother's casket."

Cassoday nodded and hustled back toward his employees still directing traffic. Mayor Frank Bridges got out of a black limousine along with Jake Pemrose, Al Meacham, Bill Marks, and Jack Stratton. They walked in quick, determined strides, pushing near the front of the crowd. The people stepped to one side to let the celebrities through. Bridges waved at Peck with a quick salute, and then turned around to nod to the people standing around him. Wherever there was a crowd, even at a funeral, Bridges was in his element.

"Folks," Joe Cassoday said over the public address system microphone, "if I might have your attention. We'd like to start and I know many of you are cold. Please step forward." He motioned for people to press closer together.

"The Peck family is going to conduct the services today. I believe they are ready to begin." He stepped back and smiled at Graham. "Go ahead."

Graham took Jackie's hand and led the family toward the head of the casket. The tent cut off the blowing wind.

"Thank you for coming," Graham began, noticing the public address system had a ringing, distracting quality. "We certainly appreciate the love and affection you've shown us." Graham clumsily adjusted the tiny microphone even though it really didn't do any good. "Ah-hump." He tapped on the mike a second time. "I'm not sure how to do this service today, but we wanted it to be our personal tribute to my mother. I've asked my wife Jackie to begin by sharing some of the details of Mom's life."

Graham watched his wife walk forward. He had always thought Jackie was beautiful, but today she was particularly striking. Her oblong, angular face surrounded by brilliant brunette hair had the features of a model. Even though Graham knew she was terrified, what he saw was a tall woman, carrying herself elegantly. The black mink coat added another note of dignity to a woman showing an air of poise that belied her apprehension.

Jackie stepped up to the microphone and began reading from a sheet of paper. Her voice cracked a couple of times, but she continued to recite the facts of birth, events, and experiences.

Is this how you do a funeral? Graham thought. *Maybe we should have opened with a prayer, but . . . forget it. Now I know why we once had preachers do this sort of thing. I didn't have any idea what we should have put in . . . Oh, my gosh! Somebody should have come prepared to read something out of the Bible. Oh, no! I missed finding a reading! Of course, we wouldn't have known where to locate anything.*

Jackie added a few personal comments and then stepped back into the family group. Matthew walked up to the microphone.

"Grammy Maria loved us," Matt said forcefully. "She cared about our family and took care of us. Every morning she started the day by fixing breakfast." He paused and sniffed. "And now she's gone."

The word "gone" hit Graham forcefully. Maria had evaporated like summer disappearing in the onset of winter. In a moment anyone of them might simply vanish. Jackie . . . one of the boys . . . Mary . . . himself . . . they could all fade into the thin air like smoke going up the chimney. Sure. It could happen in the snap of a finger. *Gone* in an instant.

No one had caught the shooter yet. The police didn't seem to have any firm leads on where the bum had disappeared to. Whoever he was, the man was *gone* as well.

As his innocent-faced children gave their talks, Graham couldn't help contrast what he saw with what was happening all over America. Moral control on erratic behavior seemed to have gone down the drain. Chicago had no idea how often the police functioned more like an army than cops. The staff at Town Hall feared criminals going wild and shooting up the metroplex. Yeah! The police would completely investigate his mother's death out of nothing more than sheer anxiety that some nut had hit the Peck home as part of a surprise attack on other city personnel. Maybe the killer had actually been after Graham!

Was such a hit really a possibility? Graham didn't really think so. Maria simply happened to be standing at the wrong place at the wrong time. The killer probably only wanted money. He was nothing but another bum trying to scratch out a living by waving a gun in somebody's face. The nation was filled with these small-time crooks who proved particularly dangerous because they were usually too frightened to pull a riskier job. This idiot failed to recognize that virtually nothing frightened Maria Peck.

Mary was the last to speak. She looked sullen and sounded almost insolent. "Funerals are supposed to be religious, but I'm not a spiritual person," she began with a critical sound in her voice, "and I don't have any Bible stuff to say." Mary took a deep breath. "I can only tell you that I loved my grandmother and . . ." Abruptly her defiant tone cracked and Mary started crying. "I—I'm sorry," she sputtered. "I know we all a-a-re s-sad." Mary's voice faded and she abruptly slipped behind Matthew as if trying to disappear from the crowd staring at her. The entire family began crying.

Graham hurried to the mike. "Thank you, family. This time hasn't been easy for any of us, but we wanted to say what was on our hearts. We're going to close this remembrance by opening the casket and letting each of you who wishes to file by and say any final farewells to Maria Peck that you might have." Graham nodded to Cassoday. "We'll start now."

Cassoday walked forward with more dignity that Graham had previously seen in the man. His employee walked with him and Mrs. Hutchinson brought up the rear. They opened the lid to the casket and began making the final arrangements.

Graham turned away and the family moved over to the side of the tent. Cassoday and Hutchinson began to send people by the casket. Some stopped while others avoided the sight, moving on quickly to shake hands with the family. Graham kept his smile fixed in place. The line shuffled past the family until the endless line of faces became a blur.

As they finished shaking hands, the mourners returned to their cars and quickly drove away. Finally only Graham, the family, and a few friends were standing by the grave while Cassoday and his man lowered the casket into the ground.

Slowly the metal rigging mechanically lowered the bronze casket into the earth. Cassoday moved quickly back and forth around the chrome rails with seeming indifference to the job. He directed two of the cemetery employees about what to do next and the men went to work immediately. No one said much, but they moved with a precision born of having done the job a thousand times.

Jackie took George and Jeff's hands and started leading the children back to the funeral home's limousine. Mary walked behind her, staring at the snow-covered ground and not speaking. Matthew lingered near the last guest's car talking to a friend. Only Graham was left by the grave.

The dirt began to tumble into the hole, splattering across the top of the metal casket. Each clot hit with a hallow thud and then broke into a hundred little pieces.

What difference does it make? Graham thought. *Maybe Mom truly is completely gone? Could she have any awareness of this ceremony today?* He shook his head.

Graham started walking away, but stopped and took one last look. All Graham could see was the hole.

CHAPTER 15

THE DAY AFTER Maria Peck's graveside service, a solemn quietness fell over the house. Mary and George went back to their schools and Jeff to his preschool. Matthew returned to Northwestern while Graham and Jackie began gathering up Maria's effects and putting them in boxes.

The move alone to Arlington Heights cleaned out tons of Maria's accumulations from over the years, but her bedroom still contained jewelry pins, broaches, artifacts, remembrances from Graham's father, and old, old clothes. The arduous task of clearing out the accumulation heaped an emotional drag on both Graham and Jackie.

After an hour, Jackie looked at him with a pained expression. "We need to get the job done before the children come home." She looked around at some of the empty drawers. "We don't want them to see us throwing out Maria's possessions."

"Yeah, but it's becoming impossible for me."

Jackie nodded and went back to placing some inexpensive costume jewelry into one of the trash bags.

"Where are we going to take Mother's clothes?" Graham asked.

Jackie scratched her head. "Good question. How about the Salvation Army?"

"They're still open? I heard they vanished about the same time when all those other people disappeared." He reached for the telephone directory. "I'll see if they're interested."

"Good." Jackie opened the closet door. "She kept some nice dresses that I'd think somebody would want." Jackie pushed several of the pieces together. "Your mother had good taste. I would think these might sell in a secondhand store."

Graham kept dialing. "Strange. No one answers at any of the numbers listed in the directory."

"Anymore you can't depend on anything! The world's filled with crazy people." She rubbed her mouth thoughtfully. "Call a nearly-new shop across town and see if they would sell the dresses."

"Look. Find a place and give them everything." Graham's voice started getting louder. "I simply want to get this job done." Graham abruptly walked out of the room.

"Wait!" Jackie reached out to grab his arm, but Graham hurried through the door like he was fleeing a fire. "Hey!" she called after him.

Graham didn't turn around, but kept stomping into the kitchen. He rounded a corner and hit the deacon's table hard. Graham grabbed his shin. The excruciating pain shot up his leg. With a swift blow, he pounded the table and then crumpled into a chair. Tears he'd been pushing back all day exploded. Graham's body shook and he crumpled up with his face in his hands. For several minutes nothing stopped the cascade of grief plunging from Graham's heart.

From out of nowhere the kitchen started to change, to rearrange itself, and for a few seconds he was a little boy back in his mother's kitchen, but the scene quickly faded. He suddenly felt Jackie's hand gently lying on his neck.

"I know this time is very difficult for you," Jackie said.

Graham could only nod.

She put her arms around his shoulders and hugged him. "Don't worry. We'll get through this struggle together. I know it won't be easy, but we will." Jackie sat down next to him. "I think it would be better if you went back to work downtown and let me finish cleaning up in the bedroom. Don't you think so?"

Graham sighed. "I don't know."

"Look, Graham. We've been through a horrendous experience. You've taken care of all of us, but now, it's time for you to get back to a more familiar world, more natural for you. Your office would be good for you. Don't worry, I can finish taking care of your mother's bedroom."

Graham drummed on the tabletop with his fingers. "It's so difficult to throw away Mother's precious possessions. They aren't worth much, but they mattered to her. It's hard to watch."

"Yes, I know."

Graham ran his hands through his hair and wiped his eyes. "I also know Bridges's reelection campaign isn't going so hot right now. Sarah Cates says that the mayor is overplaying his hand in some affluent areas of the city and not paying much attention to the problems of the poor. It hasn't gone well this past week."

"I can see the scene. Bridges has his excessive moments."

Graham wiped his eyes, but didn't speak.

"And that's why I think you need to get back to the office. Whatever is wrong with Bridges, he's better than the opposition. You need to make sure all the pieces in the puzzle are falling into place so he'll get his job back."

Graham shook his head. "It's a hard decision, but I think this is an important time in the reelection office."

Jackie held his hand and looked deeply into Graham's eyes. "Darling, I need to be honest. Your eyes look more troubled than merely tired and stressed. Your mother's death has left all of us depressed. Don't you feel like a dark cloud has descended over your head?"

"No, of course not!" Graham snapped.

"Well! I'd say that answer came way, way too fast. Sounds a little defensive to me."

"Well, aren't you depressed?"

"Of course."

Graham started to speak, but stopped. "I don't know," he mumbled.

"I do know. Here's another reason to get you back to the office; hard work might help lighten your depression."

"Yes, obviously I feel like a truck hit me."

"That's what I mean. You need to be in your office."

"You're probably right."

"One other thing." Jackie kept squeezing his hand. "I believe it would be good for both of us to join some group that would help us get beyond ourselves . . . maybe, a growth group or a grief encounter session."

"Heavens no! Jackie, you know I'm not an honesty freak; I certainly don't need to air any dirty linen, particularly during this political campaign."

"I wasn't thinking about sharing anything negative, but simply being with some good people. They tell me new groups have sprung up since all the churches closed." Jackie brightened. "They're calling these meetings Sunday Encounter Times."

"*Sunday Encounter Times?*" Graham grimaced. "*You're serious?*"

"Sure. Apparently many people are floating around out there that once went to Sunday services at some church every now and then. They find the Encounter Times to be helpful."

"What in the world do they talk about in those places?"

Jackie leaned back in her chair. "Well, I hear they explore timely topics like investing money, taking vacation trips. All kinds of activities."

"Sounds bizarre to me."

"Come on, Graham. We never got into the habit of going to church, but many people did. They met friends."

"That's what a church was about?" Graham winced. "Good times?"

"I don't know." Jackie shrugged. "I never went, but I can see how a good atmosphere might provide a nice place to meet people if you were new in the community."

"Doesn't sound like me and I'm certainly not new around here."

"Graham, you're being obstinate. I understand they have motivational speakers and self-help classes. Maybe something of that order would be good for depression."

"Jackie, I know you're trying to help me." Graham leaned over and gave her a kiss on the cheek. "I appreciate your concern, but I think you ought to attend by yourself and see if these Encounter Times do anything for you. You can bring back a report and then I'll think about it."

"Just be open to a new possibility. Okay? What do you think about that option?"

"I think I need to go back to the office. Getting back in harness would be a far better way to help me start going again."

Jackie went back to cleaning. Graham walked to his closet and started putting on a tie and his suit. He moved with lackluster speed, but eventually got himself together. Thirty minutes later, Graham felt ready to leave the house.

"Jackie!" he called from the front door. "I'm going to the office now."

Jackie came out of the bedroom. "I turned on the television a few minutes ago. I think you ought to look at this before you leave."

"Television?" Graham walked over and flipped on the set. "What are you talking about?"

"Watch."

The gray of the screen faded and an announcer was standing in front of the Museum of Science and Industry Building off Fifty-fifth Street. Flames shot out of the windows and smoke roared up from the roof into the sky.

"As we reported a few minutes ago, a bomb went off in

the basement of the museum while sightseers were packed in the building. You can see that the damage is extensive and many people have been killed."

A black limousine drove up a few feet away from the announcer. Frank Bridges and Jake Pemrose jumped out of the car and rushed toward the burning building.

"Mayor!" the announcer yelled and stuck out his microphone. "Please, can you make a statement."

Bridges stopped and nodded.

"What can you tell us about this explosion, sir?"

"It's too early for me to make any judgments." Bridges spoke briskly. "Of course, we are deeply concerned."

"We have some sources with the fire department saying they believe this is the work of terrorists."

The mayor shrugged. "I will be listening to their discoveries and have a comment as soon as we have the data. The people of Chicago can rest in the fact that their elected leaders are on top of this problem and will communicate with them hopefully by this evening. Thank you." Bridges hurried toward the burning building.

"There you have it," the announcer said. "The mayor will possibly have a full statement on our nightly news. We will continue to follow these developments. Please be calm. There is no reason to panic."

Graham stared at the television set. "That's a bad sign. Looks like they will definitely need me at the office. Maybe it's a terrorist attack and then again, maybe not. Call Sarah Cates and tell her I'm coming down."

Jackie kissed him on the cheek. "Be careful."

Graham nodded. "Sure." He hurried toward the door

and then stopped. "Oh, yes. Turn on the security system as soon as I walk out of the door."

CHAPTER 16

G RAHAM RUSHED into the reelection head-quarters and walked toward his office. Jackie had already called Sarah Cates from their home, saying she should be ready for whatever the mayor would have them do in light of the explosion at the Museum of Science and Industry. Without glancing at anyone in particular, Peck closed the glass door behind him and hurried past the secretaries. People normally straightened up when he walked in, offering warm "hellos"; but this time, no one looked up. It didn't strike him as odd until he walked about twenty feet; only then did he realize that the secretaries looked away as he passed. He slowed his pace, expecting to hear something, anything, but no one seemed to notice.

For a moment, Peck thought he had turned into the invisible man, or become a mist, a vapor, floating down the hall toward a chimney. Graham walked completely through the office without anyone speaking.

"Oh! Hello, Graham," one of Al Meacham's assistants sitting at the end of the room said nervously. "Glad to have you back." The man stood up and immediately walked toward the water cooler. A secretary smiled perfunctorily and then ducked her head.

Graham turned the corner and saw Sarah Cates sitting at her desk typing.

"Graham!" Sarah immediately stood up. "You certainly got here in a hurry."

"Sounds like we've got a problem over on Fifty-fifth Street," Graham said.

"Big!" Sarah's eyes widened. "Terribly big. I got a call moments ago from the mayor and he was extremely pleased you would be here today. He wants you to call him on his personal cell phone immediately."

"I'll make it in my office."

"He changed his phone number a couple of days ago to prevent any media intercepting his calls." Sarah handed Graham a piece of paper. "I wrote the new number down for you."

"Thanks." Graham took the note from Sarah and closed his office door behind him. He punched in the numbers and put the phone to his ear. "Mayor, this is Graham Peck. I'm in the office."

"Good! Excellent!" Bridges shot back. "I'm on my way back to the office. We will have a staff meeting when I get there. Shouldn't be fifteen or twenty minutes from now. We have some urgent problems to discuss."

"I'll be there." The phone clicked off.

For a few moments Graham didn't move, holding the telephone in his hand. The mayor hadn't mentioned Maria's death either. His rapidly spinning world had come to a shrieking halt; he had never felt so lonely as he did in that moment. Obviously, no one in the building wanted to speak to him. Had his mother's death turned him into a pariah? Was there something about him that was different from all of those other uncountable days he had walked through the office just as he did this morning?

He reached over and punched the intercom button. "Mrs. Cates, please come in."

Moments later the door opened and the secretary walked in with a notepad in hand. "You called. What can I do for you this morning?"

"Please sit down."

Sarah Cates kept the warm smile firmly in place. Her eyes looked far less assured and she seemed slightly nervous.

"Sarah," Graham began uncharacteristically, "level with me. What's wrong out there?"

"Out there?" Sarah shrugged.

"Look. I walked in here today and nobody even looked at me. No one has said a word about what happened in my family, and even you seem a little tense."

The smile disappeared from Sarah Cates's face. She didn't answer.

"So, tell me." Graham leaned forward across his desk. "Why am I getting the distant treatment?"

Sarah looked down at the floor for a minute and then took a deep breath. "No one knows what to say, Graham. Death is . . . a . . . well . . . one of those things we simply don't talk about. No one knows how to think about dying and then one of us has a family member killed." Sarah cleared her throat nervously. "They're all good people, but they don't know how to respond *to you*. That's the problem."

"My mother's death has made me *an outcast?*"

"Look, Graham. None of the staff has any negative feelings toward you personally. It's just that they don't want to talk about death." Sarah shifted nervously in her chair. "The truth is that they don't even want to think about dying or disappearing."

Peck slowly leaned back in his chair, staring at his secretary. "This is the way we deal with death these days?"

"Graham, no one knows what's happened to millions of people that disappeared in an instant. We don't want to think about it, remember it, see it, much less talk about it at work."

"I see," Graham said slowly and deliberately. "Death is now the final obscenity. We shouldn't use the word in polite company?" He pushed back from his desk. "Thank you for your honesty." Graham pointed toward the door. "Please call me as soon as the mayor is back here for the staff meeting."

"Certainly." Sarah stood up nervously. "I'll call you at once." She hurried out of the room.

For a few moments Graham stood at his desk, shaking his head. "I can't believe it," he said to himself. "My mother dies and everyone is so frightened that they won't even give me a simple 'Sorry to hear it.'" He sat down slowly and stared at the wall.

CHAPTER 17

TWENTY MINUTES LATER Graham walked briskly into the large conference room in Mayor Bridges's office. "Good morning," he said in a flat voice.

Jake Pemrose had already staked out his usual seat at the table with Jack Stratton sitting across from him. Bill

Marks came in ahead of Graham. The men shook hands, made polite conversation, but no one mentioned Maria Peck's death. Moments later Frank Bridges marched in with Al Meacham. Bridges was wearing Dockers and a pullover sweater. The attack obviously caught him by surprise. The men sat down quickly and silence settled over the room.

"Graham, I appreciate your being here this afternoon," Bridges opened the meeting. "We obviously have another crisis staring us in the face. The explosion this morning was a terrorist attack of some order." He shook his head. "A bomb was set off in the basement that destroyed much of the museum and killed several hundred people. Maybe more. I got a call on my way here from the president that slowed me getting to this meeting. He'll send us any assistance that we need."

"You're sure it was a terrorist attack?" Graham inserted the question forcibly.

"You always ask the jackpot question," Bridges answered. "We're not certain. The issue will keep the police and the Homeland Security people busy until it's answered definitively."

"Then, it could have been a local extremist?" Graham leaned back in his chair. "Possibly an accident?"

Bridges pulled nervously at the sweater he was wearing. "I doubt it," he said with cold resoluteness. "But we can't breathe a word on this subject." He looked slowly around the room at each man. "Are we all clear that no one can allow any leaks on Graham's question?"

"Sure, boss!" Al Meacham answered. "You know you can trust us."

"This is a sensitive issue," Bridges said. "We can't afford any slip-ups. My opponent is going to scream that we aren't providing citizens with adequate security. We've got to face this problem before it avalanches." He looked at Graham. "How would you answer that one, Peck?"

Graham blinked a couple of times. "I'd ask him if he thinks that the president of the United States was not guarding the country when the bombs went off on the boat in the Long Beach harbor. Does he think he's smarter than the American military?"

Bridges stared for a second and then broke out in a broad grin. "Graham, you're a genius! Excellent answer."

Murmurs of approval drifted around the room.

"I like that answer!" Bridges said enthusiastically. "I'm certainly glad I *thought of it*."

The men chuckled again.

"Okay!" Bridges walked to his blackboard. "I've been thinking about how we'll respond to the entire problem and I've already talked with the president about this idea." The mayor picked up his laser pen and bounced it up and down in his hand. "I've got a word I want to make sure you all know." He started writing on the blackboard. "Nanotechnology," Bridge said as he wrote. "It's the most radical technology in human history. We're talking man-made machines about the size of 100 nanometers or about 100 billionths of a meter. That's a device one thousand times smaller than the diameter of a human hair."

"A human hair?" Jake Pemrose sat up in his chair. "*Man-made?*"

"You've got it!" the mayor answered. "These tiny machines are, in effect, miniaturized computers that can literally crawl through arteries. Nanomachines are able to lighten or darken your skin. These creations can literally be painted on your arm and no one would ever know it's there!"

"Are you talking science fiction?" Bill Marks asked skeptically.

"No," Bridges answered. "The government has been secretly spending billions of dollars a years to perfect these gadgets. They've got a few nanomachines working now that could transfer garbage dumps into energy. The president tells me they've got nanomachines that can be coated on your house to generate electricity. How does that hit you?" Bridges smiled broadly.

"Where you going with this?" Graham asked cautiously.

"Citizens want security," Bridges answered. "They are terrified—they want to know what the city is doing to fight these attackers. It doesn't make any difference if they're local or international. They want to know that we are providing adequate coverage. Now we've got it."

"How?" Peck pushed.

"We can coat an easily accessible part of their bodies . . . say their foreheads . . . with a solution that carries nanodevices; they will tell us if that person is security approved. We can cover the entire population of the metroplex with invisible security. What do you think of that idea?"

"Are you serious?" Pemrose asked. "I mean is this another political gimmick to keep people happy for a while?"

"No!" Bridges snapped. "I'm talking about a way we can actually create a quick system to tell who is acceptable to our police officers and who isn't. We would be able to identify a terrorist immediately."

"Remarkable," Jack Stratton said. "And it only takes someone painting these nanomachines on a forehead?"

"They'll never wash off," Bridge insisted. "Once the device is on the skin we can find anyone by simply punching in their social security numbers on a computer and they'll come up like a flashing light."

"How would we come at this politically?" Pemrose asked. "That's a sensitive issue for this current campaign." He lit a cigar. "People might be cautious about such an unusual idea."

"Cautious?" Bridges grinned. "I'll tell you exactly how we'd turn fear into our ally." He started pacing back and forth. "We'll let our worthy opponent make his attack, scaring people to death. Then, we'll be ready to hit him right between the eyes. We'll come back with our promise of providing total care for every citizen. All people have to do is come to a nanotechnology center and have an invisible dot painted on their foreheads. In a second, they will be protected for life. Mayor Frank Bridges has provided them with an immediate answer."

"Brilliant!" Meacham said. "We give our opponent the rope he needs to hang himself. Then, we go riding off into the sunset with him swinging from a tree."

"And who would you vote for under those circumstances, boys?" Bridges asked confidently.

"Are these nanomachines available right now?" Graham asked.

"There's still a few problems they are ironing out, but

the president tells me he can provide us with the security devices in around two weeks," Bridges said. "He's thinking about using them all over the country anyway. In a very short time we could cover this city. Other than the time it takes to stand in line, people would have this nanomachine put on their heads with the touch of a cotton swab. Bingo! It's done."

"How much time will it take before our opponent hits this fear theme?" Stratton asked.

"I'd give him twenty-four hours," Bridges said cynically. "Let him scream and holler for a couple of days. That's about all it will take to get this show started."

"Sounds right to me." Pemrose tapped his cigar into an ashtray. "During the next two or three days we'll be secretly getting our operation set up to spring on the public." He pounded his fist into the palm of his hand. "We've already talked about adding more surveillance cameras. I say, let's do it!"

The men nodded their approval, but Graham sat quietly pondering what he was hearing. The idea might be political dynamite and it frightened him. This nanotechnology business was a door into a dream world that could turn into a nightmare. They were playing with the possibilities of technological disaster.

"I appreciate your affirmation, gentlemen." Bridges smiled broadly, but he kept watching Graham, obviously noticing his reluctance. "I'll be talking further with the president this afternoon. Let's see where this takes us. Remember! For the time being, everything is confidential."

Pemrose and Meacham got up and hurried toward the

door. Marks and Stratton followed them; only Graham stayed seated. Bridges erased what he had scribbled on the board, but kept looking over his shoulder. Graham knew he was watching him.

"You seem to have some reservations?" Bridges turned around from the board.

"Frank, are we moving a little fast here?"

"What do you mean, Graham?"

Graham smiled at the typical Bridges retort. "We could be opening a can of mechanical worms that'll chew our heads off."

"Explain." Bridges kept smiling.

"What about the security aspect of these nanotechnology machines, Frank? After these devices are in place, wouldn't everyone be under the constant surveillance of the government? I mean . . . couldn't the police instantly grab anyone who comes up on the computer as a suspect for anything under the sun?"

"Well, Graham, I'm not even remotely considering putting people at risk. My idea is to isolate the terrorist."

"I understand. However, in terms of surveillance the result is actually the same. People would no longer have privacy."

"Have you talked with anyone about this?" Bridges asked.

"No, of course not. I just heard you present the idea a few moments ago."

"Let's not spread this concern, Graham. It could create the wrong response."

"I understand and I'm not trying to wave any red flags.

I'm simply asking you a question. Wouldn't this make people easy targets for the government?"

"I'll think about it," Bridges said slowly, "but right now our concern is to keep people from getting killed. That's our big problem. Security!"

"Security today—arrest tomorrow?"

Bridges smiled. "That's a little dark, isn't it?"

"My question is whether it's a possibility or not."

"I think we need to put that problem on the back burner, Graham. Let's keep it between us." Bridges winked. "Okay?" He waved and headed for the door.

"Whatever you say, sir." Graham slowly stood up. "Sure. We can talk about it later." He watched Bridges disappear.

Graham started back down the hall, watching people nod and smile to each other, but saying nothing to him. The silence bothered him, but he kept thinking about the mayor. He didn't like the possible involvement with Borden Carson and the Royal Arab Petroleum Company, but he was far more terrified about the nanomachines. They could be walking into a dark, dark tunnel.

CHAPTER 18

MATTHEW PECK slowly closed the door to his dormitory room and started the long walk down the dim corridor. Over the decades thousands of outstanding students had lived in the hallowed halls, lending an atmosphere of studiousness and honor to being there, but today none of the accoutrements of accomplishment touched Matthew. His grandmother's death had shaken him to the core, killing his usual desire for one of the campus pubs. Rather than his normal brisk step, Matthew slowly dragged himself through the dormitory.

"Hey man, sorry to hear about the tragedy in your family." A student stepped out of his room.

"Yeah." Matt nodded to the young man who lived several rooms down from him. He still didn't know the guy's name. "Thanks." He kept walking.

"Everyone's talking about the ... ah ... shooting," the student said over his shoulder. "What a bummer."

"Yeah." Matt walked faster.

The last thing he wanted was to be the topic of local conversation, the poster child for home violence. He didn't want notoriety and being the subject of everyone's rambling speculations was at the bottom of his "to do" list. Ducking out the dorm's side door, he hurried across the parking lot, hoping to avoid anyone who might have heard the tragic story.

Ten minutes later Matt walked into the library and found a table by the wall next to the stained glass windows and out of the flow of students entering and leaving the library. Slinking down in his chair, Matt pulled out his economics textbook and thumbed through the pages. For the next hour, he studied persistently without looking up.

"Hi, Matt."

Matthew looked over his shoulder. To his surprise a girl was standing behind him.

"Oh, hello!"

Jennifer Andrews sat down next to him and laid her books on the table. "I heard about the terrible shooting," she said sympathetically. "I was so sorry."

"Thank you," Matt said. He had known Jennifer since high school. Although they hadn't spent any time together, she had always been a warm, friendly face. "I appreciate your kind words."

"I don't really live that far from your house, you know. Well, maybe you don't know. Actually, my parents' home is probably about a mile away from Crown Point. My folks moved to that end of town to try and get away from the mob moving out of downtown Chicago. Looks like we didn't move far enough."

"The bums are everywhere. Since the economy got so tight, there are far too many people roaming the streets. I guess my grandmother just didn't see this thug coming."

"How tragic," Jennifer said. "I know this has been an extremely painful time for you." She smiled with warmth and understanding. "I understand."

Matt thought it strange that he had never really paid any attention to this attractive young woman with the dancing blue eyes. He vaguely remembered her as being uninteresting a couple of years ago, but that had obviously changed. Jennifer had turned into an alluring young woman.

"Dealing with someone's death is so, so hard," Jennifer continued. "You have all of my sympathy."

"Th-thank you," Matt mumbled.

"I mean it. My grandmother died of a heart attack a year ago. We didn't see her that often, but she was such a warm, caring person and I deeply felt her loss."

"My grandmother lived with us."

"Oh, that makes everything much more difficult." Jennifer took a deep breath. "Well, if I can be of any help please let me know." She smiled. "I mean it."

"Jennifer, I don't want to be presumptuous . . ."

"You won't be."

"Did you ever think about what happens to a person when they die?"

Jennifer blinked several times. "Sure. It's a scary thought."

"I don't even know how to imagine what's happened to my grandmother. Where's she gone? What's become of her? I can't believe she disappeared into nothingness without a trace."

"I understand," Jennifer said. "After all of those people disappeared six months ago, it really terrified me. No one had any insight or knowledge about where they had gone. Yeah, I thought about it a lot."

"And?" Matt motioned with his hand for her to say more.

"And I started looking for anyone who could tell me something. My folks finally told me to buzz off, but then I stumbled across a group right here on campus. No one has helped me as much as these students."

"Students? What would they know?"

Jennifer grinned. "More, much more than you would expect. They have really helped. And there's a few adults that add tremendous insight."

"Rather unusual for kids to have anything to tell you."

"Well, these kids really are good! They have opened my

eyes to concepts that I didn't know existed. Death was one of them. I think they could help you."

Matt rubbed his chin thoughtfully. "I must have missed the notices of their meetings. Usually they're posted on the dormitory bulletin boards somewhere."

"Oh, these people's names would never appear in public." Jennifer leaned forward and spoke more softly. "They don't publish the meeting places. They are more of an underground group."

"Really!" Matthew grinned. "Now that really gets my attention. What are they called?"

"*New Seekers*." Jennifer lowered her voice.

"Awesome. I like the sound of the name."

"You'd like the people. They are an honest, inquiring group. They talk about questions like living and dying, what's going on in the world today. You'd be surprised at the book they study. New Seekers has helped answer some of my most important questions."

"Jennifer, you've got my attention. In fact, you're the first person who's given me any direction. The people at the funeral home just blew me off. Everybody else seems to see me as a curiosity."

"I think you'd be surprised by what this group has to say about the meaning of existence. You can really talk to them."

"When do they meet?"

"As a matter of fact, the group will be meeting this evening. I'd be glad to have you come with me."

"Excellent! I'd love to sit in on a discussion. When do they meet?"

"You got a car?"

Matt nodded his head. "You bet."

Jennifer started scribbling on a piece of paper. "Here's my address where you can pick me up. Make it about seven o'clock."

"Where does this group meet?"

Jennifer smiled. "Actually, it's a secret. They only want people to know about them who share their concerns. To avoid publicity they move the meeting place around and never announce it except just before the meeting. Sometimes having people know about you can get you in more trouble than you want."

"Hey, this really is formidable."

Jennifer squeezed his hand. "Sorry about your grandmother." She picked up her books and started toward the door. "I'll see you tonight."

Matthew waved and watched Jennifer disappear down the aisle. The door at the other end of the library closed behind her, but he kept looking. "Can't believe it! What a lead!" he said softly to himself.

CHAPTER 19

I WAS JUST ABOUT to call you," Dr. Paul Gillette said. "Yes, I'll come right down." He hung up his private phone and rushed out of his seldom-used back door without informing his secretary.

Gillette uncharacteristically hurried down the hall of

the University of Illinois Microfabrication Research Laboratories toward the unit used by Dr. Allan Newton and his associates. The gray-haired scientist maintained a worried look on his face. He pushed open the door to the lab and trotted in.

Newton looked up from the asphalt-covered table where he was working with David Hughes, an assistant. "Ah! Dr. Gillette, thank you for coming so quickly."

"Paul, I need to talk with you alone." Gillette gave Newton's assistant a "get lost" look.

"Sure." Hughes turned and walked some distance away.

"When you called, I had barely gotten off the phone with the president of the United States," Gillette blurted out. "Your calls nearly coincided. He wasn't a happy man."

Dr. Newton took a deep breath. "Really?"

"They want to use your nanorobots for immediate security purposes." Paul Gillette ran his hands nervously across his face. "He left a veiled hint that if we couldn't produce, our failure would dramatically affect our funding. What am I going to tell him?"

"David!" Dr. Newton called to his assistant. "Please bring me the device we've been working on."

"Certainly." The young man hurried back with a coin-shaped device in his hand. "Here it is." He carefully placed the object in Newton's hand. Two buttons in the center dominated the top.

"What do you have?" Dr. Gillette asked.

"Let me show you." Newton motioned for Gillette to follow him. "I've been thinking about the security problem we discussed since the other day. I'm not sure that I've got the answer, but it might make a difference. We assembled this mechanism only a short while ago." He pointed toward the electron microscope. "Watch."

"What is it?" Gillette's eyes narrowed.

"I have been following the work of researchers in Munich as well as in California. These scientists have been working on memory storage and computer processing using quantum dots. Of course nanocomputing or nanoelectronics is about microscopic refining of materials that could be as small as a handful of atoms."

Dr. Gillette nodded. "I am familiar with the research, but I know little of the actual application."

"Remember what happened when the nanorobots attacked the amoebas I released into their realm?"

Gillette shuddered. "That's what worries me!"

"Take a look at the microscope." Newton adjusted the lens. "You can see some of my gizmos zooming around in the solution."

Gillette looked in the lens. "Yes, I can see them quite vividly. Ugly-looking devices."

"They could be as lethal as they appear. Their hooks might devastate whatever they attack."

"You're suggesting these robots could be used for security purposes?" Gillette looked up.

"They could be."

Gillette's frown deepened. "You're not offering me much reassurance."

"Here's the new twist. Working with a quantum computer, we have experimented with sending photons aimed at nanorobots to make them more predictable. As you know quantum mechanics differs radically from the laws of classical physics."

Gillette nodded. "Certainly."

Newton put the small circular device in Gillette's hands. "I believe this device could equip us to force a troublesome nanorobot to cease functioning. We could render these robots inactive."

Paul Gillette bounced the small metallic circular piece in his hand. "This thing is about two inches in diameter," he said. "Will it work?"

"Look through the microscope."

Gillette leaned forward and stared. "I can see them moving."

"Push the green button," Newton said.

Gillette slowly pressed the green button. "Good gracious! It knocked those nanorobots right out of the picture. Excellent!" He straightened up. "Good work."

"You'll notice there is a red button."

Gillette looked again. "Hmm."

"Paul, as we both know, quantum mechanics still has problems we are struggling to understand. When a photon is released, its behavior is strange to our way of thinking. Such a particle can travel down two paths simultaneously. We are still working to understand how this might affect these nanorobots."

"I'm not following you." Gillette again looked at the red button. "What do you mean?"

"If these gizmos found an opening in the skin or chose to bore one, they could still turn deadly." Newton pointed at the red button. "I believe that application switch will cause these robots to turn in the opposite direction and attack the human entity."

Paul Gillette blinked several times. "I'm still not sure where this is going."

"David, do you have that experiment with a sample of meat still set up?"

"Yes sir," the young man called across the lab. "Whenever you're ready, Dr. Newton."

"We'll use his microscope." Newton beckoned for Gillette to follow him. "You'll see the nanorobots moving on the surface of a slice of beef."

Gillette looked in the lens again. "Yes," he said slowly. "They seem to be gliding across the surface of the meat."

"At this point, the nanorobots are in a form of suspended animation on the exterior of the meat. Watch what happens when I press the red button."

Gillette looked carefully for several seconds. "They've all disappeared!"

"No," Newton said. "They instantly bored into the meat. The robots are tearing a hole through the beef."

"Exactly what does this experiment mean for guaranteeing the security of using nanotechnology to protect the public?" Gillette asked sternly. "Remember our funding is on the line!"

"We can offer greater security, but we have also discovered how to turn this invention into a deadly device that would kill anyone. All it takes is a push of the button."

CHAPTER 20

NIGHT HAD FALLEN over the city when Matthew picked up Jennifer and sped off to a warehouse near the edge of Evanston. "Never been to this end of town," Jennifer said. "We meet in some strange locations." Matthew answered with a perfunctory, "Yeah," and stared straight ahead.

Matthew didn't say much. He didn't feel like talking and let the conversation drop. Jennifer apparently didn't mind. She seemed to be as comfortable with the silence as with talking. They pushed on through the night as if they'd traveled this new route a thousand times.

Matt kept glancing out of the corner of his eye. Strange he'd never really noticed Jennifer before. Her blue eyes sparkled and she had beautiful blonde hair. Occasionally she noticed his glance and smiled, making him feel more relaxed. Jennifer had the ability to put anyone at ease. Matt couldn't help being attracted to her.

After winding through an industrial park, the street turned into a narrow road ending in front of a large three-story brick warehouse. Most of the windows were opaque, giving the ancient building an unsettling appearance framed against the black sky. Overhead the moon cast a crimson glow over the scene. A few cars were parked along the train tracks, but the rest of the parking lot was empty. They pulled up and got out.

Appearances said the old warehouse had been used for many things before becoming a storage building for crates of merchandise waiting for shipment around the country. Boxes were stacked up on top of each other and many of the windows had steel bars over black painted panes. It nearly took a guide to lead someone through the maze of crates filling the dusty building, but Jennifer walked quickly almost as if she knew where she was going. With few lights on, the entire structure glowed eerily. Walking through the antiquated warehouse felt more like a journey through a haunted house.

Matt silently followed Jennifer until they turned the final corner behind a pile of refrigerator crates and found a group of fifteen students standing around talking to each other. Matthew didn't know any of them.

"Hey, Jen! Great to see you." A tall student gave her a hug. "I see you brought a friend." The young man kept smiling.

"Meet Matt Peck," Jennifer said.

"Welcome to New Seekers!" The student extended his hand, but didn't give a name. "I believe you're a freshman. Am I right?"

"Yes," Matt said. "You're right on target."

"Good. Hope you enjoy the group." He waved and backed away, turning to another person to talk.

"Thank you," Matt said awkwardly.

The young man disappeared and other students came by. Anonymity seemed to be the order of the day. With equal enthusiasm, they shook Matt's hand, but no one gave their name. While they talked casually, their questions probed Matt's motivation for attending. Eventually the chatter of the group settled down and the students sat down on top of some of the smaller boxes. Matthew looked around the large warehouse and studied the people who comprised the New Seekers group. Most of the group looked like average college students. A few older people sat on the outer edge and listened as the meeting unfolded. One woman with black hair had an unusually striking appearance. Matt didn't remember ever seeing anyone quite like her. The rest didn't look any different from a group meeting in Matt's dormitory.

"We don't announce our location," the leader began, "because of security reasons. We don't want anyone to run into trouble for being part of our discussions. We're not strange, but some people might consider our topics to be on the exotic side."

Members of the group laughed.

"You have to get to know us before we share our names. After all, you might not like us."

The kids laughed again. Everyone seemed to be quite at home.

"We obviously live in troubled times and that requires more care on our part," the leader continued. "If this is your first visit, welcome."

Matt's eyes narrowed and he squinted at the speaker. Sure. The times were perilous. His grandmother had been shot to death, but what were these students doing that required seclusion and secrecy? The hiddenness of the group both attracted and repelled him.

"As we all know, tonight we will again study the only

book in existence that explains what has been occurring lately, and clarifies what happened to all the people who vanished. Obviously, we are living in strange times and need something more than a little touch of sociology or a dab of psychology. We believe this singular, ancient work has the explanations to all the questions anyone is seeking to answer. This evening is another opportunity to find the hope you need in today's world."

What was this guy talking about? A secret book explaining the disappearance of all those people? What a bizarre idea! What in the world had he gotten into! A local nut group?

CHAPTER 21

HASSAN JAWHAR RASHID glared across the top of the massive desk at the general in front of him. His eyes searched the man's face for even a hint of inconsistency.

Afternoon was falling in Ribat Qila. Located at the tip of the triangle where Iran, Afghanistan, and Pakistan met, the foreboding desert town made a perfect place for Rashid to meet a Russian official secretly.

"As I said," General Vladimir Trudoff repeated himself forcefully, "the Russian Army has been oriented according *to your instructions*. The attack will proceed as *you have directed*."

Rashid's eyes did not move from scrutinizing the general. He probed like a mind reader. "You are sure the missiles are aimed exactly as I have directed?"

"I have overseen the calculations myself," General Trudoff insisted. "The matter is settled. You have nothing to worry about."

Rashid abruptly smiled. "Nothing to worry about?" He leaned back in his large leather chair. "Here we are in a desert surrounded by crimson and black mountains where a few rupees buy anything and you see no problems? My dear general, the world is filled with matters that we should all have apprehensions about. Your role is to minimize my concerns." Rashid drummed on the top of his desk. "No one in the entire Russian military knows anything about our relationship and plans?"

"Of course not," Trudoff snapped. "Our relationship remains between us. Matters will unfold precisely according to your wishes," the general insisted.

"Okay!" Hassan Rashid shot forward in his chair. "I will expect the conflict to unfold *exactly* as you have described. The matter is concluded." Rashid stood and pointed toward the door.

"Ah . . . there is . . . one more matter," Trudoff said hesitatingly. "The business of payment for these services has not been discussed."

"I believe I agreed to pay you two million dollars."

"Exactly." Trudoff bowed his head ceremonially.

Rashid tapped the corner on his desk. The door opened and a man dressed in a black suit hurried in. "Yes, sire!"

"I want you to prepare a check for our friend for five hundred thousand dollars and give it to him immediately."

"Yes, sire." The man marched out as fast as he came in.

Trudoff's mouth dropped. "But you said . . ."

"I will pay you the remaining one and one-half million when the conflict is satisfactorily completed." Rashid glanced at his watch. "If you are correct, that business should only take a matter of hours."

"But, but . . ."

"Please return when the assaults are completed and the personal check will be here for you." Rashid smiled and again gestured toward the door. "You retirement is still secure, Vladimir."

General Trudoff pursed his lips and bit his cheeks. His eyes became hard. "I will be here shortly," he growled, turned on his heels, and marched out of the room.

Rashid chuckled. "The fool shouldn't have underestimated me. We shall see if the Russians do as they were told. If not, Trudoff will be paid in lead, not gold."

Rashid walked to the other side of his office and opened the door to his immense conference room. Sitting around the long table, six military leaders from assorted countries appeared poised to act on whatever Rashid commanded. They snapped to attention when Rashid walked into the room.

"Everything is in place, gentlemen," Rashid said in Farsi. "Prepare for the assault."

The military leaders instantly rushed out of the room.

CHAPTER 22

THE SKY WAS STILL DARK, but a few rays of sunlight crossed the Pecks' bedroom. The explosion in the museum threw everyone into confusion and Graham came home depleted. Attacks and turmoil kept the city careening like billiard balls after a fast, hard break; Bridges's reelection campaign seemed to have picked up some steam and he was staying ahead in the race. At the least, Graham's return to the reelection office had helped, but last night he had gone to bed exhausted.

The weather had radically changed again. The moon was still red, but an Indian summer burst across Chicago, melting the snow and sending the thermometers soaring up the scale. Citizens were left in disarray. The air felt more like early spring.

"You're all right?" Jackie asked quietly.

"Oh! Yes. It's a little early for you, isn't it?"

"I didn't sleep well." Jackie rolled over to face Graham. "You were restless last night."

"Nothing seems to be easy these days," Graham said.

"You're telling me! How did people treat you at the office?"

"No one mentioned a thing about Mother's death. Even Sarah Cates kept her head down."

"*Really?*" Jackie sat up in bed. "You've got to be kidding."

"I don't want to talk about it."

"Graham, good heavens! I've never heard anything so absurd."

Graham got out of bed and picked up the clicker to turn on the television. "Let's get the news."

"I'd rather talk about what happened at your office."

Graham didn't answer. With a quick snap, he turned the television on and instantly the screen filled with the face of an announcer reporting the morning news.

"We switch now to our correspondents in Chechnya for the latest information on the continuing rebellion inside Russia," the announcer said. "At this time we're receiving reports that the Russian Army has abruptly swept to the south in an attempt to bring revolting Muslim areas back into line. The war apparently has spread as far as Turkistan."

"What is this?" Graham pointed at the television set. "Do you know what he is talking about?"

Jackie shook her head. The television scene shifted and another face appeared.

"This is Ivan Cransky in Grozny. Many of our details are sketchy, but we are receiving reports that the Russian Army made a surprise move last night and released a missile attack that apparently has started a major military conflict now spreading rapidly across the entire region. Many sources are concerned that the war could spill over as far south as Israel and into adjacent Arab countries."

"I can't believe what I'm hearing!" Graham sat down on the side of the bed. "Overnight the world has erupted into another war!"

"I had no idea such an attack was even imminent." Jackie put her hand to her mouth. "No idea *whatsoever!*"

The television station switched back to the original local reporter.

"And now from the United Nations, we have a report from Siegfrid Swiggum, our special reporter on assignment from Norway. What are you hearing, Siegfrid?"

Standing in front of the United Nations building, the face of a tall, thin man appeared drawn and worried. "Reports coming into the United Nations are still incomplete, but we are receiving confirmation that a major world conflict has been sparked by the harsh actions of the Russians. Apparently, Middle Eastern countries were already poised to protect their oil holdings and responded with unexpected swiftness when the Russian attack began. We are not clear yet as to the amount of damage that has been done, but it is considerable. However, the Security Council is currently in a secret meeting. The stakes are high and the war could certainly deepen."

Graham stared at the television. "That's all we need! In the middle of every other crisis going on in this city and country, suddenly a war is explodes in our faces." He shook his head and swore. "No telling what this conflict will do to the supply of petroleum and hydrogen products we must have in our country! Mayor Bridges won't have any quick and easy answers for this problem."

"The world is absolutely coming unglued, Graham. People have gone nuts, irrational, berserk!" Jackie crawled out of her side of the bed. "You must get to your office as quickly as you can. We need to know all the details of what is going on."

Graham nodded his head. "Yes. No question about it."

Without touching the transistorized music system, Graham hit the shower and was out in a minute. He wasted no time in dressing. Grabbing a bagel, he rushed out of the back door to catch the next Metro Express downtown. He didn't have any idea what he could do, but he would be available to help if anything consequential was needed. The train had only just pulled out of the station when his cellular phone started buzzing.

"Graham Peck here."

"Graham, it's me, the mayor. Where are you?"

"I'm on my way to the office. On the Metro."

"Excellent. I guess you know about the war?"

"Got the first report of the war on our television this morning."

"It's bad, Graham. I talked to the White House a few minutes ago and they believe this crisis has already spun out of control."

"You're certain?"

"They're telling me that Russian nuclear missiles have already been fired at Middle Eastern countries."

Graham took a deep breath. "Oh, man. It doesn't get much worse than that! Do you know what's happening in Israel?"

The mayor paused. "This is totally confidential." He lowered his voice. "The Israelis may be firing missiles back at the Russians."

"Why?"

"Looks like the Russians missed a target near the Lebanon border and hit the Israeli town of Sharm-el-Sheik. The Jews panicked and shot back."

"This is terrible, simply terrible."

"Graham, I'll be in the office when you get here. We're looking at another red suspenders day down here. I need to be on television. We've got to come up with an immediate press release proclaiming our stand behind the president of our country. Jake Pemrose is already working on some ideas."

"At the speed the Metro travels I'll be there in short order. I'll try to come up with something new for you to consider."

"Good. See you when you get here." The mayor's phone clicked off.

CHAPTER 23

G RAHAM STUCK the small phone back in his pocket. Only then did he notice people on the Metro Express staring at him. They had been listening to one side of his conversation with the mayor almost as if he were a television correspondent. He looked away and started scribbling on his electronic notepad. The Metro Express roared on through the city, passing the intermediate stops while Graham wrote; he avoided eye contact with the people around him. Obviously the war had left everyone unsettled and nervous.

At the reelection office, Graham walked past the empty desks and silent computers. At least no one was there to ignore him. Sarah Cates wasn't in yet so he didn't pause at her desk, but walked straight to his office. Graham flipped on the light switch and sat down at his desk to organize his thoughts for a moment. He drummed on the desk with a pen tip and tried to clear his mind. Only then did he become aware that he was also running away from something with breakneck speed.

Maria Peck's picture still sat on the corner of his desk. The world might be blowing apart with the crazies bombing each other with nuclear missiles, but inside him another war was raging. He still felt as deeply depressed as he had when he stood beside his mother's casket at the cemetery. Her loss gnawed at him; Graham felt empty and lost like a child wandering through a blizzard. For a moment his mind felt frozen and his stomach as empty as the Sahara desert. He sank down in his desk chair.

"Got to get a grip on myself," Graham said to himself. But he couldn't get his mother off of his mind. He wondered where she was and what she was doing. Was she still alive out there somewhere in the beyond or had she simply become nothing more than a dried, hard substance beneath the dirt and forever gone? Was she no different than last summer's grass?

Graham flipped on his computer and waited for the screen to come into focus. He had never realized how much he loved his mother until after she was gone, but Maria had been stability, permanence, the guarantee of continuity. Maybe all of those assurances of security and endurance were now gone as well.

He put his hands on the keys of his computer keyboard and took a long deep breath, but nothing came to mind. Only the thoughts of Maria crowded out other reflection from his memory. The telephone rang.

"Peck here."

"Graham, I'm here in my office now. How's your work going?"

"Mr. Mayor, I'm trying to get a few ideas down on my computer screen. Of course, I know nothing about this war."

"None of us do, Graham. However, I'm getting ready to talk with Borden Carson in Istanbul. I hope to get some insight."

"Turkey?" Graham felt his voice rise in pitch. *"Carson?* You've got to be kidding."

"No. Let me see what I can find out and then I'll give you some ideas. I appreciate your being here at this early hour." Bridges hung up.

Graham slowly put the phone back in the cradle. Borden Camber Carson on the phone with Bridges like they were old buddies? Graham frowned. He didn't like the sound of the entire scenario.

For the next hour Peck hammered away at his keyboard, trying to find some fresh new angle. In the end, he decided that the most important position the mayor's office could take was an unqualified support of the president of the United States. He pared his thoughts down and came out with a terse two-page statement essentially saying that the mayor stood with the president regardless of the circumstances.

The office door opened and Sarah Cates walked in. "I'm sorry to bother you. They told me you're working on an important statement for the mayor."

"Thank you," Graham said without looking up. "I'm nearly done."

"Mr. Pemrose just came by and said you have a meeting in the conference room in five minutes. I thought I should remind you."

"Thank you." Graham kept staring at the paper. "I'll be there."

Sarah Cates retreated toward the door, but paused. "I hope you're feeling better today."

Graham looked up, surprised by the kind concern he heard in her voice. "Well, yes. Thank you. I appreciate your interest."

"Just know that I care." Sarah smiled and shut the door behind her.

Graham stared. She was the only person in the office who had said anything personal or caring to him since the funeral. He wasn't sure what it meant, but thoughtful words helped. Picking up the sheets of paper, he hurried out of the room.

CHAPTER 24

WALKING into the conference room, Graham nodded to Jake Pemrose and Jack Stratton. Both men sat at the mahogany table with sheets of paper in front of them and sullen scowls across their faces.

"Tough morning?" Graham said.

"You bet," Jake snapped.

Graham nodded and sat down. "You boys have obviously heard about the war."

No one answered, but they nodded their heads.

"Good morning, men." Frank Bridges hustled into the room. "I appreciate the fact you are here so early. We are looking at a major international crisis this morning."

Graham studied the mayor. The casual look was gone and Bridges appeared much more formal. It was a red suspenders day, which meant the mayor needed to look powerful. Trouble and television time were ahead.

"I received a report from Washington during the night," Bridges continued. "They aren't sure why this war has blown out of all normal proportions, but a baptism of fire is storming through the western edge of Kazakhstan and down into Turkmenistan as well as into Georgia and into Iran." Bridges took a deep breath. "They know Iraq got hit."

"That's a significant amount of territory," Graham said.

The mayor nodded. "And that's not all. Syria has gotten into this fray and a missile hit Israel. Of course, the Jews have fired back at everybody in sight."

Pemrose rubbed his chin. "Sounds nasty."

"Yes," Bridges answered. "That's the reading I got from Borden Carson. He is better informed than the White House."

Graham cringed, not grasping why even the mention of Carson's name affected him so much, but it deeply troubled him that this one individual appeared to be in control of such a large amount of sensitive data. The pieces of the puzzle weren't fitting together right.

"Carson told me that the exchange has become nuclear. It looks like the Russians are really taking it on the chin, but the Muslims have gotten hit hard enough that the radioactive fallout is going to be with them forever."

"What are we saying here?" Graham cut in. "You're talking about vast areas being turned into a nuclear wasteland?"

"I am afraid so," Bridges continued. "Apparently, Damascus got bombed and portions of southern Russia experienced nuclear damage with some areas probably becoming uninhabitable. We're fortunate they didn't shoot at us."

Pemrose cursed. "This whole thing is nuts! I don't understand how these incursions could have gotten so far out of hand."

"Frankly, I don't either," the mayor agreed. "It's like the sudden appearance of a tornado, but wars don't usually happen on this basis. There were signs and signals, but none of them showed up on our radar screens."

"What do we do next?" Graham pushed.

"We've got to make an intelligent statement backing our president," Bridges said, "and of course, we need to put ourselves in a good political position. We don't want our opponent making any hay out of this problem."

"I have a declaration." Pemrose pushed his papers toward the mayor.

"I have one too," Graham said.

"Excellent!" Bridges gathered up the pages. "Let's see what we can put together."

For the next hour the men exchanged ideas. Thoughts were fired back and forth and debated. Slowly a general statement emerged. Bridges seemed to be pleased and the project moved forward. Just as the second hour of discussion began, the door suddenly burst open and Sarah Cates rushed in.

"I'm sorry and I know it's inappropriate for me to burst in like this, but I must talk to Mr. Peck!"

The mayor blinked several times. "Something's happened?"

"I apologize for bringing bad news, but I just received a call from Mrs. Peck and . . . oh, my goodness . . . you must call her at once."

Graham shot up out of his chair. "What's happened?"

"There's been a gunfight of some sort at the Computer Control Center near your children's school," Sarah said. "Apparently, the gunmen, the terrorists, whoever, escaped and have holed up in your kids' school."

Graham grabbed the table. "You're sure?"

"The police are already out there," Sarah continued, "but apparently the school has turned into a battleground."

Graham slumped. "No! Not my kids!"

"Graham!" Bridges rushed to his side. "We'll get a police car to take us there. I'm going with you. We've got to get the city's best officers into this operation." He turned to Pemrose. "Jake, get us a police car downstairs immediately. We're on our way." He stopped. "Oh, yes! Alert our newspaper contacts."

Graham felt like his heart would burst out of his body. His head seemed to spin and he suddenly became light-headed. "I've got to get to the school," he shouted, trying to catch his breath. "Right now!"

CHAPTER 25

GRAHAM DASHED OUT of the conference room, leaving the mayor trying to catch up with him. "I've got to run," he shouted over his shoulder.

"Your wife has her cell phone with her." Sarah rushed along side Graham. "She'll be waiting for you to call her back."

"I will." Graham headed for the exit. "From the car."

"This way." Bridges pointed toward the elevators. "It'll get you out of here quicker."

The elevator ride down to the street and the dash toward the police car flashed by in a blur. Graham tumbled into the backseat and the siren screamed as the car shot down the street toward the freeway. Graham dialed his cell phone.

"Hello?" Jackie sounded like a child lost in a forest.

"It's Graham! We're in a police car."

"Graham, the police have surrounded the school and it sounds like a war. I'm nearly out of my mind worrying."

"Where are you?"

"About two blocks back of the police line. I heard about the attack from a television bulletin I saw by accident at the beauty shop. Terrorists attacked the Computer Control Center near the school, but the alarm system went off. The

TV announcer said gunfire followed and that's when these men fled toward the school."

"I understand," Graham said.

"What will we do if . . . if . . . anything happens to . . ."

"Stop it, Jackie! Pull yourself together."

"I'm trying, but I keep thinking about your mother."

"Don't! I'm going directly to the school. Don't worry! Some way or the other, I'll get inside."

"Graham, I'm frightened—something terrible could happen to you, too."

"It won't," Graham snapped. "Jackie, be calm."

"Do you realize that both George and Jeff are in there?"

"Yes, Jackie. I'll get them out."

"Do you think you can?"

"Definitely. We're flying down the road way over the speed limit. We'll be there shortly. I've got to hang up, now."

Graham snapped the phone off. He didn't need any more anxiety. His entire nervous system was already on overload. Sinking back into the seat, Graham realized if there was anything in the entire world that he wanted, it was that those two little boys would not be hurt. With Maria's death so close behind them, he couldn't bear the thought of his innocent children falling in a volley of wild gunfire.

By the time the police car reached the outskirts of Arlington Heights, the driver knew exactly which streets to take from his satellite guidance system. He slowed only slightly as the car shot down the main street and made an abrupt turn to the left. Graham could see the police cars surrounding the school. The driver slowed and the mayor turned around.

"Don't worry, Graham. We're going on through this blockade. We'll get as close to the school as we safely can."

Graham nodded. "Step on it."

A policeman near the blockade of patrol cars pointed to a side opening and their police car slipped inside the front line of vehicles and inched closer to the school. Everywhere Graham looked, he saw policemen with guns pointed at the school.

"I'm going in," Graham announced peremptorily. "We're city officials. I have a right to enter the school."

"Graham, it's dangerous inside that building." Bridges shook his head. "We need to leave this matter up to the police."

"I want a Mylar vest and a helmet." Graham's eyes narrowed. "Understand me?"

Bridges grimaced. "I don't know . . . you're talking about a job that policemen wouldn't want."

"I mean it," Graham growled. "Let's get me in there *right now.*"

"Well . . . whatever you say," Frank said slowly. "We've got protection in this car?" he asked the driver. "Anything to keep a man from getting shot?"

"Sure. We've got some equipment, but nothing that guarantees a man won't get shot somewhere."

"The man's saying a bulletproof vest won't save you."

"That's all I need!" Graham ripped his tie off and unbuttoned his shirt. "Let's get the gear on me."

Bridges looked down at the seat for a minute. "Frank . . ." He started to say more but stopped. "Okay, officer. Let's get this man rigged up immediately."

"Whatever you say, sir." The driver nodded and pulled up close to the big entry door into Harding school. "You're the boss."

The one-floor red brick building appeared to have long halls and a gymnasium located behind. An eerie quietness had settled over the building. No heads appeared in any of the windows. Graham huddled beside the car and put on the protection gear.

"Look, Graham. You've got to be careful. Very careful."

"Don't worry, Frank. I know what I'm doing. I was in the military once."

"Just don't get yourself in an impossible bind," the mayor warned.

Graham took off in a hard run. Just as he reached the entrance a burst of gunfire echoed down the hall from somewhere far off in the direction of the gym. Graham dived at the floor and slid across the hallway. He heard the knee to his pants rip and felt a burning sensation on his leg. A quick look revealed only a minor skin burn. For a moment he crouched against the wall, trying to get his bearings. The lights had been turned out and probably all the electricity was off. For as far as he could see, the halls were empty, but he could smell gunpowder in the air. Cries and moans echoed up and down the halls. The sound of the shooting faded away and the foreboding silence returned.

Slowly and carefully, Graham crept up to the first door and peered around the corner. Computers sat on their desks and the children lay on the floor, covering their heads with their hands. They looked smaller than George, but larger than Jeff. Some of the children were crying. His boys

couldn't be in this room. The room was secure, but it just wasn't the right place. He quickly pulled away and rushed down the hall toward the convergence where the hallways made a T. Graham cautiously looked around the corner, but couldn't see anyone. Off in the distance he could hear shouting, but the halls remained empty. The yelling sounded like policemen giving directions to each other.

Crawling on his hands and knees, Graham turned to his right and started down the corridor. As best he could remember, George's room was down this hall. Thirty feet away was the door to a classroom. He slipped up quietly and cautiously peered into the room. Ten feet from the door a teacher lay on the floor, clutching two children next to her body. The rest of the students huddled together on the floor around the room. They looked the right size.

"Is George Peck in here?" Graham asked quietly.

"No," the teacher said. "Are we still under attack?"

"Yes," Graham said. "Everybody stay down."

"George is in the next classroom," the teacher said. "Down the hall."

"Thank you," Graham answered. "Keep everybody away from the windows." He slipped past the door and ran for the next room. Graham was only three feet from the door when the terrifying rattle of machine gun fire exploded through the building. Instantly, he hit the floor and covered his head. The gunfire was so loud it sounded like the battle was just behind him. Handguns answered with quick, sharp blasts. Suddenly an overwhelming boom roared through the building, shaking the windows. The walls quivered and white tile fell from the ceiling. An engulfing cloud of dust

and smoke rolled up the hall. The echo of the bomb rang in Graham's ears and for a moment he could hear nothing but the rumble. Pieces of crumbling plaster tumbled from the wall and bounced off of his helmet. The moaning and crying of the children increased. Rushing to the door, he jerked it open.

"Is George Peck in this room?" he shouted.

"Yes," a boy's small voice answered.

"George? George, is that you?"

"Daddy?"

"Son, I'm here!"

George leaped up off the floor and ran for his father.

"Mr. Peck? Are we okay?" the teacher asked, standing up.

"I don't know," Graham answered. "I'd suggest that you don't move until we know what happened in that explosion. I have to find my other son."

"Dad!" George grabbed Graham around the waist. "I'm so glad you're here." He hugged his father fiercely. "Jeff is in the opposite hallway."

"Okay." Graham grabbed his son's hand firmly. "I'm going the other way. You stay here until the authorities lead you out of the building."

"Yes sir."

Graham looked at the teacher. "You're all right?"

"I think so," she said. "If we can get out of here."

"Don't worry. It'll be all over soon." Graham dashed out of the room.

Running in the direction from where he had come, Graham could see that the explosion filled the hall with ceiling tiles and cracked several of the walls. The smoke was heavier, which meant he had to be getting closer to the fighting. A burst of gunfire filled the air and Graham dived to the floor again. The sound was much louder, which meant he was running into the area where the men were fighting.

Graham took a deep breath. Jeff had to be closer to the explosion. He couldn't even let himself think about the consequences. At the T in the hallway, he pressed forward and kept walking. Settling into a squatting position, he peered into the rooms, and once satisfied Jeff wasn't in any of them, Graham pressed on until he came to another corner.

There hadn't been any shooting during the entire time he ran down the hall. Carefully, he looked around the corner. The hall had disappeared in a cloud of dust, but he could hear men walking behind the dust and smoke. His heart nearly stopped as he realized it could be the attackers. Suddenly he heard the voices of children and the noise of small feet coming toward him. Graham cautiously looked around the corner again.

Out of the cloud of dust a policeman led children toward him and out of the building. Graham stood up and inched around the corner.

"Hey, I'm with the police!" Graham yelled. "Do you need help?"

"Yes," a voice answered. "We're sending a classroom of preschoolers toward you."

Graham stepped into the center of the hallway and suddenly saw Jeff's teacher. Covered with dust, Mrs. McElroy's hair stood out in disarray and covered her eyes. She looked panic-stricken, but was leading her classroom out of the debris. Five children behind her, Jeff was holding a little girl's hand.

"Jeff!" Graham screamed. "Jeff! It's me! Your dad!"

Jeff broke ranks and ran for his father. "Daddy!" he screamed. "Help me!"

Graham dropped to his knee and held his arms out. "Son!"

"Daddy!" Jeff slipped into Graham's arms and hugged him. "Oh, Daddy! I was so afraid."

"It's okay now, son. We're all okay."

A policeman hurried up. "Can you take these kids out of here? We shot the attackers, but we've got to get everybody out of the building."

"Sure," Graham said. "I'll take them out."

"Thanks." The policeman hurried back into the smoky hallway.

"Oh, thank God!" Graham gasped. "I'm so relieved." He hugged Jeff, pulling him as close as possible. "Thank heaven you're all right."

"What's happened to us?" the teacher asked.

"I think we've been struck by an attack of mass insanity, ma'am. People have gone stark raving nuts!" Graham started sliding down the wall toward the floor. "Absolutely crazy." He pulled Jeff even closer and felt tears sliding down the side of his son's dusty cheek. "The world is falling apart."

CHAPTER 26

MARY RETURNED HOME from school late to find George and Jeff sitting around the kitchen table with her parents. The stillness that had settled over their home following Maria's death remained throughout the house. Mary didn't like the insular feeling and always tried to turn on loud music when she came in. One glance at the kitchen table said tonight wouldn't be a good time for the raucous soundtrack of *The Blasters*, her favorite.

"Hey, what gives with the long faces," Mary said, and placed her palm-sized computer on the kitchen cabinet. "Someone d—" She started to say "die," and then stopped.

Graham slowly looked at her in dismay. "You haven't heard?"

"Heard what?" Mary maintained her usual tone of indifference intended to make anyone arguing with her sound stupid. "What you talkin' about?"

Graham grimaced. "Only a teenager could say such a thing."

"Your father is surprised you haven't heard about what occurred at the boys' school today."

Mary looked more carefully at George. That sickly look had returned in his eyes that had appeared after Grandmother's shooting. He seemed detached and distant. "What happened?"

"There was a terrorist attack on the school. Men got

killed and a bomb went off," her father said. "Got it? Your brothers were square in the middle of the battle!"

Mary's negativity, her sense of detachment vanished. Giving her parents a bad time for the sake of irritating them melted and she was drawn back into the vortex of the family world.

"Oh my gosh!" Mary blinked several times. "Good heavens! I went out for basketball practice after school and didn't talk to anyone. No, I didn't know."

"Your father rushed into the building and helped bring the children out," Jackie said. "He helped save people's lives."

"No, I didn't," Graham said quietly. "You're overstating the facts."

"My goodness!" Mary looked at her father. "We're proud of you, Dad."

"Sit down, Mary," Graham said. "We need to talk."

"Sure."

Graham stared out the window. "Our lives have been turned inside out and upside down by attacks, assaults, and wars. Not only was the school hit today, but there's a war raging tonight."

"I heard about the war," Mary interjected defensively. "We heard some reports over the school's television system."

"Whatever you heard is an understatement," Graham said. "The war is serious and people are getting killed at this moment. We live out here in the suburbs where we should be protected and look at what's happened to us!"

"I can't even walk out in the backyard anymore without being terrified," Jackie said.

"I don't know what we are going to do," Graham answered, "but we've got to find some alternative."

No one answered and the quietness became ominous. Mary kept glancing back and forth between her brothers and her parents.

"We need help." Graham finally broke the silence.

Jackie nodded her head. "Graham, we haven't tried any of the Sunday Encounter Times group. Maybe if we . . ."

"P-p-lease, Mother!" Mary protested. "If there's one thing we don't need to get into, it's a bunch of religious nonsense. That's the last thing I want to hear about!"

"Why?" Graham asked. "You got a better idea?"

"Look," Mary said confidently, "we studied about religion at school. It's nothing but a superstitious way to hide from your problems. I don't want any goofy spiritual talk around the supper table. None of this 'talking to the sky' and calling it god or heavenly father of some kind."

"Then, what's your alternative?" Graham pressed.

Mary didn't like her father pushing her in a direction she didn't want to go. "You didn't like going on Sunday either," she retorted. "How come you've gotten so big on the idea?"

Graham glowered. "You've certainly got on the smart-mouth side of this argument, Mary. We're not trying to argue with you. We are looking for an alternative."

Mary slumped back in her chair and decided she would be better off if she kept her mouth shut. She wasn't going to get anywhere by fighting with them. Mary looked down at the floor.

Jackie reached out and touched Graham's hand. "What about the Encounter groups?"

Graham shook his head. "I'd go if I thought they would do me any good. The trouble is I don't need a fun and frolic time on Sunday morning. I need someone to tell me the hard truth about why the entire world has gone crazy. Where have all of those people gone? Why has the moon turned blood red and the weather gone berserk? Why did a creep kill my mother and how come the Russians, the Muslims, and the Jews are all blowing each other up? I don't want to know how the skiing is this weekend."

Silence fell over the room again. Jeff slipped off of his chair and snuggled next to his mother. She put her arm around him.

"I was afraid." Jeff's voice sounded high and tense. "The bad men came, started shooting and I thought they would kill me."

Jackie patted his head. "I know, son. We all understand."

"We could hear them screaming and shouting," George added. "And then all the lights went out. Our teacher started to go outside in the hall, but she rushed back in and told us to get on the floor. She looked very afraid." His voice trailed off into silence.

"We all could have been killed," Graham said. "We're just lucky you boys weren't in the other end of the building."

Mary didn't know how to respond to what she was hearing. On one hand, it was all true, and yet she didn't want to get religious about what had happened. None of them had been killed so leave it at that.

"Something has gone terribly wrong with the world," Jackie concluded. "Never in my life have I seen anything like what we are living with today."

Graham nodded his head. "That's what is so hard to put together. Values, morals, hopes, dreams—they've all gone down the drain like yesterday's cold coffee. Everywhere I look people are in a panic. There simply has to be something more to hang on to than what we've experienced."

"Get tough!" Mary said almost before she meant to speak. "We've got to buckle down. Watch out for ourselves. What else?"

"Getting tough won't do it, Mary," Graham said. "It's like an evil force has been loosed on the world and I can tell you that I'm not up to doing battle with some monster that I can't even see."

"Don't talk like that," Mary protested. "I don't want to hear nonsense about all of this good and bad stuff. Before long you'll be telling me to look for angels and to watch out for devils. Stop it!" she said with more force than she intended.

"I am your father!" Graham snapped. "Don't talk to me with that disrespectful sound in your voice."

Mary crossed her arms over her chest and glared sullenly back at her father.

"You're right, Graham," Jackie said. "It seems like what is happening to the world is different from anything I've ever known in my life. I don't know what it means to talk about evil, but I get the feeling whatever that thing is, it is has crawled under our house and made its home in the basement."

The telephone rang. Graham picked up his remote control and punched the "on" button. "Hello."

"Dad!" Matthew's voice boomed out from the remote speakers attached to the kitchen walls.

"Yes, son. The entire family is sitting here around the table."

"Listen, everyone! I've just discovered the most amazing things that I've ever heard."

Mary looked at her father. Graham's face had switched from the dismal look of despair to a flash of optimism. What in the world was Matthew talking about? She frowned.

"I went to a meeting with a girl I knew from high school," Jeff said. "They call themselves the New Seekers. Wow! You won't believe what I learned. I need to talk to the whole family as soon as possible."

Her father leaned forward. "Sure, Matt. We want to hear the complete story. When can you come home?"

"I've got to study for a test tonight. Is tomorrow night too soon?"

Graham laughed. "Not for us! We've been sitting here hoping that someone could tell us something to clarify what is going on out there. You heard about what happened at Harding School today?"

"No. I've been in the library all afternoon and haven't seen a television."

"You'll see the news on television tonight. I'll tell you my version tomorrow."

"How about seven o'clock tomorrow?" Matt asked.

"We'll be looking forward to seeing you," Graham said. "Take care." He clicked the phone off.

"Let's hope Matthew has learned something important

for us," Graham said. "Maybe this is the spark we've been looking for."

Mary didn't like Matthew's ideas in general and this one didn't sound encouraging to her. Maybe she could find some way to avoid being at home tomorrow night. She had twenty-four hours to work it out and would start immediately looking for the exit door.

CHAPTER 27

S INCE MARIA'S DEMISE and the school attack, the possibility of unexpected death had almost become an obsession with the Peck family. Graham awoke at three o'clock in the morning after a painful dream about the entire family getting lost in an endless maze inside an impenetrable forest. The Metro train ride to work seemed little more than an extension of that nightmare. For two hours Graham struggled to write various alternatives for the mayor to present when he spoke at a rally in the ghetto off the Eisenhower Expressway.

A loud buzz jarred him. Graham glanced at his computer. The red light on top of the small QuickCam video camera flashed that someone wanted a face-to-face conversation. He switched on the Web camera attached to his computer and the screen sprang to the life. Mayor Frank Bridges's face loomed across the monitor.

"Graham," Bridges began in his usual demanding tone of voice. "We've got to do something more about these attacks. Your home situation was frighteningly close to what many other people have experienced recently."

"Really," Graham said with a twist of irony in his answer.

"Graham, I think we need to guard ourselves at all times. Who knows when any of us could get hit next."

"You are just now getting concerned?"

"Come on, Graham. I went with you to the school yesterday, remember? You know I've been worrying about these problems ever since those terrorists' bombs exploded out there in Long Beach harbor."

"Okay." Graham nodded. "What's up today?"

"I want you to spend some time thinking about new ideas for how we can improve security around our city. Then, you and I are going to have a private conference in my inner office."

For a moment Graham didn't answer. Seldom had the mayor held any conferences in his inner sanctum. He always used the big conference room. This issue was different.

"Something new happened?" Graham asked.

"No! I think the time has come to up the ante. That's all."

"Okay, Frank. I'll be there in about thirty minutes."

Graham flipped the camera switch off and the screen faded. He had spent too much time with the mayor, and developed a sixth sense about whatever Bridges said. Something was going on and Bridges wasn't being completely candid with him.

Graham hit the buzzer on his intercom. "Sarah, please bring in my file on the Chicago city security systems."

"Yes sir. I'll be right there."

Graham booted up his word processing software and got ready to type, but he couldn't. An image of Maria's face emerged from out of nowhere and he could only sit there, blankly envisioning his late mother.

"Here you are!" Sarah Cates came bounding through the door. "I think everything is here." She handed him a computer disk. "Hope this helps." She smiled affectionately.

"Thank you." Graham avoided eye contact. He quickly stuck the disk in his computer.

"Let me know if you need anything else. I'll be here in a flash."

"Thank you," Graham repeated himself without looking up.

The file opened, laying out various kinds of apparatuses they had used in the past. Graham studied the electronic devices, surveillance equipment, and computer systems for identifying people. Thirty minutes passed quickly. Switching off the computer, Graham got up and walked quickly down the back stairs.

"Good morning," Graham said to the secretary. "The mayor is expecting me."

"Certainly." The young woman pushed a button on her desk and a wall panel slid open, revealing a hallway. "Please go on in."

Graham walked through the opening and the wooden panel closed behind him. The hallway was covered with a thick-pile carpet and elk horn lamps hung on the walls, but the corridor still left him with a sense of foreboding, as if he were only a piece in some gigantic human puzzle. Ten feet ahead he walked through a large ornate wooden door.

"Graham!" the mayor said. "Come in, my boy! Sit down."

Graham had not been in the mayor's private office many times. The large room had only a few objects, but the office had such lavish furnishings that it felt daunting. Mahogany wallboards from the floor to the ceiling concealed the bookcases behind them. One punch on the computer panel on Bridges's desk could open up any section of the room.

"I want us to talk about an upgrade of security, a more comprehensive surveillance of our population," Bridges began. "We discussed turning to gadgets the size of one hundred nanometers to be painted on people's forehead. Brilliant suggestion! I think the moment is overdue to crack down."

"Yes sir." Graham sat down on the severely stylized chair in front of Bridges's desk. "Why are we talking privately?"

"I trust you completely, Graham. I can't say that about many people today. Our considerations can only be known within an extremely limited circle. Only my secretary knows you are here."

"I see," Graham said slowly. "I appreciate your trust."

Bridges leaned forward over his desk with his hands folded in front of him. He had on his red suspenders and a tie designed to give him an aura of power. "You will be only one of three people who know about the electronic surveillance system I'm about to put in place." He lowered his voice.

"Yes sir."

"Most Americans are unaware that a couple of decades ago the government linked these systems together in an interconnection that would assist in the technical prerequisites for a national surveillance system. Not long after the turn of the century, the government came up with a program called Total Information Awareness that was operated through the Defense Advanced Research Projects Agency, or DARPA, as the government called it."

"I know very little about these matters, sir."

"And you're an insider, Graham. Most Americans *know nothing.*"

"Of course."

"During the last couple of decades, the government made remarkable progress in tying all of the information in these computerized systems together." Bridges leaned back in his chair. "The first generation of computer work was the simple transfer of information across the Internet where electronic mail was sent around this country. The second generation increased the outreach around the world via the World Wide Web."

"I am aware of these systems."

"But you never heard of the transformation of the Total Information Awareness project into the Complete Alert Complex?"

Graham shook his head. "No!"

"This latest system now connects computers to computers with the capacity to access data and sort out what is being communicated. Buzzwords are fed into the system and any transgressions in those areas will come up in government computer systems."

"Really?" Graham frowned. "Doesn't that tread on the invasion of privacy issues?"

The mayor shrugged. "We've been manipulating data for years, son. Is this really any different?"

"I think so, sir. We're talking about the ability to enter people's homes through their private computers."

"And that's the beauty of the system, Graham. We now have the ability to check on what *anyone* is doing! It's like we have planted the big eye in everyone's living room."

Graham leaned back in his chair. "I take it this is basically secret material?"

Bridges nodded. "You bet!"

"How'd you learn about this system?"

Bridges beamed. "Graham, back at the turn of the century a software designer who also was the inventor of the Lotus Notes operation came up with an approach that allowed analysts within government agencies instantly to share intelligence data. Since then, computer experts have figured out how to break into isolated databases and access that information. They do it all the time."

"Frank, where did you find out all of this information?"

"That's one of the reasons I invited you in here today, Graham. I want you to know what is going on." He punched a button on the panel inlaid in his desk. Instantly an entire wall panel shot up into the ceiling. A strange, black electronic unit sat about two feet off the floor behind the panel. It looked like the bottom of an old electric blender. "Take a look."

Graham stared. "What am I seeing?"

"It's a holographic transmitter." Bridges flipped a switch and a brilliant beam of light shot up out of the base. "You're looking at a new means of communicating around the world on an extremely personal basis. We are about to talk to a person whom you will see in three dimensions via laser transmission." He stood up and slipped his coat on. "Now, doesn't that beat anything you've ever seen?"

Graham stared in amazement. "You actually talk over this thing?"

"Not only do I talk, we converse with a light image like friends sitting in a restaurant, even though the individual is on the other side of the world."

Graham blinked several times. "Exactly what are you saying?"

Bridges winked. "You need to know precisely what my plans are." He glanced at his watch. "We've got an important holographic call coming through in a few minutes, but I want you to know all of this is part of a much larger plan. Graham, I'm looking far beyond this coming reelection. I have larger plans that could possibly involve the presidency of the United States."

Graham's mouth dropped. *The presidency!*

"Many things have been happening behind the scenes, Graham. I have been contacted by some powerful people who want to push me forward. It's one of the reasons that we need to win the reelection campaign by a big margin."

Graham realized his earlier suspicions were being confirmed. Bridges hadn't leveled with anyone; the man was working from another agenda altogether.

"And that's the reason we are having a conference today over the holographic transmitter. You'll note that the man's image will be in color. It's time for you to meet the key player in this big game." Bridges began pushing buttons. "You will find this man to exceed your wildest expectations of what a human being can be." The light shooting upward from the base of the machine became more intense. "I want you to meet Borden Camber Carson."

"*Carson?*" Graham blinked several times. "You're kidding?"

"I realize no one knows what he looks like, but you're being given entry into quite a limited circle."

The laser beam abruptly took on a greenish glow and a shape began to appear in the center of the light. A man emerged wearing a coat with a high formal collar that buttoned around his neck like a Nehru jacket, sitting in a large leather chair. His hair appeared to be black and his skin dark or deeply tanned. He was handsome and had black eyes with piercing intensity. His nationality was not obvious, but he had a Mediterranean appearance that could have allowed him to pass for an Italian, a Palestinian, a Jew, or someone of Arab descent. He smiled and instantly radiated a magnetism that drew everyone toward him.

"Dr. Carson." Frank Bridges stood and bowed at the waist. "We are so pleased you could spend this time with us."

"Frank," the deep resonant voice almost had a lyrical musical quality, "it is my highest pleasure to see you once again. I trust all is going well in Chicago?"

"We are having our problems, sir, but we are enduring."

"You are a man of strength and cleverness, Frank," Carson said. "I know you will be able to handle these trying times."

"Thank you, sir." Bridges bowed his head slightly. "I want you to meet one of my closest colleagues, Mr. Graham Peck."

"Welcome, Graham." Borden Carson extended his hand. "I welcome you to the fraternity of the Inner Circle."

Graham felt himself being strangely drawn to this figure appearing out of the dancing light. "Thank you," he answered awkwardly.

"Mr. Peck, these are most difficult times for all of us," Carson continued. "Those of us chosen to direct the affairs of nations must be armed with prudence as we seek to thwart the intrusion of diabolical opponents. I am sure you will appreciate the complexity of these difficult matters."

"Of course," Graham answered.

"Sir," the mayor said. "Can you update us on what is happening with this terrible war that has broken out with the Russians fighting Muslim terrorists. We understand it has spilled over into Israel."

Carson nodded knowingly. "You are correct. For some time now we have been concerned that our oil fields could be vulnerable to attack. For that reason, we encouraged many of the countries in this area to arm for a possible missile response. The Russians simply overstepped themselves and got reckless."

"And the Israelis responded?" Bridges asked.

Carson smiled with a cynical grin. "We always knew that the Jews had nuclear weapons hidden in underground silos. Like a flyswatter killing gnats, they hit the land of Gog with an awesome blow. Only animals of prey would dare venture into those radioactive parts of Russia where their missiles exploded. The Russians will never again be a problem."

Graham stared. This man was talking like he ran the world with the same skill Graham drove a car. His answers carried such authority it suggested he might have data that the United States had not yet gathered.

"Frank," Carson continued, "we are currently centralizing databases across the world, fusing them together into a single system which will allow us to ferret out all suspicious and potentially dangerous intrusions happening anywhere in the world. We will be able to monitor a surveillance system with almost universal control. I believe the time has come to move the entire metroplex of Chicago into this unit and give you access not only to your city, but the region." Carson maintained his engaging smile. "Soon you will be responsible for the entire United States."

Frank Bridges swallowed hard. "Thank you, sir, for such a vote of confidence."

"I always expect you to perform with such skill," Carson said. "You gentlemen should also be aware that we are installing a new system here in Istanbul with a type of 'black box' surveillance that will alert us to all suspicious patterns of behavior in your country. We will soon be positioned not only to control but to anticipate hostile behavior, stopping terrorists from striking with nuclear weapons. Apocalyptic fanatics traveling around with secret means of mass destruction could be an ultimate danger to the entire globe. Prepare yourself, gentlemen. The clock is speeding up!"

Borden Camber Carson smiled and nodded his head. The image faded and he was gone.

Graham stared at the blank stream of light, almost unable to grasp what he had just seen. While he was apprehensive about Carson in the past, in a few moments the man overwhelmed him with a serene sense of confidence, control, and intelligence.

"I know you are surprised," the mayor said, "but I have been consulting with Borden Carson for some time. He has chosen Istanbul to be the center of his oversight of the petroleum industry stretching across the world. However, Carson is changing his focus and moving very quickly in the political world. He has told me confidentially that within a few weeks, he will be propelled to the office of prime minister of Turkey. As you know the Turks have chosen a secular road and no longer have a religious agenda although they were formerly of a Muslim orientation. He will be in a highly influential position to affect the entire region as well as the world."

Graham shook his head. "I don't understand what any of this has to do with American politics?"

"Politics can no longer be regional, Graham. We can't limit ourselves to one hemisphere. For example, we must work out an oil agreement to save our city vast amounts of money. Carson has assured me we will be given special consideration on pricing. That's how the world works today."

Graham took a deep breath. "We're not just trying to get you elected in Chicago," he concluded. "You're talking about a worldwide power base with all of us under the surveillance of an all-encompassing eye."

Bridges smiled confidently. "Graham, play your cards right and I'll take you to the top, and that peak is getting up there above Mount Everest!"

CHAPTER 28

FLYING DOWN the Metro's tracks, Graham wondered if Carson had already given Bridges instructions on implanting electronic surveillance devices that the mayor hadn't told Graham about. He certainly had plans to wire the whole city. Maybe the "big eye" was already operating in his train car. Obviously, Bridges had elaborate political plans he hadn't told anyone about, and the idea disturbed Graham.

But Borden Camber Carson left him confounded. The man's eyes danced with intense intelligence. As he reflected on their surprise holographic conversation, he realized that the man pierced Graham's external defenses like a CT scan peering into a human heart. His voice had been eminently enticing, but his eyes had a penetrating quality of mystery as if they concealed a vast amount of clandestine information. Carson had read him like an open book. He didn't know whether to fear such a man or to be delighted to be considered as one of his Inner Circle. More than confounded, Graham felt apprehensive.

Graham shut the front door of their home behind him. Graham had tried to put everything he had heard in perspective, but the pieces didn't fit. The faces of Maria,

George, and Jeff had been pushed aside by Borden Camber Carson's beaming countenance.

Through the years Carson had been sequestered and managed to keep his face out of the newspapers and off the television. While he nearly became a household word, virtually no one actually knew what the man looked like. Graham was surprised by both his handsomeness and charm. The man's face seemed almost timeless; that made it difficult to guess his age. He could be in his late thirties, his forties, maybe even older, but it was a guess.

He walked into the kitchen. "Son!"

"Hi, Dad." Matthew turned and opened his arms.

Graham hugged his son. "Hey, we're glad you're home." He glanced around the room. Jeff was playing on the floor. George sat in a chair by himself next to the corner. "You boys okay?"

Jeff said, "Yes." George nodded his head, but looked disconnected. Graham hugged George. The boy didn't speak.

"It's going to be okay," Graham said. George didn't smile.

"Don't worry."

George nodded his head, but still didn't say anything.

Jackie walked in. "We're glad you're home safely. I told Matt about yesterday. I hope today was successful?"

"Very strange," Graham said thoughtfully. "Maybe we can talk about it later. Where's Mary?"

Jackie shook her head. "She called from the school and said she had a late drama practice tonight. She wants us to go ahead without her."

"I told her to be here." Graham's voice turned hard. "In fact, I demanded we all hear what Matthew has learned."

"I reminded her, but Mary said she had no alternative," Jackie said. "I pushed her, but she hung up on me."

"I don't like it." Graham rubbed his chin. "I guess we don't have any choice, but she'll answer to me when she gets home."

The family sat down together and quickly ate supper. Matthew talked about his classes and Jeff asked some questions. George said nothing. Jackie kept glancing at her eight-year-old son and Graham could see the worried look on her face. The battle at the school had spun George back to where he had been after his grandmother's death. It would take love and a considerable amount of talking to bring him back around.

"I'm sorry Mary won't be here," Matthew finally said. "You know she's not too crazy about my ideas anyway."

"The issue is that I gave her no alternative," Graham said, "but I know you've got to get back to the university tonight, so I guess we don't have any choice but to start without her."

"I'm sorry," Matthew said. "What I have discovered is the most important information that I've ever heard in my life. She needs to hear these facts."

Graham stood up. "Whether she likes it or not, we're going to record everything that's said tonight and she can listen to it later. We're not going to be outfoxed by little Miss Mary." He hit the switches on a box next to the telephone. "I'm taking the phone off the hook. We'll record through it and that will also keep us from being interrupted by any calls."

Matthew pulled up a small briefcase and set it on the table. "I have something in here to show you," he began. "I think I have stumbled across the most amazing information in the world." He reached inside the briefcase. "This may be hard for you to accept, but I've found the answers to some of the most difficult questions we have all been facing."

"Son." Graham scooted closer to the table. "What do you have?"

"Will you and Mom please hear me out before you make any final judgments?"

"Sure, Matt." Graham looked at Jackie. "We'll agree."

Matthew pulled out a black leather-covered book. "It's *the Bible.*"

Graham's eyes widened. *"The Bible?"* He looked at Jackie. "What are you talking about, Matthew?"

"As strange as it sounds, I met with a few kids and some adults who have found in this one book answers to what's going on in our world. As I listened to them talk, I found the answers to why the world has gone crazy."

Graham stared at the book. "Sure. I've heard of the Bible. Mother had one she kept somewhere but I've never read it."

"Matt, you don't really mean that this book has explanations for what is happening in our world today?" Jackie shook her head. "It was written ages ago. This doesn't make any sense to me."

"Mom, let me show you something." Matthew started

thumbing through the pages near the back. "Haven't we all wondered why the color of the moon has changed to a reddish glow? We've heard the weathermen scramble for answers, but nothing fits together." He stopped and opened up the Bible. "Listen. 'The full moon became like blood.' See, there it is." He pushed the Bible toward her.

Jackie looked at the words. "My goodness."

Graham frowned. "Matthew, you could have found a quote like that in a book of poetry . . . any book for that matter."

"But it jars you, doesn't it?" Matt picked up the Bible and started thumbing back through the pages. "Let me show you something else. You've wondered what happened to that multitude of people who simply disappeared. Right?"

"Of course," Graham conceded.

Matthew put his finger under a line in the Bible and started reading again. "Listen carefully. 'Then we who are alive, who are left, shall be caught up together with them in the clouds to meet the Lord in the air; and so we shall always be with the Lord.'" He looked up. "That's what happened to all of those people. They were Christians; they were raptured."

"*Raptured!*" George spoke virtually for the first time that evening. "I've never heard of that word before."

"It's how some Christians describe the experience that they anticipated would happen," Matt explained. "At the end of the age, they believed they would be taken out of this world just before a time of wars, strife, and terrible tribulation."

"Stop!" Graham said. "You're telling me that all of those people were simply jettisoned up and out of this world?"

"Dad, that's why the churches are empty." Matt grinned. "It makes perfect sense. These Christian people left and the churches are empty even today."

Graham kept blinking. "It makes sense but . . . I . . . don't . . . know."

"We haven't believed in this sort of thing," Jackie said. "You are talking as if you came in tonight from another world."

"I have, Mom. Most of these people in the New Seekers group already knew a great deal about the Christian faith before this Rapture happened, but they weren't committed to Christ. Several of these people are Jewish and they knew the Old Testament inside out. That's what has bound them together in such a secret group."

"I don't know, Matthew," Graham said. "You've found a couple of amazing answers, but that doesn't prove the Bible is correct or even comprehensive."

Matthew flipped back through the pages again. "I want you to hear some more. Listen to what Jesus promised was coming. 'And you will hear of wars and rumors of wars; see that you are not alarmed; for this must take place, but the end is not yet. For nation will rise against nation, and kingdom against kingdom, and there will be famines and earthquakes in various places: all this is but the beginning of the sufferings.'"

Graham could feel the blood draining from his face. "Lately we've heard of nothing but strife, fighting, killings."

He shook his head again. "Right now we are in another war."

"Want me to tell you about this war that just broke out?" Matt said. "We studied it last night."

Jackie's mouth dropped. *"You studied it?"*

"Adah Honi is Jewish," Matt explained. "Her family was caught up in one of the wars around Jerusalem and she came to the United States to study even though she's older than the average college student. Adah has an amazing grasp of the Old Testament."

Jackie ran her hand nervously through her hair. "I don't even know what to think about what you are saying, Matthew. Good heavens! What did this woman say about the current war?"

"Look." Matthew put his finger in a section of the Old Testament. "At least five hundred and fifty years before the Christian era, Ezekiel wrote these words. That's two thousand and five hundred years ago. In those days they called the regions that are now Russia by the name of Gog and Magog. Ezekiel 38 and 39 predict the time when Gog and Magog or Russia attacks Israel. Here's what's going to happen to the Russians."

"You're telling me that this last war was prophesied centuries ago?" Graham blurted out.

"Listen to it, Dad." Matthew started reading. " 'You shall fall upon the mountains of Israel, you and all your hordes and the peoples that are with you; I will give you to birds of prey of every sort and to the wild beasts to be devoured. You shall fall in the open field; for I have spoken, says the Lord God. I will send fire on Magog and on those who dwell securely in the coastland.'" He stopped. "Isn't that what just happened?"

Graham started to speak, but stopped.

"Well," Matthew pushed, "hasn't every word that I just read to you happened in the past six months? We have been living through the final chapter of human history."

The countenance on the faces of both George and Jeff changed. Depression was replaced by fascination. The two boys kept shaking their head.

"You bet!" George said with new enthusiasm in his voice.

"I guess I didn't expect anything quite so dramatic, so final," Graham said. He took a deep breath. "I don't know what I was expecting." He stood up and started pacing back and forth. "Matthew, how many people know about what this New Seekers group is teaching?"

"It's a small group, but I think it's going to grow fast. When this word gets out, it's going to create a big stir."

"Look, son. The times are going to get worse, much tighter with far, far greater security. You've got to be careful. Some people would be very upset if they heard these explanations."

"Why?" Matthew frowned. "We're not doing anything but studying an ancient book."

"I know. I know, but the world is spinning out of control, and there are some people out there who want to bring it under their domination. You have no idea what they might be willing to do to stop the spread of this story you've just told us."

Matthew leaned back in his chair and frowned for the

first time. "Maybe that's why this group is so secret. Someone has already figured out that we could get into some kind of trouble."

Graham put his hand on Matthew's shoulder. "Take them seriously, son! This is no time to be playing with explosive and dangerous ideas!"

CHAPTER 29

THE BALLROOM of the Mid-America Exposition Center only blocks from the reelection offices of Mayor Bridges overflowed for the celebration of the local and national election results. Balloons floated across the gigantic room and streamers hung from the rafters far overhead. Around the mammoth room, monitors placed at the top of the ceiling flashed the returns from across America as well as Chicago. Periodically a local band would break into a number and people would start dancing. Secluded in the back of the building, Bridges huddled with his closest advisors.

"We've clearly won." Jake Pemrose sorted through the numbers coming in on his monitor. "No question about it." He puffed on his black cigar. "We're the big winners."

"But what's the margin?" Bridges pushed. "Just winning isn't enough." He stood up and walked over to a mirror to look at his tuxedo tailored in a turn-of-the-century style that reflected the stability and prosperity of another day.

"Man, you're tough tonight," Al Meacham said. "After all a win is a win. Isn't it?"

Bridges shook his head. "Not tonight."

"Hey!" Jack Stratton said with a cynical twist in his words. "Frank, we can keep our machine running. What more could we want?" He gulped a beer sitting in front of him.

Bridges shot a cold-eyed glance loaded with meaning at Graham Peck. In an instant Graham concluded that Stratton and Meacham knew nothing about the arrangement Bridges had made with Borden Carson. The mayor's interest in the White House wasn't obvious to them. Pemrose might know, but he was the only one.

"I'm not going out there to make any statements until we are at least fifteen points ahead of the margin I won by in the last election," Bridges said. "I have something special to say and I want that big of an edge to make my point."

Stratton rubbed his forehead nervously. "That's a pretty good swath, Frank. I don't know."

"That's where I'm standing," Bridges said emphatically. "Let me know as soon as we get those numbers."

"I'm going outside to talk to my wife," Graham said. "If you need me, buzz me on my pager. It may be hard to hear out there."

The mayor nodded. "Enjoy yourself, Graham. You've done a great job on the campaign. Have a good time."

Graham quickly walked out of the room. He didn't like the smoke-filled conferences and Pemrose's arrogance bothered him. The noise in the ballroom was better than sitting around in the cigar smoke generated by Bridges's boys.

Looking for Jackie, he walked into the back of the ballroom. On the south side of the hall the national election numbers were pouring in over the television screen. Clearly their party was also carrying the U.S. Senate.

"Graham!" Jackie yelled. "Over here!"

Just beyond a wild conversation among a crowd of celebrants, Graham could see Jackie sitting next to one of the exit doors. Pushing through the people, he grabbed her by the hand and pulled her outside into the night air.

"I can't even think in that riot, much less talk," Graham said and kissed her on the cheek. "You look gorgeous tonight."

"Thank you, Graham. I wore this gown just for you."

"It's beautiful." Graham smiled. "I'll be glad when the big party is over and we can get out of here."

"Yeah, me too."

"Did you make sure Mary listened to the recording of our conversation with Matthew?"

"She groaned and complained, but I made her listen to every word. Of course, none of her friends' families function as a unit. She wants to be a lone wolf like her buddies."

"And?" Graham motioned with his hand for Jackie to say more.

"Religious ideas turn Mary off. She got rather nasty and I was forced to stand firm."

"I don't care what she thought," Graham retorted angrily. "We are a family and Matthew has come up with information that we can't ignore. She'll listen whether she likes it or not."

Jackie nervously ran her hands through her hair. "I

don't know what to think of it myself. Everything Matthew showed us makes sense, but who takes the Bible seriously?"

"Millions of people once did, Jackie. Maybe that's where we started going wrong."

"I can't put it all together. I am terrified by what the world is turning into. On the other hand, the Bible seems like such an antiquated, ancient book to have anything to say in our contemporary world."

"I know," Graham said. "I know, but Matthew has given us more concrete direction than anyone and it came out of that book. We can't overlook the facts." He glanced at his watch. "I think we ought to go back inside."

Jackie slid her arm inside his. "Okay, let's join the hullabaloo."

Walking back inside, they found the gathering had only grown in size. Balloons kept popping and some of the streamers from high up on the ceiling broke loose and drifted toward the floor, adding to the sense of organized chaos. Most of the people had been drinking and were talking or shouting far too loud. Jackie and Graham stayed close to the back door.

Television screens flashed the numbers, suggesting a national landslide and, for Bridges, smashing returns from all over Chicago. Fifteen minutes later an anchorman announced that Frank Bridges would appear momentarily.

"Is Frank descending from heaven or walking on water when he enters?" Jackie asked cynically.

"He's arriving in a chariot of fire."

Suddenly Mayor Frank Bridges burst through a curtain in the center of the ballroom. Instantly, his face appeared on every television screen along with his wife and two adult children. For five minutes, he marched back and forth across the platform like a triumphant gladiator while the mob screamed their applause.

"He's the big winner," Jackie said. "No question about it."

"You've got it," Graham answered dryly. "On to Washington!"

The noise started to subside and Bridges began motioning for people to become silent. It took another full minute for the throng to settle down.

"I just received a congratulatory phone call from my opponent wishing us success in the next term," Bridges began and the herd shouted their acceptance.

"We cannot afford to sit on our laurels." Bridges's voice instantly changed from the sound of a winner, to again becoming the serious candidate selling his audience a new set of ideas. "The times are too dangerous!"

The crowd murmured their concurrence.

"As we have seen in recent days, Chicago is vulnerable to attack. As many as a thousand boats float into our harbors nearly every hour. Possibly only two percent are inspected." Bridges shook his head emphatically. "A dirty bomb smuggled in on one of those vessels and detonated in our harbor could contaminate this entire metroplex for a century! Anyone can see our problem."

Once again the mob moaned and groaned. Obviously, they were completely with Bridges.

"Petroleum needs continue to be pressing." Bridges stopped and let the pause settle. "But I have anticipated these needs and have already prepared a response."

The crowd exploded in cheers and applause again, sounding like he could propose they walk off the edge of the universe and all would join lockstep behind him.

"Many of you are acquainted with Borden Camber Carson and his petroleum empire. Mr. Carson has assured me that our needs in the Chicago metroplex will receive his personal attention and we will be supplied at the lowest possible price."

Once again Bridges's supporters rocked the room with wild, enthusiastic applause. The noise of their support was being transmitted across America via the television networks and it sounded like Bridges was Everyman's messiah of the hour.

"Further"—Bridges cleared his throat and waited for the noise to subside again—"I have already put in motion a series of steps to further insulate you from attack. We are going to make Chicago the safest city in the world by installing a system of increased surveillance to make sure no one can be attacked without that information being instantly transmitted to the police headquarters. In addition, Mr. Carson will help us with the expense."

The crowd shifted from radical support to near mass hysteria. Bridges had in effect just said "I won, and I'm taking over everything in sight," and the public had screamed their acceptance.

Sitting in the corner with his wife, Graham remained silent but he kept looking around the room, wondering if the election headquarters had turned into an insane asylum.

"What do you think?" Jackie asked, putting her mouth to Graham's ear.

"I'm troubled, deeply troubled. We need to get out of here. This place is a nut house. I've got a great deal to think about tonight." Graham reached for Jackie's arm and headed for the exit.

CHAPTER 30

THE DAY-AFTER-THE-ELECTION party at Mayor Bridges's headquarters rolled on with the same raucous blowout that had erupted the night before. The mayor had conveniently ducked out of the office, but the staff and secretaries kept the wild binge spinning. Graham Peck arrived at the office an hour late because he didn't expect much work to get done that day. When he walked in, the party was going full tilt.

"Happy days are here again . . ." One of the men stood up on his desk and sang the old political song as loud as a drunken sailor. Several other rather well-looped men surrounded him and hummed along. The group looked like a fraternity quartet, preparing to launch into an interplanetary orbit.

Graham watched the scene for a moment, thinking it looked almost like at any moment the entire office would turn into a Roman orgy. To Graham the scene seemed to show how drastically the society had changed in the last thirty years. Increased casualness and loss of significant personal relationships had turned into a world where frivolity, spontaneity, and pleasure ruled the day. Any opportunity for amusement or diversion was seized as a personal right. Looseness invaded every encounter. Men and women stood intertwined and sequestered in the dark corners of the office. Graham didn't like the picture, but he realized there was nothing he could do on this "morning after" blast except get out of the way.

Ducking his head, he hurried to his office and shut the door behind him. At least, his suite was secluded. Graham stood there in the silence and thought about what he heard Bridges say last night and shuddered. Those stupid local supporters of the Bridges's campaign had no idea that they were wildly applauding the installation of "the eye" in every corner of their lives. Their homes, their offices, the streets, stores, and even subways would be wired with cameras watching everything. Rather than applaud, they should be boarding up their windows.

Abruptly the door burst open. "There you are!" Sarah Cates giggled. "You should have gotten here earlier. What a party!"

Graham studied her for a moment. She had obviously been drinking heavily and looked well past the edge of sobriety. Sarah had a wild, carefree gleam in her eye.

Shutting the door behind her, Sarah grinned. "What's up today, boss?" She sauntered across the room toward him. "Surely, we're not going to work this morning."

Graham cleared his throat. "Well, I guess most of our

work is finished as far as the election goes, but I know there will be other . . ."

"*Really?*" Sarah suddenly slid directly in front of him and lightly stroked the side of his face. "Graham, the only thing wrong with you is that you're always so distant."

Graham felt the warmth of her hand caressing his cheek. He had carefully avoided sending Sarah any suggestive signals, but she was a very attractive woman, too attractive to be standing nearly on top of him. "Wh-what?" he sputtered.

"You've enticed me like . . . I believe they once said . . . like a moth to the flame." Sarah's voice settled into a husky, lusty quality. "*You always have.*" Her other hand gently touched his tie and then moved up to the other side of his face. "And I don't want someone as gorgeous as you to disappear." Sarah pulled his head forward and kissed him passionately on the mouth.

Graham didn't move. At first he was shocked and then he realized how much he enjoyed the kiss, but his wits kicked in and he pulled back. "Sarah . . . please." He caught his breath. "You've been drinking too much and we're both married." He pointed at the door. "I want you to go back outside and we'll both pretend this didn't happen. Understand?"

Sarah's eyes widened and she blinked several times. "I'm not playing with you, Graham. Everyone has lovers today and here I am offering myself to you."

Graham rubbed his chin. "Sarah, please go back to your desk." He stumbled at choosing the right words.

"Now?"

"Yes." Graham nodded his head. *"Right now."*

Sarah started backing away with a hurt look on her face. "Look. I wouldn't tell anyone and we both know everyone does this sort of thing today," she pleaded. "You really turn me on and I just knew that . . ."

"I'm married and that puts me off limits. Please go back to your desk."

A cold soberness returned to Sarah's eyes and for a moment anger flashed across her face. Shaking her head, she walked out and closed the door with a slam.

Graham dropped into his desk chair like a boulder falling off of a mountain. He had never given this woman even a hint of interest, and she had walked in like the office paramour, sent to him like an order from the delicatessen up the street.

On second thought, Sarah had been flirtatious, occasionally, but she had sounded like she truly cared. He remembered other times when the woman had been warm and genuine.

Reaching into his bottom drawer, Graham pulled out a bottle of bourbon Frank Bridges had given him over a year ago and untwisted the cork on the bottle. He started to pour himself a drink and then heard explosive laughter and women giggling in the outer office. He stopped. The last thing he needed was the same addled brain as those people in the outer office.

Graham started to get up and take a peek out of his door, but decided against it. He put the cork back in the bottle, set it back in the drawer, and closed it.

For the next couple of hours, he worked on some unfinished paperwork and tried to ignore the sounds of the pandemonium and hubbub going on beyond his walls. No matter what he heard, he wasn't going out until the uproar subsided.

A quiet knock on his door interrupted his thoughts. "Come in," he said.

The door opened slightly and Sarah Cates stuck her head in. "May I speak to you?"

Graham braced himself.

The woman's entire countenance had changed. Sarah had sobered up and looked almost like she had been crying. With her head down, she quickly slipped into the chair in front of his desk. "I want to offer you an apology."

Graham studied her. Sarah looked more broken than disingenuous or manipulative. "Yes?" Graham tried not to sound abrasive.

"I was drinking, but I should never have said what I did." Sarah bit her lip. "I am sure you may want to replace me or move me to another person's office and if you do, I will understand." She stopped and looked at the floor. "I'm very sorry."

Graham said nothing partly because he couldn't think of what he ought to say.

"I care about you." Sarah looked up slowly with pain in her eyes. "But you are right. I want you to know that I respect your sense of propriety and I won't ever do anything like this again." A tear ran down her cheek. "I should never have been drinking."

"Sarah," Graham said with sincerity. "Let's both go

back to work and forget this happened. I hope we can go on down the road without this encounter damaging either of us."

Sarah nodded. "Yes . . . yes . . . thank . . . you." She walked out of the room with her head down.

Graham heaved a deep sigh. He had never been a party boy and his mother had imparted a sense of right and wrong that sometimes got in his way, but he was more than relieved that this unexpected road jam seemed to have been cleared away. He would need to avoid all appearances of impropriety in every possible way. If Bridges did run for national office and these contacts with Carson kept coming, Graham knew he couldn't afford anything but the best of reputations. He didn't want to go from being the office pariah because of a death to having the reputation of the office playboy. This was not a good morning.

CHAPTER 31

M INUTES BEFORE NOON Jackie phoned. "Matthew called and wants to bring a friend to our house for supper tonight. He says she is a Jewish woman in his New Seekers group."

"Good! Excellent!"

"Matt thinks we could have an important conversation with her."

"And I don't care what Mary comes up with this

evening or what the school assigns, you tell that girl to be at the table with the rest of us."

"I will. Graham, are you all right? You sound a little on edge."

Graham started to be candid, but stopped. "I have many things on my mind," he said. "I'm struggling with what's happened to our family."

"Don't worry, Graham. I want you to know that I've made my peace with what Matthew is telling us. I'm open to whatever the Bible says."

"Well, that's the best news I've heard this morning! Good. I'll look forward to this evening. See you then." He hung up the phone. Maybe the morning would turn out better than he thought.

At three o'clock in the afternoon, Graham took the back stairs out of his office and left for Arlington Heights. Most of the staff was long since smashed and nothing was going on that involved him. He didn't want any more nonsense and needed to think alone. Walking along the river in the Ship Canal would give him time to make sense out of everything happening to him.

From what he had seen in the last week, it was now clear to Graham that the mayor would do anything that Borden Camber Carson told him. The idea of attaching nanomachines to people and adding more surveillance cameras had fit a plan already unfolding when Graham entered the discussion. The bottom line meant Chicago would actually be run out of the back pocket of this Middle Eastern oil magnate. Wiring the city with an all-encompassing surveillance system would give Carson an extraordinary ability to control all of Chicago. The thought remained almost unimaginable. At the least, he would make sure his family stayed unmarked.

The buzzing of his cell phone stopped Graham. He pulled the phone out of his pocket.

"Peck here."

"Graham, this is Frank. You've let the office?"

"Yeah, we seem to be having nothing but an endless party today. I cut out."

"Know what you mean. That's why I left. Graham, I'm deeply concerned. Something terrible has happened overnight."

Graham took a deep breath. "Not again!"

"Fortunately not in Chicago," Bridges said, "but I got a report from Israel. You know those missile attacks that started the nuclear exchange?"

"Of course."

"Apparently something else was at work. Smallpox has broken out in Israel and is sweeping through Jerusalem."

"Smallpox? I thought the last time anyone talked about that disease was back when we were getting ready for war with Iraq when Saddam Hussein was alive."

"That's my recollection, but it's happened. They tell me that only Russia and the United States kept samples of smallpox in their germ warfare laboratories, but other countries may have gotten hold of the germs. Looks like someone also shot a missile loaded with the disease into Israel."

"Oh, no! That's horrible."

"They tell me about one-third of all the victims die and that the disease leaves terrible effects on survivors. It's highly contagious. I'm terrified it could come our way; virtually nobody is immune today."

Graham cursed. "That idea is too awful even to think about."

"You can see what could happen if one suicide bomber flew in here from some rogue country armed with smallpox. Before anyone knew what was happening a third of this country could be dead!"

Graham shifted his cellular phone, pushing it closer to his ear. "What are you going to do?"

"I've already contacted the White House to see if any vaccine is available and they are scrambling to find out. At the least, we need to quarantine our city from Middle Easterners until this is settled."

"How can we do that? We have airplanes coming and going all day long from Israel, Jordan, Saudi Arabia, you name it. Are you going to shut the airport down?"

"What else can we do?" Bridges asked.

"I don't know, but I don't think that option will work."

"Graham, I want you to think this through. Late tomorrow morning I must talk on the holographic transmitter with Carson. I need to have something meaningful to say to him."

"This is going to be tough. I'll have to sleep on it."

"I understand," Bridges said. "Don't hesitate to call me if you wish. We've got to have some response in the morning."

"Okay," Graham said resolutely and flipped the cell phone off.

The river bounced against the walls of the canal in a

leisurely flow. The current seemed to move in a peaceful, gentle roll as if these waters forever remained indifferent to the globe's problems. Bridges could say what he wanted, but possibilities of the outbreak of smallpox were everyone's nightmare. Where would it ever stop?

Graham turned back toward the entrance to the Metro train station. Today he would not take the Express. Maybe the long ride would be good for him. He hoped this woman called Adah Honi that Matthew was bringing with him would have something important to say.

CHAPTER 32

PEERING AROUND THE EDGE of the kitchen door, Jackie watched the living room while Matthew talked with Jennifer Andrews and the unusual woman he called Adah Honi. No one had met Jennifer before and the young woman looked like a good friend for Matthew. Jackie knew Matt had girlfriends during high school, but he had not been big on dating, which was a relief to his parents. Obviously, this little blonde caught his eye with her sparkling personality.

But the Jewish woman was a complete unknown. Speaking with an obvious, but pleasant accent, the woman had a long, narrow face with a fashion model's profile. Adah was small, but walked with authority as if she knew where she was going at every moment. Her fingers were long and narrow, with an artistic flair. Her black hair had been combed back in a straight line that accentuated her high forehead. Penetrating black eyes imparted a striking appearance and gave the impression that nothing went unobserved.

"Jackie!" Graham shouted from upstairs. "I'll be down in a moment."

"We have plenty of time," Jackie called back, but wished he would hurry up. She really didn't want to say anything because Graham had been under plenty of pressure and he didn't need any more at home. On the other hand, the food could cool.

Jackie worried about her husband. His world had been scattered and no one seemed to pay any attention to the way the breakup had affected Graham; those crazy people at work wouldn't even talk to him about Maria's death. The incident at the children's school must have pushed him nearly over the edge, and now this smallpox epidemic was staring him in the face. Graham had always been the stiff-upper-lip type who pushed on regardless of what happened around him. He bore the load no matter what anyone else said or did, but he tended to be oblivious to certain emotional considerations, like failing to notice the feelings of others. He could wall the world out, but it was still there . . . like their daughter Mary.

"Hi, Mom!" George yelled from the back porch. "Here comes Mary. She's home!"

The back door slammed and Mary came in looking like a typical fourteen-year-old trying to appear twenty-five. "Do I have to be a part of this religious circus tonight?" She slammed her books on the table. "I'd rather eat by myself."

"Stop it!" Jackie demanded in a whisper. "You try that line on your father and you'll go to war with him. Get your stuff in your room and be back in here in two minutes."

"Oh, Mother!"

"And get that excessive lipstick off. I swear you seem . . ."

Mary shot out of the room, apparently having forgotten to wipe her lips off before she came in the back door.

Graham came down the back stairs and hurried into the kitchen, kissing Jackie on the neck. He had changed into a gray sweater. "What a day!" he sighed. "You'd think winning the election would be enough, but I tell you . . ." He stopped. "Enough about the office. Let's go in and have supper with these people Matthew brought with him. I want to hear what they have to say."

After a couple of minutes of polite conversation, the family and their guests settled around the dinner table. Mary sat to one side with a frown on her face, but no one paid any attention to her, so she didn't have the effect she intended.

"Well, I'm ready to start." Graham smiled and reached for a bowl of beans. "Anybody hungry?"

"Dad," Matt said. "I think we ought to say a blessing tonight."

"A blessing?" Graham blinked several times, trying to grasp what he had heard.

"A prayer," Matt said. "The people in the New Seekers group pray before they eat."

"Oh, yes!" Graham puckered his lip and tried to act like

this was an old family custom. "Yes, indeed! A prayer? Well! Who would like to say it?"

"Why don't we ask Adah?" Matthew suggested. "She's a special guest tonight."

"Certainly." Graham nodded to the young woman. "Would you do the honors?"

Adah smiled and bowed her head. "Blessed art thou, O Lord God of the universe who gives us bread. We thank you for the food we eat today. Amen."

"Well, that was easy enough!" Graham said with too much enthusiasm and began passing around the bowls of food. "Adah, I understand you came here from Israel to study?"

"Yes, Northwestern offered opportunities."

"Good!" Graham started the meat around. "You had some sort of family problem if I understand correctly. Have I got that right?"

The smile slowed faded from the young woman's face. "Yes, Father was a merchant who always built good relations with the Palestinians. In fact, Abba worked near the West Bank town of Nazlat Issa." Adah spoke in a flat, factual voice as if she were describing the scenery. "Mother went with him when an altercation broke out with Israeli army officers. The soldiers fired tear gas and rubber-coated steel pellets and then someone opened up with a machine gun." Her steady tone started to fade. "Both my parents were killed in the battle." She looked down at her plate.

"I see." Graham's happy-go-lucky ringmaster voice ceased. "We understand," he said soberly and reached over to pat her on the top of her hand. "I suppose you know about what happened in our family?"

Adah took a deep breath. "Yes, Matthew told us about the death of your mother. Our hearts are heavy for you."

"Adah," Jackie said. "I don't think we ought to waste any time. Matthew has told us some of what he has learned from your group. We didn't grow up in the church—we've never heard of these strange ideas, like a 'Rapture' or the moon taking on a red glow. Matt showed us in the Bible the passages about today's wars and terrible struggles happening everywhere. We don't know what to make of this."

"Neither did I," Adah said. "I carefully studied Torah as a child, but it was not until after my parents' death that I started discovering the rest of the story. I married a Christian Jew." She giggled. "Asa Honi. I must say the marriage almost made me an outcast with my family and friends, but Asa and I were very happy. I thought Asa's strange beliefs were unusual, but they fascinated me. My husband taught me about these Christian ideas of end times." She nodded her head soberly. "I listened, but of course, I didn't believe any of it."

CHAPTER 33

THE FAMILY KEPT EATING while Adah Honi talked. Jackie shot a glance at Mary. She was listening, but had an arrogant, detached look on her face that her father hated. At least she was paying attention.

"You mean you heard all of these ideas from your husband before any of these events happened?" George asked. "Wow! That must have wrecked your bike?"

"Yes," Adah said slowly. "I suppose an American might put it that way." She shook her head soberly. "My husband disappeared with all other Christians." She lowered her head gently. "That forever changed my life."

Silence fell over the table and even Mary appeared shaken.

"You lost your parents in a war and your husband *through the Rapture?*" Jackie asked.

"I am afraid so." Adah forced a thin, sober smile that bordered on a grimace of pain. "But these experiences prepared me for the role today I have with students. If my husband had not made me read the entire Bible, I would be of no use to anyone."

"I must tell you," Matthew said. "No one has given students the guidance that we have received from Adah. We thank God for her every day."

Graham pushed his plate aside. "Adah, we have looked at some of these images in the Bible, but we simply don't understand what we see. We read about white horses, red horses, black horses, on and on. How do we make any sense out of this?"

"It is not easy, Mr. Peck. Some of the Bible is literal and some of it is symbolic. You must have instruction to know how to pull apart some of these strange passages, but I tell you that the key to understanding them is in the Old Testament. That's where clues are found."

"The Old Testament had been like reading Plato's dialogues until Adah helped us understand how straightforward it actually is," Matt said. "She taught us to look at how the New Testament's use of colors and symbols—like rainbows and trumpets that first appear in the original order of God's plan in the Old Testament. That's what started me putting the pieces together for myself."

Jennifer nodded and smiled thinly.

Jackie watched Graham's face. For the first time in weeks his eyes twinkled. He was cutting through the darkness with a new light he had never seen before.

"We have seen already nature spin out of control," Adah continued. "You have noticed the moon? Yes! And the seasons have changed radically. No? One can see God warning us."

"How fascinating!" Graham interjected. "I don't want to sound like a doubter because you are making sense out of the past, but if this method is true, you ought to be able to tell us something about what is ahead. Can you give us any prophecies about the future?"

"I can," Adah said with understated honesty.

"I don't believe it!" Mary suddenly blurted out. "Give us an example or two."

"I think I know what the next step in this chaos will be," Adah said. "It may not happen in the next day or so, but very soon it is coming."

Graham leaned over the table and motioned with his hand as he often did. "Tell us more. Don't stop now."

"I believe we will soon see the Anti-Christ start to arise if that has not already happened. He will be compelling, handsome man who will draw unto himself the world and he will have great power."

Out of the corner of her eye, Jackie saw Graham's face turn pale. His mouth dropped slightly. His eyes quivered momentarily like they did when he was severely jarred.

"The Bible speaks of this man uniting a pact of nations European into a form of a new Roman Empire." Adah shrugged. "Of course, the number ten is a Jewish unit like counting from one to ten and then starting all over again. It is a symbol for unity, completeness. It simply might be the Bible's way of saying that this Anti-Christ will form a solid confederation of nations that in complete unity will act under his control. They would become his mouthpiece."

Jackie watched Graham slide back into his chair with a colorless, panicked look on his face. She instantly realized that he knew something she had not heard yet. He stared at the wall as if he was reading something on the other side of the blank wallpaper. The look in his eyes was unmistakable; Graham knew who this Anti-Christ might be!

"I believe this incredibly attractive man will start to take over our society entire probably through the use of electronic surveillance of some variety or the other," Adah said. "The book of Revelation suggests 666 will be his name. I am still working on what that means but I would expect this to happen in the immediate future."

"That's weird!" Mary protested. "How could anyone be named 666?" She slumped back in her chair indifferently. "That's a number."

"Numbers often also are symbols for ideas in the Holy

Bible," Adah said. "Perhaps, we simply have not figured out for what idea the number is a symbol." Adah didn't seem to be offended by Mary's scornful attack. "Give me a while on it to work."

"Graham," Jackie asked thoughtfully, "I sense you find what Adah has said somewhat confounding?"

Graham slowly shifted his vision from the wall toward his wife with a vacant, distant stare. "Yes. I am highly unsettled."

George looked at Jeff, who didn't seem to be quite putting everything together. "Oh man, I love this weird talk. Adah, you are really neat."

"One more thing," Adah added. "From the Scripture I get a hint that a serious illness might in Israel soon break out."

"I don't like it!" Mary protested. "I think it's all nonsense."

"No," Graham said firmly and looked hard at Mary. "You've just received the most important information you've heard in your life. We must understand everything Adah can teach us." He stared at the Jewish woman. "I don't know what you will tell us, but we must learn everything you know. We must!" He suddenly reached across the table and grabbed her hand tightly. "I warn you to be extremely careful. You should be aware that electronic surveillance is increasing and people will be watching." He looked straight into her eyes. "Our lives depend on it."

"Let me tell you something, Mr. Peck," Adah said politely, but with forcefulness in her voice. "I am no longer afraid to die. This is not with me an issue."

Jackie watched Graham catch his breath. Adah's answers had taken all of them by surprise, but Graham had been struck straight between the eyes. Jackie could tell he was clearly staggered by her audacious answer.

"I—I—don't think that I understand," Graham mumbled.

"As I have read the Holy Bible through," Adah continued, "I have found that the great people of faith did not fear death because with them they knew God was. Jesus the Messiah brought life to us. We need to be confident in what for us he has accomplished."

Graham blinked several times, not saying anything.

"You are telling us *not to be afraid of death?*" Mary pushed.

"Yes." Adah smiled. "You do not need anyone to fear who can kill the body. Fear those who can take your soul." She leaned toward Mary. "That is . . . if you know Jesus."

CHAPTER 34

GRAHAM WAS NO LONGER preoccupied with thoughts about what words should be placed in the mayor's mouth to make him sound appropriate and intelligent. One visit in front of his holographic transmitter had radically changed Graham's perspective on Bridges. He might not always express himself clearly, but the mayor knew exactly where he was going. Time spent the night before with Adah Honi and Jennifer Andrews had also changed Graham's mind. His priorities were cast in an entirely different light. He must now concentrate on his family's survival. Smallpox was loose in the world.

The big party and the hangovers were past. The re-election committee had officially disassembled and the personnel already been absorbed back into the staff of the Chicago mayor's office. No one changed desks or secretaries; only the sign on the front door of the office was repainted to indicate the shift. The newspapers and television stations didn't report the change. That was it. Life went on.

Beyond his office door, Graham could faintly hear Sarah Cates pounding away at her computer. She had been distant since her apology and avoided personal encounters. Sarah remained all business and that satisfied Graham, but he knew her expressions of affection, though slightly drunken, had been genuine and that remained dangerous.

Graham glanced at his watch. In a few minutes he would sneak out the back door and grab the Metro train that would take him through Lincolnwood and into Evanston. He had an appointment with Adah Honi that nothing in the world would keep him from attending. Whatever this woman knew, he wanted every piece of her data stored in the front of his brain.

A knock jarred his thoughts. The door opened slightly and Sarah stuck her head in. "I'm sorry to bother you. I think you'll want to see what I understand is about to be announced on television." She quickly ducked out.

Graham hit a button on the corner pad on his desk and a television screen the thickness of a picture hanging on the wall jumped to life. He pushed a second button and the screen filled with the face of a newscaster.

"Moments ago we received this report from Istanbul. While Borden Camber Carson has again avoided being photographed, he just released this important statement. We are going live to Steve Miller, standing in front of the administrative offices of the Royal Arab Petroleum Company. Steve, what have you learned?"

A picture of a gray-haired man appeared in front of a massive opulent building shaped like a huge medieval Turkish mosque with a minaret. The camera zoomed in on his face.

"I am reading sections of a prepared statement released only moments ago from the administrative offices of Mr. Carson. Because of the recent attack on the Middle Eastern oil fields controlled by Royal Arab Petroleum, Carson has now issued a challenge to the world to join him in protecting oil production; he has also called on European nations from Poland to Spain to form a confederation to guarantee the safety of all shipping. It is not clear whether he is speaking of a cartel or an actual merging of governments, but Carson is otherwise specific. He demands an immediate joining of armed forces to protect these supply lines. We will report the response of the European nations as we receive them." Miller stopped and looked away from the camera for a moment. "This is obviously an extremely serious move on the part of an international company which seems to have its own military capacity to enforce these concerns. Of course, the entire world is fearful of what the loss of any amount of petroleum could mean. Back to you in New

York." The picture faded and the first announcer reappeared.

Graham punched the mute button. He had heard more than enough. Everything about this telecast sent shivers down his spine. Adah Honi had made a prediction on one night and the next day the television issued a report so remarkably similar that it chilled him. It could not be a coincidence that she was so absolutely correct on these matters!

For a few moments, Graham stared at the silent screen, trying to order his thoughts. No question about it! He needed to talk to Adah as soon as he could get on the Metro. He punched his intercom phone line.

"Mrs. Cates, I don't want to take any more phone calls today. I'm going to be tied up in a research project. Thank you." He flipped the switch and turned on his private line to the mayor's secretary.

"Please tell the mayor that I'm working on a research project," Graham said. "If there is an emergency, he can reach me on my private cell phone number."

"Certainly," the woman said with a professional sound. "I will let him know."

Graham grabbed his overcoat and headed for the back exit. The weather had suddenly gotten much colder with the temperature dropping into the single digits. These abrupt weather changes along with a reddish moon every night seemed to sound as if nature was shouting, "The world's coming unglued! Nothing is like it once was."

In 2015, the Metro train from the downtown to Evanston had been built on tracks above the city landscape. Why

they hadn't plowed through the slums and cleared out the
rabble remained a mystery to Graham. In the last twenty
years the gap between the affluent and the poor had
widened enormously and what had once been middle class
areas had now turned into dilapidated sections of rat-
infested neighborhoods. Maybe that was why the train had
been lifted high above these poverty holes? It was dangerous
to get caught down there in those dark alleys at night. Slum
people could get savage, but then again, they weren't any
worse than what appeared to be unfolding in the Middle
East. The world was turning cold with a temperature drop
the sun couldn't lift.

While the train roared down the tracks, Graham
thought about Mary. No matter what was said or done, his
fourteen-year-old daughter wasn't moved. Undoubtedly, the
influence of her friends at school took precedence over
everyone else. Kids functioned like that these days, but it
was still irritating that this girl couldn't get her head on
straight.

The train hurled across Chicago Avenue and slowed for
Evanston at the Northwestern University stop. Graham
could see the blue waves of Lake Michigan bouncing up toward the shore and for a moment the beauty of the cold,
massive lake seemed like a peaceful reprieve. The Metro
pulled to a halt.

Graham hurried out the door and clomped down the
steps toward the small café where Adah said she would
meet him. Cold winds forced him to turn up his collar and
cram his hands deeply into the pockets on his overcoat.
Ahad had said that La Baguette Bistro, a French restaurant,

would provide a quiet corner where they could talk unobserved.

The Bistro had a quaint look with a large sign above the entrance and hanging plants in the windows. Waiters walked back and forth with towels stuck in their belts for aprons. Graham paused and glanced through the large plate glass windows. The striking black-haired woman was already sitting near the back sipping coffee. He hurried in.

CHAPTER 35

ADAH HONI looked up from the restaurant table. "Ah, Mr. Peck, I hope you had no trouble in getting here." She pointed at the chair across from her. "Thank you for coming."

"Make it Graham." He quickly removed his topcoat and hung it on a rack behind them. "And I appreciate so much you're taking the time to talk with me." He slid into the chair.

"You are an important person," Adah said. "Everyone knows of your relationship with the mayor. Talking to you is an honor and for me a privilege." A waiter walked up.

"I'll have a cup of espresso," Graham said. "That'll do fine." The waiter walked away as quickly as he had come.

Graham smiled. "Well, let's dig in. I have many questions."

"I am not sure that I can answer, but I will try."

"Have you seen the television today?"

Adah shook her head. "I must be frank. Much of your American news is manipulated, managed. The broadcasts and contents are slanted to project a correct viewpoint politically. I avoid these government expressions so my mind clear will remain."

Graham rubbed his chin. No one had ever put the matter so succinctly. She was right. The waiter set a cup of espresso in front of him.

"I hope this does not offend a politician like yourself."

Graham shook his head. "We must talk on a completely honest and open basis. Whether something you say offends me or not is irrelevant. I want the truth."

Adah sipped her coffee. "Good. This is the only way I can talk now to anyone."

"You must tell me more about what the Bible said about the Anti-Christ forming a coalition of nations to promote his plans. This is extremely important for me to understand."

"I see," Adah said slowly and carefully. "You see the Scripture is not clear about whether the Anti-Christ will be a political leader like, say, the head of a country, or simply a person of great personal persuasion. However, let us read the book and see."

"You have a Bible?"

Adah reached in her purse and pulled out a small black leather-covered volume. "I study every time I get the chance, this book. Right now I am trying to correlate the insights of the ancient prophet Daniel with the book of Revelation, the last book in the New Testament. In these we find explanations about this kingdom coming." She opened the Bible and quickly flipped through the pages.

Graham leaned over the table to see. "Show me what you find?"

"In the seventh chapter, Daniel explains his vision of a terrible frightening beast with iron teeth. In the twenty-fourth verse he says, 'as for the ten horns, out of this kingdom ten kings shall arise, and another shall arise after them; he shall be different from the former ones.'"

"What does this mean?" Graham asked.

"Let us now turn to the Revelation and see what it says." Adah quickly flipped through the pages. "Listen to how the thirteenth chapter begins. 'And I saw a beast rising out of the sea, with ten horns and seven heads, with ten diadems upon its horns, and a blasphemous name upon its heads.' Do you see the similarities?"

"Of course!"

"Even though Daniel was written centuries before, the writer of Revelation had surely studied his work." Adah pushed back her coal-black hair. "These passages written millenniums ago are now about to be fulfilled."

"You said the number ten might not be an exact head count?"

Adah nodded. "Yes. Ten is a Jewish symbol for completeness. The number could mean that this Anti-Christ simply assembles enough nations his purposes to complete. I could accept that interpretation. The point is that talk of beasts, horns, and diadems is a symbolic expression of what is coming. The original meaning had to be put in symbolic language because such talk was politically dangerous. For this reason, both Daniel and John wrote their messages in a highly colorful language to confuse spies watching them.

Perhaps, you will remember that both the Jews of Daniel's time and John's day were under extreme political oppression."

"Yes, I studied history in college."

"Now, Graham, this vision of ten nations has an extremely important point you must not miss. This final king will eventually rule over the entire world and speak against the true God. This man will attempt to set aside the long-accepted laws and customs that have stood for centuries." She paused and shook her head emphatically. "This man will also attack and persecute God's people."

Graham took a long drink of espresso. "Persecution?"

"Indeed! Revelation chapter thirteen tells us more about the world government coming. We will not only have a beast, but a false prophet. I believe this may well mean that the Anti-Christ will have an assistant who will help him control society." Adah thumped on the table with her index finger. "This Anti-Christ man may be extraordinarily handsome, but never forget *he is a dragon*, a fire-breathing threat to righteous people."

Graham could feel his stomach knotting. "I want you to hear something. Even though you don't listen to television newscasts, you should hear what's happened today." He reached inside the breast pocket of his coat and took out a small, flat device the size of his cell phone. He pushed the "on" button. "This is a pocket television with the capacity to bring in everything broadcast from satellites. I can get at least one hundred and fifty channels." He pushed in several buttons. "Let's see what we can bring up on CNN." Graham pushed the tiny speakers into his ears and listened momentarily. Pictures appeared on the small screen of an announcer sitting behind a desk. "Ah, they're about to replay what I heard at my office an hour ago. Listen carefully."

Adah placed the speakers in her ears. Leaning back against the chair, she closed her eyes to concentrate. Graham watched her face intently. For thirty seconds, Adah listened with the visual world tuned out. Slowly, she opened her eyes and stared at the small screen. Her lips parted slightly and shock registered on her face. Adah took a deep breath and stared out the large glass windows. Her chin dropped even further. As the pictures of reporter Steve Miller faded, the Jewish woman pulled the speakers from her ears.

"What do you think?" Graham asked.

Adah shook her head. "It has started!" Adah sounded stricken. "The end times tribulations have truly begun. The dragon is now among us."

CHAPTER 36

GRAHAM CONTINUALLY THOUGHT about what Adah Honi had shown him in the Bible. Jackie found a copy of the book in Maria's possessions and Graham put a newspaper cover over it to keep anyone from recognizing what he was reading. Everywhere he looked, Graham saw nothing but disconcerting evidence that what this woman had told him was true.

Across the city of Chicago and throughout the suburbs

workmen were climbing light poles and working over the entrances to buildings to install more surveillance cameras and keep the city wired. Mayor Bridges had not wasted any time in upping the ante on security. Television reports constantly blasted the public with stories of what Carson was reported to be planning to protect oil production. Belgium and Hungary responded immediately, pledging their feeble support behind the Royal Arab Petroleum Company's intentions to form an international union. The big guns in Germany and France were still pondering their options, but Italy and Greece were assumed to be in because of their proximity to Turkey. Not once on the televised reports did Carson show his face.

Chicago citizens seemed relieved that Frank Bridges would continue in office and they were reported to be highly pleased with the increased number of electronic eyes. Ships sailing in from Lake Michigan were inspected more often now, which put people at greater ease. The smallpox outbreak in Israel was contained within the country and the United States did not appear threatened for the moment.

However, no one could tie the explosion in the Museum of Science and Industry to any group. An assumption floated around the city that the attack on the Computer Center that spilled over to Harding School and the blast at the museum were linked, but no one could show solid evidence. After a thorough examination, the bodies of the gunmen killed in the school were identified as Arab terrorists, but there was nothing new in the discovery. Middle Eastern terrorists had been attempting attacks for decades.

The general conclusion was that these onslaughts were simply the usual periodic episodes. Murder, attacks, explosions, and terrorism had become so common that most of the people quickly forgot what just happened while waiting for another explosion.

Not Graham Peck.

Graham now had far more time to sit in his office and stew. He could order police reports and several times he reviewed all the evidence compiled to date. Far from forgetting, he couldn't understand why any of the government security agencies hadn't found something more significant. The FBI, Homeland Security Department, and the Chicago Police Department all used the best electronic devices and the most far-reaching means of identifying terrorists. The fact that nothing had turned up left Graham confounded.

However, Graham's mind was more unsettled about what was happening on the other side of the world. The dragon was indeed on the loose. Yet what could he do? In a bizarre twist of events, he had been plunged into the center of an unwinding plot that struck at the heart of the destiny of the world.

The buzzer on his computer sounded. Graham hit the buttons and Frank Bridges's face loomed on his screen.

"Graham, I want you to come down to my office immediately. Something important is about to occur."

"Yes sir. It will take me a couple of minutes."

"Good. No one knows you are coming. Knock on the panel entrance and I'll open it from the inside."

"I'm on my way."

Graham flipped the computer off and hurried out the back entrance. When he arrived in the mayor's office, the secretary was not there. He gently tapped on the door panel and it quickly opened. He hastened down the hallway to Bridges's office.

"Graham, thanks for coming so quickly." Bridges had on his formal attire with suspenders. "Time is important." He slipped on a suit coat.

Something important was imminent. With a quick glance, Graham could see that the holographic transmitter was open and ready to be used. "Of course." He forced a smile.

"I am going to talk with Carson in a moment and wanted you to be part of this conversation. Ready?"

Graham clenched his teeth and took a deep breath. "Yes."

"Relax. You are talking with a friend."

Graham again made himself smile.

Bridges hit the buttons on his desk and a brilliant beam of light shot up out of the base of the machine. In a few moments the illumination took on a green glow and the shape of a man emerged out of the column of light.

"Welcome to the fraternity of the Inner Circle," Carson said. The green illumination solidified and Carson's black hair and tanned face appeared in the three-dimensional shape of a person sitting across the room. Once again wearing the Nehru jacket, Carson now appeared to be sitting behind a large wooden desk. "I am delighted we can talk this afternoon."

"Thank you, sir." Bridges bowed formally. "We are looking forward to your response to the adjustments we have recently made."

"You have done what I expected you to do, Frank," Carson began. "As I told you earlier, I was extremely pleased with your solid validation in the election. We are now ready to move forward rapidly. I am also delighted with the speed with which you are getting the surveillance systems in place."

"Thank you, sir." Bridges maintained a solemn countenance. "We are moving ahead even as we speak today. The city is almost wired."

CHAPTER 37

WATCHING THE CONVERSATION between Carson and the mayor, Graham tried to listen as if he were a distant observer, but Borden Carson's magnetism almost instantly drew Graham toward him with an aura of trust and affirmation. The man had an uncanny ability to present himself as the embodiment of truth and hope. Even though he listened to what the mayor said, Carson seemed to know everything before the words were even spoken. He was the complete master of their conversation.

"Therefore," Bridges concluded, "I believe our new level of electronic observation will be completely in place by this Friday afternoon. If not, it will be done by Monday morning."

Carson nodded his approval. "Excellent. I will present

your name before a national political council in twenty-four hours. I anticipate your winning margin will add new weight to our future projections. It is mandatory if we are to meet our goals."

"Yes sir," Bridges said with a broad smile, "I am fully prepared. As you can see, today I have my associate Graham Peck with me again. He is prepared to assist me in this work. Your suggestion is our command."

Graham froze. Bridges had not yet asked him to do anything more than listen. He was being dragged toward a pit that Graham desperately wanted to avoid. Bridges's casual commitment of Graham to tasks that he knew nothing about frightened him, but it momentarily broke any hold Carson had over him. Graham could feel himself retreating.

"Good!" Carson said and turned his head toward Graham. "Mr. Peck, the time has come for immediate action." Carson's black eyes stared at Graham with piercing intensity. "We will assemble a new governmental structure in Europe. It will require Mr. Bridges to make a number of trips. I want you to be in control of all activities of government in the Chicago area during his absence. Are you prepared to accept such important responsibilities?"

Graham wanted to say no, but couldn't. Once again, Carson mesmerized him back inside the man's circle of control. Almost mechanically, Graham answered. "Yes sir."

"Excellent." Carson smiled and turned back to Bridges. "My true portrait will be released to the public in the immediate future. I am sending you a secure, top-level, hand-delivered package with materials that I want distributed across your city. The time has come for the citizenry not only to recognize me but also to understand that I am fully prepared to protect them from aggression. I will be their defense against the terrorist attacks you have experienced in recent days. Be prepared for immediate distribution of these materials. Are there any questions?"

Graham instantly shook his head.

Bridges bowed in formal respect. "No sir. We are prepared to act immediately upon your request."

"Excellent." Carson held up his hand in the form of a salute. "We move forward."

The technicolored image disappeared back into a green light. In a blaze of brilliance, the shape dwindled and disappeared. The color turned into nothing more than an intense white light.

Graham blinked several times, clearing his eyes. He took a deep breath.

"As always, Borden Camber Carson was brilliant!" Bridges said. He had a detached look in his eyes almost as if hypnotized. "Magnificent!"

Catching his breath, Graham took a step backward. He wanted out of the office as quickly as he could run. "Anything else?" he mumbled.

The mayor walked slowly around his desk again and sat down in a careful, if faltering manner. "I don't think so," he said mechanically. "Thank you for coming."

"Yes sir." Graham kept walking backward. "I'll be leaving the office shortly."

"Yes, Graham." Bridges's voice was flat and distant. "I will call you if a need arises."

"Thank you." Graham hurried out of the room and darted down the hall. Without returning to his office, he went down the back stairs and ran toward the Metro station.

CHAPTER 38

W HEN MARY ARRIVED home from school, her brothers had already been there for an hour and were upstairs playing. Graham was sitting at the kitchen table with Jackie, waiting for her.

"Oh!" Mary blurted out. "I'm surprised to see you home so early, Dad."

"Sit down, Mary." He pointed to the chair across the table. "Your mother and I want to talk with you."

Mary grimaced. "I haven't done anything," she instantly protested. "I mean, no one at school has even . . ."

"Mary," Jackie cut her off. "No one has accused you of anything. Your father and I have some important matters to discuss with you. Please sit down."

Mary looked suspiciously back and forth between Graham and Jackie. "Okay." She slowly sat down.

Jackie reached over and took her hand. "We have something important to talk about."

Mary recoiled. "Has someone died?"

"No," Jackie smiled. "I'm glad to tell you nothing has happened to anyone we know."

"But the matter is just as serious," Graham said. "We need to have a confidential conversation."

Mary pursed her lips. "*Confidential?*"

"Which means you cannot talk with anyone about what we say. Is that agreeable?"

"Sure."

"I mean your brothers, anyone you know, but especially your friends at school."

Mary frowned and made a face. "No one?"

"Absolutely," Graham said. "I've always trusted you. Can I continue to do so?"

"Well, sure. Of course, I can keep a secret."

"Good," Jackie said. "We want to talk about the conversation we had the other night with the woman from Israel. The New Seekers group has become important to us."

"Oh, no! *Not her.*" Mary shook her head. "I wouldn't let anyone in the world know those creeps came to our house. I hate that quasi-religious stuff they're into."

"Mary, it is far from nonsense," Graham said. "We need you to give serious thought to these matters."

"*Serious?* Listen, Dad. I don't want to hear about this nonsense much less talk about it to *anybody.*"

"It's no longer an option," Graham said. "This matter has become extremely serious."

Mary crossed her arms over her chest defiantly. "The last thing in the world that my friends want to hear about, and I mean anything about, is religious junk. Whatever you believe is fine with me. Just leave me out of the loop."

"Mary, we won't be able to do that," Graham explained. "I expect serious changes to happen quickly."

"Good for you! You and Mom believe whatever you

wish and do whatever you think is right, but I don't want to be any part of it."

Graham looked at Jackie and shook his head. "She doesn't get the picture."

"No," Jackie said. "She refuses to listen. Okay, Mary. We'll leave you out of the picture for the moment but . . ."

"*But nothing!* I don't want to know any of these ideas and I sure don't want my friends hearing about your plans. Let's just leave this issue as a truce. You go your way; I'll go mine."

"I don't think we can," Graham said, "but for the moment we'll agree to leave you out of these discussions."

"Your father believes something critical is about to happen," Jackie said. "If we're wrong, then it won't make any difference. If he's right, it will make all the difference in the world."

"Whatever." Mary stood up. "I need to go upstairs. Is that all right with everybody?"

"Go on," Graham said, lowering his head into his hands and sighing.

Mary stood in the doorway, staring at her parents and their strange behavior.

"We did our best, Graham." Jackie patted him on the back. "I'm sorry, but Mary simply isn't with us."

"The day is coming when she will have to be," Graham said, "and I'm afraid the time is growing short."

This scene is way too much, Mary thought and turned toward the stairs up to her bedroom. *I think my parents are completely unzipped. I'm living in Nutsville.*

CHAPTER 39

D URING THE WEEK that followed Graham's attempt to confront his daughter, the European nations began to fall in line behind Borden Carson. Turkey declared its total national support for Carson as its new prime minister. Working behind the scenes, the oil magnate lined up Italy, Hungary, and Slovenia immediately. Romania and Poland pledged to unify with him in a few days as did Croatia and the Netherlands. France and Germany held out, waiting to see what the rest of Europe did, but Greece seemed to be a pushover. Political disunity for well over a decade in Europe had shoved these nations apart. Carson's challenge had a sudden jolting affect, reeling them back in. None of these changes affected Mary Peck one iota. The fourteen-year-old never watched the news on television or got it anywhere else. She shut her ears and avoided all talk of what was going on in the world. While she and her friends wouldn't admit it, they worked to avoid hearing about incidents of terror exploding all over the world. Affluent and happy, she had no intention of upsetting her apple cart.

George and Jeff listened carefully when their parents talked about a rising world leader who could prove dangerous to their family. Jeff quickly tired of chattering about family problems and the five-year-old went back to playing, but his bright mind still picked up and retained the details of what was going on. George remained fascinated and was willing to talk constantly. His world had turned into an exotic movie offering a thousand strange plots for him to think about and giving George constant diversion.

With Thanksgiving only a few days away, the weather abruptly turned unusually warm. Matt called to ask what the family would do for the holidays if it stayed hot. Matthew generally called home in the evenings to inquire how the family was doing. He shared what he was learning in the New Seekers group and exchanged worries with his father. The growing reach of the security cameras that were now almost everywhere concerned him. Graham kept him informed about the areas of the metroplex that were wired and that he should avoid if Matt wanted to stay away from the big "eye."

"Dad," Matt said over the phone, "if this heat wave stays, have you considered going to the summer place at Tomahawk? The woods in Wisconsin are great in hot weather."

Graham laughed. "Usually Mohawksin Lake is snowed under at this time of the year. It's a thought, but who knows, by tomorrow the temperature may drop below freezing."

Matt lowered his voice to nearly a whisper. "We are going to have an important meeting tomorrow night. The president of the United States is going to speak on television and many of the students feel we should listen as a group. Would you and Mom would like to join us?"

Graham thought for a minute. "Do these people know who I am? My involvement in politics?"

"Jennifer and Adah do, but the others don't. We still keep our identities under wraps."

"Good. As a matter of fact, I'd like to hear what your friends think about this presidential address. Yes, your mother and I will be there."

"Excellent! I'll let you know where the meeting will be tomorrow. We keep the place secret until the last minute, but it will be somewhere with a television."

"Thanks, son. We'll look forward to seeing you."

Graham had barely hung up when his private cell phone rang. He clicked it on.

"Graham, we need to have a special meeting early in the morning." The familiar voice of Frank Bridges boomed over the tiny receiver. "At the crack of dawn."

"How early?"

"Can you get here by seven o'clock?"

"Certainly."

"As our Middle Eastern friend would say, this is an Inner Circle meeting so you'll need to come up the back way."

"I'll be there."

The phone clicked off. These special meetings inside Bridges's inner sanctum always proved disconcerting. If there was anything Graham didn't want, it was another holographic conversation with Carson. The man frightened him and Graham now had plenty of evidence to fear whatever it was that this Middle Eastern oil tycoon was doing. Maybe he was the "dragon" Adah feared or possibly the man was simply an international opportunist; nevertheless, he had personal capacities that were too powerful to be treated lightly. Graham would not sleep well that night.

CHAPTER 40

A T PRECISELY seven o'clock, Graham walked down the hidden hallway into the mayor's office. Jake Pemrose was already sitting in front of Bridges's desk smoking a cigar.

"Ah, our star athlete of the behind-the-scenes maneuvers," Pemrose greeted him. "Welcome."

Graham's eyes squinted menacingly. "Good morning," he said solemnly.

"Surprised to see me?" Jake quipped and blew a big cloud of smoke in the air.

"Every morning the sun comes up on a new day," Graham said. "Can't ever tell what to expect next."

"Now, now, you boys put your swords away," the mayor said. "We're all playing on the same team. I haven't revealed any other identities to you, Graham, because it's been important to keep our work in complete secret."

"Oh?" Graham said.

"Sit down, Peck," Bridges said. "Before you arrived, Jake and I were discussing some of the details of what will be unfolding in the next twenty-four hours. I believe that today will prove to be a major turning point for the entire globe."

"*Really?*" Graham said. "What do you mean?"

"Come on, boy!" Pemrose said in a condescending tone. "You should be able to guess what's on the table."

Graham shot a hard glance at Jake, but said nothing. The fact that Pemrose had arrived earlier meant the man was at least one step up the ladder from Graham and maybe many more rungs.

"Peck," the mayor began, "between now and Christmas you will see amazing things happen across the world. Borden Carson has already talked with me about most of what will be developing and tonight the president of the United States will start the big ball rolling."

"Please be more specific," Graham said.

"Electronic surveillance is not only in place around Chicago but across the entire country," Bridges began. "Computer systems in this country have been meshed with the operations fronted by the Royal Arab Petroleum Company. Surveillance is now positioned on anyone who resists our control. Understand me?"

"We've made some other adjustments," Jake said and tapped his cigar in the ashtray. "Our local police department is going to have direct access to everything in the State Department's records. At the flip of a switch on our computers, we'll be able to look at anyone's Visa, MasterCard, and any other credit card data as well as any criminal records even from overseas. The Chicago Police Department will be part of a global network. We've got our finger on everybody."

Graham frowned. "Really?"

"No matter how solid our political leadership is, someone is always out there trying to wrestle control away from the central leaders," Bridges said. "Carson now has a plug in that bottle. Anyone trying to stop him can be identified quickly."

Graham turned nervously in his chair. "What kind of group are you talking about? Terrorists of some sort?"

Pemrose shook his head vigorously. "Naw. We can handle those people quickly enough. What you have to watch out for is religious groups, the nut cases who always spark trouble."

Graham blinked several times, trying to carefully frame his question. "You talking about those Sunday Morning Encounter Groups springing up around the country?"

"No, no," the mayor said. "Those gatherings are little more than hot air conferences of navel gazers, individuals with too much time on their hands and too many worries in their heads. You have to watch the extremists. Those are the people who might throw a wrench into the machinery."

"Look," Pemrose continued his tirade. "Freedom of expression is going to be a thing of the past, Peck. We can't have people running around saying whatever pops into their heads. The government's going to put a clamp on those loudmouths."

A cold sensation ran down Graham's back and fear grabbed his throat. These two men were talking about a group like the New Seekers, now considered subversive and vulnerable to arrest. His own son could get hauled in for nothing more than showing up at the wrong place.

"Religious subversives corrupt normal people!" Pemrose spat harshly. "True believers always have started revolts.

We've got to wipe these people out and I say the sooner we start the better!"

"Now, now, Jake. You're getting the wagon ahead of the horses. The whole plan has to unfold in stages, and our first step is to get people acquainted with Carson's face. Tomorrow his portraits will be released—they'll be all over the papers and television. We are on the verge of working out a petroleum deal with Royal Arab Petroleum that will be extremely worthwhile for this city. At this moment I want to make sure both of you are fully aware of what's coming. It's time to buckle your seat belts." Bridges looked Graham squarely in the eye. "I haven't said it before, and I'm sure it's not necessary to say today, but I want to make sure that you and Jake understand how serious these matters are. One breach of security and either of you could be on the butcher table."

Jake chuckled. "You're suggesting we'd get carved up like a side of beef?"

"You've got it," the mayor said cynically.

Graham's eyes narrowed. "Either of you men really know anything about death?"

"What?" the mayor asked.

"You're talking about death like you and Jake have all the answers. I wondered what you knew."

"I don't want to talk about death," Bridges bore down. "I'm suggesting you boys keep your noses clean. Get me?"

Graham didn't move or say anything. Bridges shrugged and asked Pemrose a question. As they bantered, Graham abruptly realized he had gone back and forth on the question of the Anti-Christ, thinking maybe Borden Carson wasn't that bad; maybe he was. This early morning meeting had pulled the rug out from under his feet. If he and Jackie accepted Matt's invitation and went to the New Seekers meeting tonight, they could be crossing a highly dangerous line. He could no longer stand along the edges and simply watch.

"You with me, Peck?" the mayor asked.

"Yes sir," Graham answered mechanically.

"Good! Now I want you and Pemrose to look at the materials I received from Carson which will be plastered all over this city in twenty-four hours. We need to make some choices and get this matter in order. Nothing will happen today, but first thing tomorrow morning the presses start flying. We're going to turn this city into Carsonland." Bridges chuckled. "Gentlemen, take a look and see." He pushed the photos forward.

Graham wanted to bolt out the door, but knew he couldn't. He would have to play this hand down to the last card, so he wouldn't accidentally sell out his son and the boy's friends. Worse still, he might betray his wife and their entire family!

"Carson is awesome!" Bridges grinned. "The man has an amazing heritage. While he looks sort of like a cross between an Arab and an Italian, Carson's lineage goes clear back to the Caesars. No one is his equal."

"Yeah," Graham muttered and stared straight ahead. "I bet so."

"One of the most important facts you want to keep in mind is that Carson actually has two names," Bridges said. "He uses the English name with the western world, but our leader has an unusual background. He has used many names in his rise to power while still keeping the name he was born with."

Graham's lips parted slightly. "He has another name?" he mumbled.

"Really!" Pemrose said.

Graham gawked. "I see," he mumbled and prepared to scribble the name on a piece of paper. "An Arabic name?"

"Only the Inner Circle know he also has an Arabic name," the mayor explained. "His closest advisors also call him Hassan Jawhar Rashid."

CHAPTER 41

THE UNUSUALLY HOT WEATHER for late November did not subside. By early morning, Chicago felt like the Fourth of July with the burning moon appearing to have joined the scorching sun in baking the entire United States. The heat only added to Graham's discomfort. Following the early morning meeting with the mayor and Jake Pemrose, Graham didn't come out of his office all morning. He told Sarah Cates to hold his calls, and she maintained a polite distance.

Shutting the world out, Graham anguished over what he had heard in the mayor's inner office. Not knowing the Bible well enough to reference any specific passages, he felt lost and bewildered, like a child wandering through a thicket in a dense forest. By ten o'clock, he could wait no longer and called Adah Honi. She agreed to take the express train and meet him halfway, at a stop at California Park around 11:30. At the least, she might help him gain some smidgen of insight.

Graham arrived before Adah's train pulled in, forcing him to wait on the station platform while the sun bore down. Fortunately, he had only worn a cotton pullover sweater, but it still felt like he was sitting under a heat lamp. Glancing up and down the platform, Graham noticed the strange assortment of people waiting for the next train. By and large, they were a poor, surly group, avoiding all contact and conversation with anyone. Most of them wore badly worn clothing, torn pants, shoes cracked and ragged at the toes. The indigent looked at him with accusing eyes as if he was far, far too well dressed for their lot. Graham turned away uncomfortably and stared up the tracks.

The Metro Express came flying into the station and pulled to a screeching halt. Passengers hurried off and the disheveled commuters pushed to get in. Adah Honi was among the last to break through the crowd.

Wearing a long black dress that buttoned at the neck, Adah didn't look like anyone on or around the train. Her straight, black hair pulled back revealed her elegantly chiseled profile that lent her a haunted appearance. Her black eyelids were half closed, but Graham realized she was surveying everyone on the platform with computer-like precision, checking all their faces. The woman looked like a polished spy in the midst of an unkempt world.

"Adah!" Graham walked quickly toward her. "Here I am."

The Jewish woman smiled thinly and only nodded slightly.

"Thank you so much for coming, Adah."

"Let us quickly walk away from the platform." Adah spoke low, almost in a whisper. "We need from any cameras to stay away."

"Of course." Graham pointed toward the steps. "We can find a place to sit down at the bottom of the steps."

"Please go ahead, and I will follow you."

Graham hurried down the stairs and spotted a bench a few feet away. He immediately sat down, and only then realized Adah was not following behind him. She seemed to be coming down the steps at a snail's pace, leisurely catching up with him almost as if she didn't know him.

"We must not look like together we came," Adah said. "One can never tell when they are being followed or observed."

Graham looked around at the trees around them. "I don't see any cameras around here."

"Good. On the phone you said you had something important to share with me. You can tell now me."

Graham shoved a piece of paper into her palm. "I discovered that Carson uses a second name in Arabic. I have written it down for you."

Adah took a deep breath. "I see." She exhaled slowly. "Very surprising."

"The name is Hassan Jawhar Rashid. I have no idea what it means to have two names."

After several moments of quiet reflection, Adah said, "I can tell you that Hassan means handsome and Jawhar is a jewel. It is like saying this man is a handsome or beautiful jewel. Anyone who knows the Arabic language would this meaning understand."

"But does this refer to the Anti-Christ?"

Adah pursed her lips. "I am not sure. I will need to spend the rest of the day working on this meaning. I can say no more."

"I am coming to the New Seekers meeting tonight. I want to hear what your members think about the president's speech."

"You must be very careful. Nothing is safe."

"You're telling me! Groups like yours are the new targets for instant police investigation. I fear for all of you, including my son."

Adah nodded. "I will hope to have an answer for you about this name by tonight." She stood up and looked around carefully. "We shall see. Goodbye." Adah quickly walked toward the steps on the other side of the tracks to return to Evanston.

Feeling like a pawn in a strange chess game, Graham watched her disappear. He waited a few minutes and then went back up the stairs to return downtown. When he came it had not occurred to him that he might be observed by a camera or someone following him. He glanced around the station, feeling naked and vulnerable. For the first time, Graham realized an unseen spotlight might be shining on him.

CHAPTER 42

GRAHAM AND JACKIE PECK pulled up to a dilapidated restaurant on the outskirts of Skokie, a perfect place for a secluded meeting. The drive from Arlington Heights down Palatine Road toward Interstate 94 had not been difficult, but they made sure they arrived slightly after the announced starting time, wanting to look as anonymous as possible. They had been told to instruct the waiter that they were with the Paul and Harriet Seeker party in the back room. The attendant at the door wore a black vest over a white shirt, but his black khaki pants were on the smudged side. The waiter walked them through the old steak house that looked like it hadn't been painted since 1990.

"This place needs more than a coat of fresh paint," Graham said quietly.

"Yeah," she answered.

The waiter shot both of them a dirty look, but didn't stop walking. Entering through a door at the back, they found a group of thirty students sitting around long tables. Across the room from them stood an old large-screen television. A tattered menu with the evening specials was thumbtacked to the wall. Most of the New Seekers group were eating quietly. Adah Honi sat next to a baldheaded man with puffs of white hair on the sides of his head. His dark, suntanned face was covered with white stubble. The older man looked up at them with black eyes twinkling with warmth and hospitality. Adah leaped to her feet and rushed toward Graham and Jackie, hugging them both.

"Bless you!" Adah effused. "I am so glad you could come tonight." She hugged Jackie. "I want you to meet my good friend Eldad Rafaeli."

"Hallo. I am Eldad." He extended a dark pudgy hand with thick fingers. Eldad might have been somewhere between forty and fifty years old, but his face seemed to be almost ageless. He could be much older. "Glad to meet you," he said in a heavily accented voice.

"My pleasure." Graham shook his hand.

"Me, too," Jackie said.

"Eldad recently came here from Rosh-Ha'Ayin, a town near Tel Aviv," Adah explained. "He worked in a Pil tobacco factory for many years."

"Yes," Eldad said. "For many years."

Graham glanced around the room. Sitting with some friends and next to Jennifer Andrews, Matt watched them. He winked at his father, but didn't move. Graham smiled back.

"He sees us," Jackie said. "Play it cool."

"Please sit down with us." Adah pulled a chair out. "The program on television begins in just a moment." She leaned over and spoke into Graham's ear. "Eldad is a new believer and one of us. You can trust him implicitly."

Graham nodded and sat down next to Jackie. One of the students at the head table stood up and welcomed everyone on behalf of Paul and Harriet Seeker. The young man paused and winked knowingly at the group; he noted that they had gathered to hear the president of the United States speak and that the program would begin momentarily. One of the students got up and turned the television on. The set flashed pictures of Washington, D.C., and the group became silent.

Graham leaned back in his chair and studied this unusual group of students. For the most part they didn't look different from any group of kids in Evanston. They had a typical university demeanor and seemed well-mannered enough. They hadn't overwhelmed Graham and Jackie and kept a polite distance. He liked their restraint. Everything felt in order.

"Looks like the show's about to start," Jackie said.

"*The big show*," Graham added, softly.

"My fellow Americans," the president began in his usual familiar tone, "let us begin by reviewing what has happened in the recent military incursions unfolding in the Middle East and with the Russians."

Graham listened attentively, but he had already heard most of what was said. Borden Carson had given them inside information with explicit details on the extent of damages and the serious nuclear fallout problems stemming from the Russians' attack. Graham watched Eldad and Adah. Their faces were stoic, giving no hint of what they actually thought of the speech.

"The time has come for the United States to stand with Borden Camber Carson's efforts in Europe," the president said. "World petroleum interests must be protected and our armed forces will support this effort. On a personal basis, I have known Mr. Carson for many years and I believe this is a man we can and must trust. Recently elected the prime minister of Turkey, Borden Carson has stepped on the stage of world leadership in the role of an overseer and a visionary."

Here it comes, Graham thought. *We are about to receive an exhaustive list of Carson's credits, then he'll ask this country to accept him as their savior.*

As Graham expected, the president continued an almost unending recitation of the accomplishments of Carson as well as the Royal Arab Petroleum empire. The president pushed for the United States to line up behind Carson because his surveillance systems offered the nation an even higher level of security. The president appeared certain that more terrorist attacks would hit America. Abruptly, he held up a portrait of Carson, wearing a tie and black business suit.

"Because of his extreme modesty and propriety," the president continued, "you have not seen photographs of Mr. Carson, but that is now coming to an end. I want you to know this man is our friend; he will, in a sense, stand on every street corner to make sure that the enemies of freedom are not able to destroy our rights. *Watch for him because he is watching for you.*"

Graham recoiled. Just as Adah had predicted, the stage was being set for this man to gain world dominance and power. Borden Carson, or Hassan Rashid, had his hands on virtually all the control switches of the American government!

"We are going to do everything in our power to protect American citizens from terrorist invasions," the president insisted. "You can go to bed tonight knowing that I have made this my number one agenda for today, tomorrow, and the rest of my administration."

With all that Graham had learned from Bridges and the holographic conversations with Carson, he knew the president was up to his neck in this ruse while the country didn't have the slightest idea about the real agenda, but the die was cast and the plan would unfold as the president, Mayor Bridges, Jake Pemrose, and heavens know who else in the "Inner Circle" expected. The telecast faded with the camera focusing on Carson's picture in the center of the screen.

Several of the student members of the New Seekers group walked to the doors and the windows in the room to make sure no one was outside listening. The rest of the members squeezed closer together.

"We made an electronic sweep of the room before we began," the young leader said quietly. "We're convinced there are no hidden mikes or surveillance equipment in here. We can speak openly and forthrightly. What do you think of this speech?"

"I think we're being duped," one of the students immediately charged. "I don't like what I heard."

"I agree," another student chimed in. "The president is selling this Carson guy as the answer to all our national problems. I don't believe it."

Jennifer Andrews said nothing, but watched the group intently.

Jackie whispered in Graham's ear, "These are bright kids."

Students spoke heatedly for several minutes with no one

supporting the president's position. Graham and Jackie listened attentively without saying anything. Eventually the leader turned to Adah Honi.

"You are our advisor, Adah. What do you think?"

"The important issue is what says the Bible," Adah began quietly. "What we think is important, but the Scripture is critical. We are all still in this world because we failed earlier to take this into account."

The students murmured their agreement.

"We know that the first step in the final plan began with the Rapture of all of the true believers. Of course, the moon has also turned red. Then we have heard of nothing but wars and more wars. This problem is right on schedule for what comes next. The nuclear defeat of Russia is straight out of the book of Ezekiel. Now we come to the next step, the appearance of the Anti-Christ. Makes sense to you? Does it?"

Graham watched the eyes of the students. Each person watched with intense seriousness registered across their faces. No one heard Adah's words with anything less that the utmost respect.

"Today I received a very important message." Adah looked at Graham as if she wanted his approval before she said anything more. "A name! A very important name! I think this is the most insight to date I have received. I have been studying this matter all afternoon." She looked at Graham again.

"Go ahead," Graham said. "This matter is too serious not to be completely honest. We have already decided to stand with you."

Adah smiled broadly. "Thank you, sir. We are deeply indebted to you, Mr. Peck, for giving me this new name."

The students glanced back and forth between Matt and Graham as if they were putting a piece in the puzzle together. Matt stared at the floor and said nothing.

Adah pulled her Bible out of her purse and opened it to the back of the book. "We must turn to the final verses in the end of chapter thirteen in Revelation to understand what this night we have heard." She read slowly and carefully from the Bible. "'This calls for wisdom: let him who has understanding reckon the number of the beast, for it is a human number, its number is six hundred and sixty-six.'" She stopped and looked around the room. "Do you not see the relationship between what we heard tonight and this number?"

No one spoke. The students looked mystified. Graham glanced at Jackie. Neither had any more insight than the students did.

"Let me put it this way." Adah reached down and ripped off a big piece of the white paper tablecloth. Taking a ballpoint, she scribbled furiously across the page. Walking to the front wall, she pulled a couple of thumbtacks off the menu hanging there and tacked the page to the center of the front wall. On the torn page a big 666 had the name of Borden Camber Carson written underneath. "What do you see?" she asked the group.

No one spoke.

"The number 666 is what the book of Revelation says is the name of the beast. This creature is a symbol of the evil power that will make war on the saints and even conquer some of them." Adah stopped and slowly looked around the room. The group sat as if they were in a trance, stupefied by what she was saying. "In the first century, Christians thought that this number was the name of Nero and it probably was in their time."

"You're saying Nero is the name of the Anti-Christ?" Matt abruptly broke in.

"No, no." Adah shook her finger emphatically. "Not *the final Anti-Christ*. No! In his time he was only *an Anti-Christ*. I am saying that some of what the Bible says is true both then and now! In the final times this beast will also have the name of 666."

"What is your point?" Graham interjected. "I'm not following you."

Adah started writing on the torn sheet of paper again. Directly beneath Carson's name she wrote Hassan Jawhar Rashid. "Do you see it now?" she asked the group.

Once again no one answered.

"Let me tell you. This Carson also goes by the name I have written here. Rashid is Arabic." Adah started tapping on each of the letters in the name. "Look! B-o-r-d-e-n," she said. "How many letters that is?"

"Six?" someone said.

"Good," Adah answered and started tapping again. "C-a-m-b-e-r. How many here?"

"Six!" Jackie suddenly exclaimed.

"Look." Adah tapped on the name Hassan in the same way. "How many letters here?"

"Six!" Graham exploded. "Every one of these names has six letters!"

"And when you put them together each name makes six-hundred and sixty-six," Adah explained. "This Carson has two names, but they both say the same thing. *This man is Mr. 666!*"

For thirty seconds no one said anything until the silence became ominous.

Students suddenly began talking furiously and the room broke into turmoil. Jackie turned to Graham, her face white and drawn. Graham could only shake his head.

"I'm horrified!" Jackie said.

"Me, too," Graham answered.

Eldad Rafaeli held up his pudgy hand. "May I speak?"

"Of course," Adah said.

"In Israel we have lived with war and fighting since the day in 1948 we become a nation," Eldad began. "In my town of Rosh Ha'Ayin it is no different. But I came here because I believed that the Holy One, blessed be His name, for some reason I cannot understand, sent me here. Now I have heard the truth I seek." Eldad's eyes widened in an alarmed stare. "This man Carson, or Rashid, is the beast we must fear!"

CHAPTER 43

B Y THANKSGIVING DAY, the weather had snapped out of the summer-like high digits and now, ominously, a new blanket of snow covered Chicago. The Pecks gathered around a sumptuous table laden with the traditional turkey, stuffing, and green beans as well as a couple of pumpkin pies. However, the Arlington Heights neighborhood remained more subdued than in previous years with the memories of Maria Peck's violent death. If anything, fear had only increased in the past few weeks.

Graham and Jackie attempted to maintain a festive atmosphere around the loaded table and avoided talking about what they were learning from the New Seekers group. Matt avoided any confrontations with Mary, but tension still hung in the air. Only once did George mention that Grammy always fixed marshmallow cranberry salad and Jeff immediately started sniffling. Everyone pushed on, attempting to avoid their own grief. Somehow, the family got through the Thanksgiving celebration without erupting either into a war or a litany of grief. At dawn on Friday, Mayor Bridges called another emergency meeting and Graham was forced to return to his office.

"You hadn't planned to go today, had you?" Jackie had a pensive sound in her voice.

"No," Graham said emphatically. "I even gave my secretary the day off. I don't expect anybody to be there."

"What do you think is going on?"

"I don't know, but it makes me extremely apprehensive."

Jackie nodded. "I agree and it makes me worry about you."

Graham hugged her. "I'm more worried about what our entire family's next step is going to be. Because of what we've learned from Adah Honi, we must make some big decisions."

"Oh, Graham. This is as frightening as your mother's death!"

"Yeah," Graham said resolutely. "This entire experience changes everything we've believed in."

"Adah told me we should learn to pray."

"Well, I don't have the slightest idea how you do it." He hugged her again. "Keep the doors locked."

As usual, Graham drove his small hydrogen-powered car to the Metro Express station and boarded the train. A picture of Borden Carson had been posted over his head on the side of the car. Avoiding the picture and not looking at anyone else, Graham thought over and over again about what he heard Adah say about Carson or Rashid. He was stuck with the man's extraordinary capacities, which left Graham feeling like Carson could crush him as easily as stepping on an ant.

Jake Pemrose was there when Graham arrived. A quick glance left the impression that the man had been there much longer than a few minutes.

"Hello, Peck," Pemrose said coldly.

"Thanks for coming in today, Graham," Bridges answered. "I want to thank both of you for the excellent job that was done in getting Mr. Carson's pictures plastered all over downtown Chicago and out over the suburbs. At this point, there isn't anyone that can say they don't know what this man looks like."

Graham gave only a slight nod.

"We also have nearly everyone in the city covered with

the mark on their foreheads that allows the nanorobots to send security signals to our computers."

Neither Graham nor any of the family made the mandatory visit to get the "mark of the beast" on their foreheads, and they weren't about to do so. It took some maneuvering, but they escaped being tagged.

"The president's speech has been well received," Bridges continued. "The motto, 'Watch for him because he is watching for you,' seems to have stuck. Our latest poll indicates the public is lining up behind Carson. That's important."

"Why?" Graham suddenly asked. "What's coming next?"

"Ah, Peck! You're always a jump ahead of me." The mayor smiled broadly and winked. "I could tell the moment you walked in here that you had something important on your mind."

Graham stiffened.

"Okay, boys. We need to move on to the next step that Mr. Carson has laid out." Bridges threw a couple of switches. "I recorded the important part of my last conversation with Mr. Carson over the holographic transmitter." A beam of light immediately shot up from the base of the machine and began changing colors. "Let's see what our leader said last night."

The greenish light turned into a form; an immobile Borden Carson appeared to be sitting behind a desk, his hands extended across the desktop with a large diamond ring sparkling on his pinky finger. Carson's black eyes flashed with intensity. The mayor hit another button and the motionless figure started to move and speak.

"The European Union has solidified," Carson said. "We have now created a military alliance with the capacity to control the world's oil supplies as well as hydrogen production. Members of this union stand unanimously with me. I have also reached an agreement with the Russians to insure the stability of the price of petroleum and maintain a predictable supply. I am well pleased."

As Graham feared, Carson had worked out a deal with the Russians. The man moved at a pace far beyond anything he would have thought possible.

"I fear your country will be faced with more terrorist attacks," Carson continued. "You will need to spread this report across your area, warning people that you intend to patrol the streets at night to protect them from these dangerous elements. I suggest that we impose a curfew of eleven o'clock with police and military personnel immediately arresting everyone on the street after that time. We need a significant crackdown in order to make your population feel secure. This should be done quickly."

Bridges hit the off button. "There you have it, boys! Our leader wants us to get the city prepared for a curfew."

"Wait a minute!" Graham objected. "No one wants this kind of intrusion. If we put it into effect, get ready for a reaction. People will be angry!"

Pemrose raised one eyebrow. "You're going to deny Borden Carson?" he asked with a surly twist to his words. "And don't forget that you're talking to the mayor who won by a record-breaking margin."

"I'm telling you that we are talking big trouble with this idea," Graham pushed back. "Yes. People are afraid, but they've never had anyone tell them when to go home and stay. Moreover, we've got people working night shifts. What about them?"

"That's up to you and Jake to work out," the mayor shot back. "I'm sure you'll come up with something that'll work."

"Me?" Graham's voice became shrill. "My answer is let's not do any of it!"

For a moment Jake and Frank looked back and forth as if sending a silent message to each other. Bridges leaned forward and looked intimidatingly at Graham.

"Graham, this is not only a test of the people. It's also aimed at us. Are we going to obey or will we be like one of these rebellious religious groups?" Bridges stuck his finger in Graham's face. "Are you on the team or not?"

Graham caught his breath. "I thought we always had honest and forthright discussions in here."

"Oh, we do," Bridges said, "but we don't contradict anything that Mr. Carson asks us to do. His wisdom far exceeds anything that any of us know. We follow without reservation."

"I—I see," Graham fumbled.

"I'll give you a hint," Bridges said. "In a few days the European Union is going to go to war against India and Pakistan because they have not complied with demands on petroleum shipments across those countries. When the bombs start to fall, we will have an ample pretext for our police action. Don't worry. The president will create a nationwide curfew system to coincide with what we are doing."

Graham shook his head mechanically.

"Never question anything Carson says," Pemrose warned. "Don't forget it, Peck."

Something was going on in this room beyond Graham's awareness and he needed to be extremely careful. A hundred thoughts shot through his mind. At best, Pemrose was telling him he was number 3 in the Chicago part of the Inner Circle, and at the least, Pemrose was ahead of him in the pecking order. Clearly Bridges and Pemrose had their own private agreements to which Graham would never be a party. He should keep his mouth shut and hold the cards close to his vest. Duck his head. The action was getting much too close to home.

"Thank you," Graham said professionally. "Anything else?"

The mayor shook his head. "No. The war with India and Pakistan will break out in two days. I want our local personnel in place immediately so we can declare a curfew. I trust such a plan will be operational by Monday."

"Of course." Graham avoided looking at Pemrose. "Anything else you need from me?"

Bridges looked surprised. "No. No. I don't think so."

"Good. If there's no problem, I'll be on my way."

"Of course." The mayor stood up. "Thanks again for coming down early."

"Naturally." Graham nodded to both men and walked out the door. He noticed that the sliding door at the end of the wall was left open. Stopping on the plush, thick carpet, Graham hesitated to listen for a second.

"What do you think?" Pemrose's voice echoed down the hallway.

"I don't know," the mayor answered. "I can't tell."

"I don't like it," Jake growled.

Graham silently hurried through the front door and disappeared down the hall.

CHAPTER 44

ACROSS CHICAGO the snow deepened, and the children were forced to spend most of their time indoors. Mary Peck steadfastly refused to talk about or listen to any conversations about the Scripture. Insisting it was the last thing in the entire world that her friends wanted to hear about, she dogmatically maintained that developing a reputation for being a "religious crazy" was not what she needed *ever*! When any spiritual topic came up, Mary retreated to her room. On Wednesday during the first week in December, Graham, Jackie, and Matt sat down around the kitchen table.

"Time is working against us," Graham began.

"What do you mean?" Jackie asked.

"In only a few weeks our world has been turned inside out." Graham slowly stirred his coffee. "What we thought was dependable, permanent, stable, has been revealed only to be cardboard. Our entire society is being used as a pawn in a game being played by people they don't even know exist."

"*Know?*" Matt's voice raised an octave. "Listen, Dad. How many people in the world even knew what Carson looked like until after you actually saw the guy? *You've* been on the inside of history's final drama."

"It's been an accident," Graham argued.

"I don't believe in accidents anymore," Matt countered. "The hand of God is working in everything that we do. Divine power has led you into the camp of the ultimate enemy."

Graham ran his hands nervously through his hair. "I'm not used to thinking theologically. I have no idea how to answer such an assertion. As far as I'm concerned, it all just happened."

"But things don't *just happen*, Dad. God has already taken his church out of the world, and now he's trying to bring people like us out of the world's turmoil. He's attempting to save us from the terrible days that are ahead."

"I don't know that all of those assertions are true, son. I'm only attempting to save our family from a web that's being spun around our feet. A dangerous spider is loose in the world and I don't want us to get bitten."

"Your father's terribly concerned that we don't get sucked into a whirlpool that will drown a lot of people," Jackie argued.

"We can't avoid what's coming," Matt said. "It's all a part of God's plan. He's the big foot that will eventually step on that ugly spider!"

"Son, you've been the key for us to all these new insights," Jackie said. "Don't ever forget how grateful we are to you."

"And I'm not arguing with you," Graham said. "What I'm concerned about is that electronic surveillance is increasing in Chicago at such a rate that we could get caught.

This whole city is wired. We've avoided being marked on the forehead, but the process is likely to catch up with us sooner or later."

"So?" Matt asked. "What are we going to do?"

"Do you think the *entire* New Seekers group is trustworthy?" Graham asked.

Matt nodded. "Down to the last person! Jennifer Andrews is only one example of how trustworthy these people are. You already know Adah Honi is straight as a stick."

"Yes," Graham said thoughtfully. "Those people seem to be honest, but we can't take any chances. I don't want our family jeopardized by talking with the wrong people."

"Outside of the New Seekers, I don't know who the right people would be," Matt said.

"Okay. That's what I concluded," Graham said. "I want you and your mother to know that we must maintain the closest attention to what happens around us. I'm worried myself that I might walk into a trap at the office. I don't trust Bridges or Pemrose. But if I'm right, we may need the help of your friends in the New Seeker's group. Is that possible?"

"Sure." Matt shrugged. "Listen, Dad. You've become a hero to these kids. They don't really know you, but you've got big time respect with them."

"What are you thinking?" Jackie asked. "I think there's something else going on in your mind."

"Well," Graham said slowly, "there's one more thing. I haven't trusted my secretary Sarah Cates for a long time, but I may need her help. She could be lying to me, and that could bring the roof down on my head if she's in cahoots with Pemrose, Bridges, or who knows."

"You really think so?" Jackie asked.

"I don't know." Graham said. "But I wanted both of you to know that I'll probably crawl way out on the end of a weak limb at the office. If something snaps, we'll have to move fast."

Jackie put her arm around Graham's shoulders. "Don't worry. We're three hundred percent behind you."

"Thanks," Graham said. "I'm about to jump on that branch. I hope I don't crash to the ground."

CHAPTER 45

ON THURSDAY, the New Seekers group met again. Following the meeting, Graham and Jackie met with Adah Honi at the back of the room. Huddled next to a back wall, they talked quietly.

"Adah," Graham said, "you've been amazingly correct. You've helped us understand why millions of people disappeared, the moon turned red, the source of the accelerating wars and conflicts, and the rise of the Anti-Christ. What do you see happening next?"

Jackie squeezed in closer to the Jewish woman. "We need your advice and direction."

Adah smiled. "I am no prophet."

"You are to us," Jackie insisted.

"If my interpretation of the Bible is correct," Adah said slowly. "I think that the climate of fear and chaos will increase as does Rashid's ability the world to control. I suspect that this man his power will consolidate. He will be a most diabolical person."

"More war, huh?" Graham asked.

"But he will make a surprising support for Israel in a short while, but the troubles for Christians, for believers in Jesus as the Messiah will only increase. If I were you, I would put my money into gold as a hedge against troubles with currency."

"We have more dark days ahead?" Jackie asked.

"I am afraid so. *Very* dark days."

Graham patted Adah on the shoulder. "We may need your help when the crunch comes. Can we call you?"

Adah beamed. "At any moment! My friend Eldad Rafaeli is also ready to help. Don't hesitate to let us know about how we can be of assistance."

"Thank you, Adah. We appreciate your support," Jackie said.

"More than we can say," Graham added. "And you trust this group of students?" He pointed around the room.

"Of course," the Jewish woman said.

"Adah," Jackie said, "I have one last question. I hear you talking about trusting God." Jackie stopped and rubbed her chin thoughtfully. "I understand the idea, but nothing seems to connect with me. Trusting someone like my husband makes sense, but God is such an abstract idea."

Adah nodded. "Yes, I understand. Let me see if I can help you." She beckoned for them to follow her across the room. Picking up a slice of bread and a glass, the Jewish woman sat them on the table in front of Graham and Jackie. "From our history each year we have the Passover

Supper, a time when we remember God delivered our people from death and set us free. We eat bread and drink wine to celebrate our trust in God."

"Y-yes," Jackie said slowly.

"Then Jesus, or Yeshua as we say, took this cup and unleavened bread and made it a symbol of himself. Christians usually took this sacrament to come into an intimate relationship with the Lord. You see?"

Graham shook his head. "No. No, I don't."

"When you eat something, it becomes a part of you," Adah explained. "It is literally absorbed into the cells and tissues of your body. Nothing could be closer or more intimate."

"Of course," Jackie said. "I understand that idea."

"You must trust the bread and wine completely if you are going to eat them, expecting such a wonderful encounter in your spiritual world. Right?"

"H-u-mm." Jackie nodded her head. "Trusting God is like deciding to eat the bread and drink the wine?"

"Exactly!" Adah said. "It is a act of saying 'yes' to everything that is to you offered."

"Thank you," Jackie said. "Yes. The idea makes more sense to me now."

Graham said nothing. The explanation was clear but had left him uncertain. Could trusting God be as simple as eating a piece of bread? He didn't think so.

On Friday Graham called Sarah Cates into his office. The attractive young woman brought her scratch pad, prepared to take notes.

"Sit down, Sarah," Graham said. "I want to talk to you for a minute."

Sarah gritted her teeth. She sat down slowly. "I'm being fired? You're moving me to another office, aren't you? I knew this wouldn't last."

Graham studied her carefully. Sarah didn't look hostile. In fact, she seemed to still have that slight gleam in the corner of her eye.

"I understand," Sarah continued. "I'm sorry, but I guess I had it coming."

"No, Sarah. A move isn't in my plans."

"Oh!" Sarah looked surprised. "Really? You're sure?"

"You said that you had some affection for me," Graham continued. "Is that still true?"

Sarah's face began turning red. "Look. I was drinking and I should never have . . ."

"I ask if you still care about me?" Graham pushed.

Sarah looked at the floor, saying nothing. Finally she said, "Yes."

Graham took a deep breath. "Good. I need your help as well as your confidence. I must be able to trust you."

The woman blinked several times. "What? What are you saying? Certainly, you can tell me anything."

Graham's eyes narrowed. "We've got some traps to set. You ready to go fishing?"

CHAPTER 46

JACKIE PECK was sitting at her desk, when the walls began to shake slightly. The desk gradually inched away from her and the chandelier swung back and forth. She looked up from the list she was making and stared at this strange movement around her. The ceiling rippled and the entire room seemed to shift. Her balance abruptly felt out of kilter. Suddenly the entire house shook and for a moment Jackie felt nauseous. She grabbed the edge of her desk for stability, but everything inside of her buckled. Thirty seconds later the frightening movements stopped.

Jackie's heart pounded. With her hand on her chest, Jackie dashed out of the room and darted through the front door. Across the front lawn a large, winding crack jagged in an ugly zigzag pattern into a cracked sidewalk. A black cloud drifted in front of the sun, sending ominous dark shadows everywhere. The wind whipped around the corner of the house and a blast of arctic air hit her in the face. Across the street the neighbor ran out her front door.

"Oh, Lord help us!" the woman shouted. "What's happened?"

"It must have been an earthquake," Jackie said. "Never in my life have I been in such a big shake. I don't think one like this has ever hit Chicago."

"Never heard of such a thing! Did it hurt your house?"

"I don't know. I suppose I'll have to wait for Graham to come home and check around the foundation."

The woman nodded. "Yes, I suppose so." She looked up into the sky. "How strange. Even the sun looks black."

People began coming out of other houses, looking around and gawking up at the sky. Jackie didn't like the exposure and went back inside.

One day there would be summer-like temperatures; twenty-four hours later a blizzard blew in. Everything was out of order. Now an earthquake had undermined their city!

Jackie walked through all the rooms of the house looking for cracks in the wall or through the ceiling. Finally, she picked up the phone and called Graham.

"Did you feel the shock?" Jackie asked.

"Yes. Our building swayed for several seconds. When I looked out the windows I could see huge waves rolling in off of Lake Michigan and slamming the piers. Looks like significant damage is being done down there by the docks. Did it hurt our house?"

"I don't think the damage is severe. What do you make of it?"

"I think the quake must have occurred out there under Lake Michigan," Graham said. "It's really created chaos downtown."

"I can't actually tell how badly the house got hit, but we do have a cracked sidewalk."

"I hope we don't have any trouble with the foundation."

"I wanted to make sure you were okay," Jackie said.

"No problem down here that I've detected yet. Have you started gathering up those items we spoke of last night?"

"I was making the list when the earthquake hit," Jackie explained. "I'll be on to it shortly."

"Good," Graham said. "Let me know if any other problems pop up."

"You bet!" Jackie hung up.

She walked back to her office. The small writing desk had moved three or four inches more after she left the room and books had fallen from the bookcase. Jackie readjusted the furniture and picked up the list she was writing.

"Flashlights, pocket knife, extra blankets, dehydrated food, a rope ladder," Jackie read out loud. "I sure hope Graham knows exactly what we need." She sat down to complete the list.

Graham's door flew open and Sarah Cates burst in. Behind her Graham could see turmoil in the outer office. Employees were shouting and some of the women were darting hysterically back and forth.

"The glass on the front door shattered," Sarah said breathlessly. "We've got a dangerous crack in the front wall! People are frightened to death."

"Okay. I'll be there." Graham walked through the doorway and leaped up on top of Sarah's desk. "Everybody listen to me!" he shouted. "The earthquake appears to be over. It's all right. Let's settle down. No one's hurt. Get back to your own desks."

The noise started to subside.

"I'll have workmen up here as quickly as possible," Graham assured the staff. "Don't worry. We're not in danger anymore."

Some of the men waved their appreciation. Several of the secretaries returned to their workstations.

Climbing down, Graham looked around the office. The truth was that he didn't know that there wouldn't be another quake at any moment, but he couldn't let the office fly out of control. He had to put a lid on a boiling kettle.

"I think the disturbance will settle down now," Graham said to Sarah. "Please come back into my office." She followed him inside and Graham shut the door behind them.

"Have you found anything yet?" Graham asked.

Sarah shook her head. "Like you said, I have to be extremely careful. I've been by his office several times but inside it only once. Mr. Pemrose has been here most of the time. No. I haven't seen anything like what you described."

"You're frightened?"

"Of course I am!" Sarah forced a smile.

"Good. Keep your eyes open for information about something that will neutralize the security devices placed on people's foreheads. Watch for any clues. Remember this search is a total secret."

"*You bet,*" she whispered.

"Okay, Sarah. Go back and look like a hardworking secretary."

Sarah took a deep breath. "I'll keep watching." She walked out and shut the door behind her.

Sarah seemed to be playing her part well. Her apprehension appeared genuine enough. On the other hand, if Sarah was a plant, she might have talent for this sort of thing and might only be acting. Should the woman balk then he'd know she wasn't trustworthy and he could believe a plot was unfolding within the mayor's offices. However, if Sarah really did come back with something revealing, he might know what Pemrose was doing behind the scenes.

Picking up his cell phone, Graham dialed Matthew, hoping that it had not been worse to the north.

"Hello?"

"Son, we got hit by a earthquake down here. Did it do any damage at the university?"

"Dad, it's been terrible. Several classrooms collapsed and the side of the library caved in."

"Sounds worse than what we got in downtown Chicago. I take it you're not hurt."

"I came out without a scratch because I was walking across the campus. If I'd been in the library, I might have been injured."

"Okay," Graham said. "I'm relieved to hear you're in good condition. Is it possible for you to come home tonight or could I meet you somewhere if the roads are open?

"*You* asking *me*?" Matthew laughed. "Now, that's a twist!"

"No, son. I'm serious."

"It would help me if you could come up here. I am supposed to have a big exam tomorrow."

"Is this afternoon bad?"

"No. Not at all."

"I'll see you at three o'clock. The regular place."

"You bet!" Matthew said.

Graham hung up the phone. Going back to the window, he watched the waves pounding against the shoreline. Like the bizarre glow of the moon, nature had spun out of control again with a quake that had unleashed terror up and down the Chicago waterfront. Workmen worked frantically on the docks with every possible tool. Wherever he looked, it seemed that God himself was screaming at the world.

CHAPTER 47

REPORTS OF INJURIES poured in from up and down the coastline of Lake Michigan with the damage up north appearing to be worse. People in the Highland Park area and around Glencoe reported severe losses. The entire Chicago train system sank into chaos while officials worried about the effects of the earthquake. The downtown Metro Express train closed while workmen checked out the overhead trusses for damage to the supports.

Graham discovered that the Kennedy Expressway hadn't been damaged badly enough to stop traffic and grabbed a taxi to travel up the Highway 94 route that wound around Skokie before a side road went east toward Evanston.

Graham watched the driver carefully. The man seemed nervous and shaken. Even his usual disheveled appearance had dropped a notch and his driving was on the erratic side.

"Where're you from?" Graham asked to calm him.

"Immigrated from Lebanon." The driver glued his eyes nervously on the highway.

"Really? You came here for more opportunities?"

"No! I came here to keep from being killed! Lebanon has turned into nothing more than an enormous battlefield. Now *this* happens to Chicago!"

"Yeah. You look like this earthquake frightened you?"

"Of course! I've been through tremors in the old country. You can get killed in an instant." He snapped his fingers. "Boom! The shakes frighten me plenty."

The shakes had certainly frightened Graham. His first reaction had been to make sure the world was still in order and keep the office under control. It was only after he found the Metro closed and got in the taxi that the full emotional impact descended on him. Fear had to be settling over the entire city.

The cell phone rang. "Peck here."

"Graham, this is the mayor. I'm concerned about what this quake has done to the city."

Graham paused and thought about his position in the taxi. He was actually *running away* from the office. "I'm heading north to check out the current situation," he finally said. "I understand damage is worse up the shoreline. The Metro is now closed."

"Closed!" Bridges said. His voice filled with seriousness. "I didn't know the train was shut down."

"I'm checking it out."

"Good. Excellent. Let me know as soon as you have a report."

"Yes sir," Graham answered briskly and clicked off his

phone. At least, he was covered with the front office, but he still had to pay close attention to what had happened around him.

The driver eventually turned down Dempster Street toward the Lake. Graham kept thinking about what this man had said about war in Lebanon. No matter where he turned, the world seemed to be in endless turmoil. On every street corner, wars and rumors of wars confounded Graham.

"Let me out at that dormitory straight ahead." Graham pointed across the campus. He could see buildings that had been damaged. "I'll walk the rest of the way." The taxi pulled up to the curb and Graham paid the driver.

Everywhere Peck looked, he saw mayhem. On one side of the street a few smaller houses had front porches bent at strange angles. Around the university cracks ran down the sides of buildings and windows had shattered. Pieces of the concrete sidewalk were twisted and tilted at strange angles. Graham hurried on toward the dormitory cafeteria where he always met his son when he was visiting on campus.

The building looked like it withstood the quake fairly well; no cracks or broken glass anywhere. Students were coming and going as Graham hurried inside. He found Matthew sitting at a back table by himself.

"Quite a day." Graham sat down across from Matthew. "I had to grab a taxi to get here. Makes for a long ride. Looks like we've had one of the most unexpected disasters anyone would have thought possible around Chicago."

"Anyone who has never read the Bible," Matthew answered. "If I am reading Revelation right, this big shake is about on schedule."

"That's what I need to talk with you about. As best I can tell, you've bought *everything* the New Seekers are saying."

Matt smiled. "I'm sure I sound on the enthusiastic side, but I can't find anything wrong with what they're teaching." Matt stretched out his legs and leaned back in his chair. "In the dorm, people are afraid terrorists will blow up the university or shoot us in the streets. I see nothing but kids running around like chickens with their heads cut off. Guys are sleeping with girls like there's no tomorrow. The place is wild and crazy. I don't find any help around here."

Graham nodded. "I know what you mean. It's the same way in my office."

"But when I'm with my New Seekers friends, it's a different world. These people are sane, sensible, balanced. They believe God is working behind all the mess and they trust Him."

CHAPTER 48

GRAHAM LEANED BACK in his chair and scratched his head. "I think that's the part I don't understand," he said to Matthew. "What does it *really* mean to trust God? Sitting here in your dormitory cafeteria at this moment how can I have confidence in Him?"

Matthew rubbed his chin and for a few moments looked thoughtfully out the window. "Dad, you drove up here in a taxi. Right?"

Graham nodded.

"You trusted that a car you know nothing about would get you here through some very uncertain circumstances. You had fears about what had happened and could occur again, but still you chose to ride in that car and believed it would get you through any obstacles along the way."

"Yes," Graham agreed.

"Trust is the same confidence that what you can't prove to be true will be able to guide and take you through hard times on to the place where you want to be. When I trust God, I know that He's going to do the same thing with my entire life."

Graham listened intently. He had thought about these issues in some way or another nearly every waking moment since Maria was killed in their garage. Sometimes he almost accepted what the New Seekers group taught and then later retreated. Then again, he found that what they taught about the Bible made more sense out of these unexpected struggles than anything he had learned in his entire life.

"You've worried about death," Matthew continued. "Grammy's death just about did all of us in, but trusting in God has given me peace even about death. I'm not afraid anymore."

Graham studied his son's face. Matthew looked confident and he truly believed what he was saying. Although Matt was hardly more than a boy, this young man was standing on firm ground and Graham felt he could trust what he was saying.

"Adah showed me what the Bible says about death, Dad. The first letter of Saint John says that God has given us eternal life and that this life is in Jesus Christ, His son.

When you trust Jesus, He's the one who opens the door into an eternal tomorrow. Jesus Christ is the answer to our fears about death. When you trust God, you can let go of worrying about dying."

Graham took a deep breath. "That's quite a statement, son."

"But it's true, Dad. When you trust God, you don't have to be frightened about what's ahead."

"Son, I came up here for something different from what you've said so far, but this one tidbit made the trip totally worthwhile. I wanted to ask you about what you think is going on in the world today. Have you been able to make any sense out of these attacks, wars, the Anti-Christ, the totally unexpected earthquake? It runs together in a blur in my mind."

"That's because of how you think." Matt grinned with a sly twist. "We all grew up that way. Mary's the worst of all."

"What do you mean, son?"

"When you look at the world, you only see one dimension. It's no more than a cause and effect place for you. What you see is what you get." Matt gently pointed his finger in his father's face. "You don't take into account *what you can't see.*"

Graham grimaced. "What?" He shook his head. "You're not making any sense."

"Oh, but I am! Dad, you don't take into account the world that you can't see."

"Can't see?" Graham rubbed his chin. "Now you are talking nonsense."

"Far from it! I'm talking about the supernatural world that is always out there around us, but just beyond us. There is a spiritual world we must also confront. While we can't see it, the supersensual world is the place where evil and good do ultimate battle. Our world is only a pale reflection of that realm where the supernormal, the numinous exists."

Graham glanced around the room to make sure no one had sat down and might be listening. "I don't know," he said slowly. "Sounds awfully far out."

"Look, Dad. When Scripture says that God gave us eternal life, the book is talking to us about something that happened in that supernatural place." He leaned forward. "I'm talking about the domain that exists between earth and heaven."

Graham felt unhinged. Obviously, Matt was no longer some high school kid spinning smoke dreams in the air. His son had learned an extraordinary amount in a very small time. Matthew was confronting him with ideas for which he had no refutation.

"Dad, listen to me," Matt continued. "Jesus Christ will open this world to you. He helps you keep one foot in this planet and puts the other one in God's world. You can't see it, but that place is just as real as this one is."

"Matt, I have a hard time believing in things that I can't see."

"No you don't," Matt fired back. "You simply *think that you do*. The fact is that you believe in trust, love, caring, and many other qualities that are completely unseen. Among them is faith. Right?"

Reluctantly Graham nodded his head. "Yes, I guess that I do."

"Dad, all of these wars and our current chaos is only

part of an eternal, heavenly battle that's an extension of an unseen war with evil. When you invite Jesus the Christ into your life, He will help you understand what you can't grasp right now."

"Do you really think so?"

Matt smiled broadly. *"I know so."*

"I wouldn't have any idea how to do such a thing."

"Look, Dad. You've been kicking around all of the ideas, the explanations that Adah has given you. You can see how they fit with what's happening, but you have a hard time *fully* believing they are true. The only way it is going to come together is when you put your complete trust in those explanations. That's what you've got to do with Jesus Christ. Put your complete trust in Him."

"But how?" Graham pushed.

"You have to pray."

Graham ran his hands nervously through his hair. "Well . . . I don't know . . . exactly . . . how I would pray."

"Dad, Jesus is here at this moment. He's not standing among us in the flesh, but the savior is mysteriously present . . . like the air. The oxygen and Jesus are both vital to our being alive. When you pray, you simply talk to Him as if you can see Him and He will respond inwardly. Praying is trusting Him to enter your life."

Graham could feel his heart beating faster. His palms felt sweaty and for a moment he felt light-headed. The idea of praying in the middle of a dormitory cafeteria seemed bizarre and inappropriate, but Graham knew he had come to a turning point. As surely as the earthquake shaking the city, God had shaken everything in him.

"There's no time like the present," Matt encouraged him.

"Okay." Graham leaned back in his chair and looked hard into his son's eyes. Matt's steady gaze called Graham's bluff. He slowly closed his eyes and for a few moments walked into the silence as if it were a huge cavern opening up to a spelunker. The stillness was suddenly filled with a fullness that surprised him.

"Lord," Graham said quietly, "I want to trust you and I'm not sure how, but I pledge to you my complete confidence and obedience. I want to believe totally. Please lead me." He slowly opened his eyes.

"He will," Matthew promised. "More than you could believe possible."

CHAPTER 49

GRAHAM'S TAXI RIDE back from Evanston felt considerably different then the ride out. The weight of the world seemed to have lifted from his shoulders. For reasons he couldn't quite define, nothing felt as oppressive. While the taxi sped down the highway, Graham remembered over and over how events unfolded since the end of October, leading him now to pray with his son. Nothing could have ever been further from what he would have believed possible.

Once again his cell phone rang. Graham checked the caller identification on the small window. Sure enough!

The mayor was calling again. This time Graham felt prepared.

"Peck here."

"Got any report on the train lines?" the mayor began. "The Metro offices are telling us they are closed."

"Until all the trusses have been checked, the trains won't run. They've got to make sure there is no structural damage. I think it will take some considerable time to be certain."

"That's what I was afraid of. When will you be back in the office?"

"If we don't run into any difficulties, I would think in probably thirty to forty minutes at the most."

"Okay. As soon as you arrive, come back to my inner office. I'm expecting a holographic call from Mr. Carson. It's important and you should hear it."

Listening to Borden Carson was the last thing he wanted to do. "I'll be there." Graham cringed.

"Good. See you then." Bridges clicked off.

Graham thought about what he had heard. While it was impossible to guess what Carson had in mind, from what Adah had said, listening to Carson was anything but good. The possibilities left Graham feeling empty, but he was no longer afraid. The taxi sped down the highway.

"Please go on back," Frank Bridges's secretary told Graham. "They are waiting for you." She pointed toward the wall.

Graham waited for the panel door to slide open, but *they* rolled around in his mind. At the least, Pemrose must be back there. No doubt, he and Bridges had already completed their own full-scale discussion before Graham arrived. The door slid open and Graham walked down the hall.

"Ah, Peck!" the mayor said. "Just in time! What did you find out there?"

Graham glanced around the room. Jake Pemrose was sitting there smoking his usual black cigar and looking like the king of the world. To his surprise, Al Meacham had been added to the group. Meacham had a tall, thin build with a long narrow face. His deep-set eyes always gave his face a sinister cast. Graham nodded to both men.

"Al's been part of the Inner Circle for some time," Bridges explained. "He's an important part of our plans. Of course, you know each other well."

Graham nodded soberly, but Meacham made no response.

"Gentlemen," Bridges said. "The time has come for us also to refer to Mr. Carson as Hassan Rashid. When we are dealing with Middle Eastern business, we will use this name. Like saying mister in English, the proper way of addressing him in Arabic is to first call him Al-sayyid. In a few moments, Al-sayyid Rashid will be addressing us. Everybody ready to hear his message?"

The men settled back in their chairs. Light emanated from the holographic transmitter and in a few moments the white beam turned light green, forming into a shape. As the last time, Borden Camber Carson sat behind a massive desk in a white Nehru jacket. His black hair and deeply tanned skin came into focus first, then Carson's black eyes appeared with piercing intensity. As had been true in previous transmissions, Carson's smile was instantly engaging, immediately drawing each man into his sphere of influence. He exuded a warmth that felt personal and intimate. Leaning forward, Carson gave a slight wave and the large diamond ring on his pinky finger sparkled.

"Al-sayyid Rashid," Mayor Bridges began. "As always, we are honored that you would speak with us."

"Thank you," Rashid answered with only a trace of an accent. "I am pleased each of you could be here this afternoon." Rashid slowly stared at each man sitting in the mayor's office as if he was measuring them carefully. "Good to see you, Mr. Peck," he said to Graham before moving on to Meacham.

When Rashid said his name, Graham felt frozen in his chair. The man spoke as if they were old friends, close business associates, when in fact, Graham had been no more than an observer in a couple of transmissions. Rashid, or Carson, had an uncanny way of setting unspoken rules, reshuffling the cards, and defining relationships in his own way. He swept Graham into the Inner Circle as if there had been a complete discussion of the terms of membership when, in fact, Graham had agreed to nothing, absolutely nothing! He reminded himself that Rashid's magnetism implied nothing on his part.

"I understand Chicago has been struck by a terrible earthquake," Hassan Rashid began. "People will be terrified so this is an important time for you to further assure them that you have everything *under your control*. You must keep the citizens under your constant tutelage."

"Yes sir," the mayor responded immediately.

"In order to create calm, I am instructing Mayor Bridges to announce tonight that I will establish a new peace pact with the Russians and will insist that all the Arab nations align themselves with me once this agreement is signed. The promise of a future peace treaty will be a welcome relief from the constant wars that have been burning around the world."

"Excellent!" Bridges exclaimed. "A most helpful announcement. When will the agreement be finished?"

"I cannot say at this time, but we are moving the parties into place in order that the document will soon be finalized."

Graham could feel Al Meacham staring at him with his dark-set eyes. For reasons that he couldn't discern, Meacham seemed to be as intent on watching him as he was in listening to Rashid.

"Please make your citizens aware that my leadership is bringing this agreement to pass." Rashid smiled a broad affectionate smile. "Our time is short, gentlemen. We must make the most of every opportunity that comes our way."

"Thank you, Al-sayyid Rashid," Bridges said. "We will set up a television appearance immediately to broadcast your announcement and we hope the results will follow soon."

Rashid once again waved his hand in a polite gesture. "Goodbye," he said softly with a gentle tone that almost sounded like a child telling his mother goodnight. "*Ma-as-sa-leh-ma.*"

Graham stared at the column of light as the image diminished. This man was a bundle of contradictions. While appearing to be an innocent apostle of the truth, he had actually been telling them that he was an international power broker. With a gentle smile on his face, he undoubtedly had a nuclear bomb in his hip pocket.

"Al-sayyid Rashid has given us the next playing card for tonight's television appearance," the mayor said. "Jake, you get the television cameras in place and Graham, you can write up a statement from what you've heard. We don't have much time."

Graham glanced at his watch. He wouldn't be leaving as early as he had hoped, but he had no alternative except to bang out the mayor's desired announcement on his word processor. Graham hated the idea that he was the voice of this monster, but for the moment he had no alternative unless he wanted to endanger his relationship with Adah Honi and the New Seekers. He stood up to go back to his office.

"You have an important assignment," Al Meacham said. Not one syllable had an inflection in it; his voice had a deeply ominous sound. "We will await the outcome of your work."

Graham studied Meacham's empty eyes. The man looked cold and indifferent. "Sure, Al. I need to get to work." He quickly walked away. Meacham was not a man he wanted to spend time with.

CHAPTER 50

BEING AN IMPORTANT city official had its advantages in little things like finding a taxi when none was available, but the ride up to Arlington Heights was not without its problems. The Highway 294 tollway around O'Hare International Airport was closed, forcing the taxi to retreat and take the 290 that pushed them a little further off course. At eight o'clock Graham finally reached home. Crown Point Street looked empty when Graham got out of the taxi. A cold wind was blowing and the snow had piled up against the curb. Turning up his collar, he hurried into the house.

"Hey, Daddy's home!" George Peck shouted when Graham walked into the living room.

Five-year-old Jeff made a hard charge across the room and tackled his father. "Got ya!" he shouted.

"Hey, the Indians attacked me," Graham said, hugging his two boys.

Jackie walked out of the kitchen. "I was really worried you might not be able to get here. I know the roads have to be bad."

"Some are; some aren't," Graham said. "The airport highway is shut down."

Mary appeared in the doorway. "You look passable," she said skeptically.

Graham gestured for her to come over. "I want to talk with all of you for a moment. Everybody sit down."

Mary rolled her eyes, but reluctantly sat on a piano bench. Jackie scooted in next to her. George and Jeff piled in around their father's feet.

"I don't want you walking off," Graham said to Mary. "What I have to say is for everyone to hear." He watched his daughter and knew she had already turned him off, but she was going to hear what he had to say whether she liked it or not. "I made an important decision today."

Jackie leaned forward. "Great. Tell us about it."

Slowly and carefully Graham detailed his trip to Evanston to meet with Matthew after the earthquake. He talked about his personal waffling back and forth on what they had heard in the New Seekers group, but finally his mind was made up. Graham described how he prayed and the difference it made. The living room became intensely quiet.

"Graham, that's wonderful!" Jackie got up and came over and kissed him.

Even though Mary worked at looking bored, the boys listened intently. "What does that mean?" George asked.

"From now on, we are going to live the Christian faith in this house," Graham said. "That's our number one goal."

"Does that mean I can't play baseball with my friends?" Jeff asked.

"Sure *doesn't*," Graham said. "It means you can play even harder."

"Great!" Jeff said.

Graham looked at Mary. "Do you have anything to say?"

She shook her head and frowned.

"Nothing?" Graham pushed.

"It doesn't make any difference what I think," Mary said insolently. "You've already made that clear. All I'd say is that you better be careful or we could all get into big trouble."

"Mary," Jackie had a pleading tone in her voice, "*Please!* Your father has done a wonderful thing."

"Look! Everybody I know thinks this stuff is wacko, but some teachers at school even consider it subversive. You could get in big time trouble messing with this off the wall stuff. I want to go to my room." Mary fixed her eyes on the floor.

"I'm truly sorry you feel this way," Graham said. "So defiant!"

"*Defiant?*" Mary nodded. "Just remember that word describes my position if this religion business blows up in your face. I want to go to my bedroom."

Graham nodded his approval. She got up and walked out. Graham didn't say anything, but silently watched her leave the room.

"Why is Mary so mad?" George asked.

"She lets her friends run her life," Graham said. "She's missing out on the greatest opportunity of her lifetime."

"Yeah," Jeff said, "because we won't let her play on our baseball team."

Graham looked at Jackie. "I told Matt to invite the New Seekers group to make their next meeting at our house. It's time for us to get totally and completely honest with them."

Jackie nodded soberly. "Graham, I'm with you one

hundred percent." She stopped. "But Mary could be right. We may be headed for big trouble."

CHAPTER 51

B Y THE SECOND WEEK in December decorations for Merry Winter were everywhere. For the last couple of decades Christmas had become increasingly secular. The birth of Jesus was not mentioned publicly; no one spoke about Hanukkah either. In the last five years the emphasis had shifted so radically that everyone called the December holidays Merry Winter. Virtually no one used the old religious Christmas ornaments, but the festival of winter was going full tilt.

Recent reports indicated that almost 90 percent of the population had been marked on their foreheads with security devices. The mayor's office speculated that the remainder were probably the homeless and wouldn't make much difference. The Peck family still managed to avoid being marked. The pressure to comply was easing, but the population remained edgy. Metro train lines opened again when damage to the overhead trusses proved minimal. Overhead in the train cars, Borden Camber Carson's picture hung everywhere, offering comfort and promise. Little comfort was taken.

Graham had been in his office only thirty minutes when Sarah Cates came in. Styled with a new twist, her hair made the woman look unusually attractive. Graham worried that the extra touches were especially for him, so he said nothing.

"I've been able to get inside Jake Pemrose's office several times," Sarah explained. "I've been working around the files over there and his secretary doesn't pay me any attention. When no one is looking, it's easy to slip in."

"Good," Graham said.

"I want to show you something strange that I found." Sarah laid a file on Graham's desk. "I was able to copy these documents using the instant-reproduction machine inside Pemrose's office. It shoots out copies almost like it was breaking the sound barrier. I was able to duplicate all of these pages in seconds. And it doesn't make a sound."

Graham pulled the file toward him. "Excellent."

"I thought it was strange that Pemrose would have such documents in his possession." She reached across the desk and opened the file. "These materials describe how terrorists are financed with American money."

"*What?*" Graham came out of his chair.

"I thought you'd be surprised."

Graham quickly started scanning down the first page.

"You'll notice this is a list of twenty-five American financiers, funneling money through Muslim charities for attacks on the United States."

"Why in the world would Pemrose have this roster?"

Sarah moved around the edge of the desk and pulled out several pages. "You'll see that the balance sheet indicates exact income."

Graham took the page from her. "My gosh! These groups have amassed some twelve million dollars in assets."

"Yes sir," Sarah said. "They call themselves The Golden Chain and their influence reaches back to the saboteurs who attacked the tanker in San Diego, the Museum of Science and Industry, and the Computer Center near your children's school."

Graham stared. The documents were beyond his wildest dreams. "I-I can't believe what I'm seeing," he muttered.

"Look at this material." Sarah thumbed through the file. "It describes a Russian terrorist attack in Turkmenistan where a subversive was paid five hundred thousand rupees— which is about nine thousand American dollars."

Graham dropped down in his chair and started rubbing his chin. "What does all of this mean? Who are these people?"

"I wasn't able to identify any documents that answer that question," Sarah Cates said. "Then, Pemrose's secretary started moving around and I had to leave, but I don't get the impression that she's in on any of this. She always has a blank sort of look on her face."

Graham folded his hands together, and shook his head. "I can't understand why Jake would have any of this material."

"There's one more thing I found." Sarah laid a small round device on Graham's desk. "I noticed a sack with about a dozen of these things so I took one."

Graham picked it up and looked at the circular golden object with a green button and red button in the center. "What does it do?"

"I don't know," Sarah said, "but the sack was marked *security protection*. I thought maybe they . . ."

Graham instantly stood up. "Maybe this is what I've been looking for. You may have found it!"

Sarah shrugged. "I don't know. You notice there's both a red and a green button. Who knows what each one does?"

"Hmm." Graham turned the strange-looking instrument over in his hand. "Very strange. You're right. The two buttons present a problem. I'm not sure what it does, but I'll think about it." He dropped the piece into his pocket.

"I hope some of this helps," Sarah said.

"Nothing makes any sense, but it's extremely important. Sarah, you need to keep digging. Use every opportunity you can get to work your way inside that office. Always have an excuse for being in there and don't get caught." He shook his finger. "But don't back off either."

"I will be careful."

For several moments Graham stared at the pile of papers. "I'll keep this file," he said more to himself. "You keep working around those file cabinets and grab every possibility to watch Jake's office. I'm sure he doesn't have any idea that anyone is occasionally dropping in to rifle through his desk and he sometimes gets sloppy. That's when you want to strike."

"I'll do my best."

"Thank you for helping me," Graham said with sincere appreciation. "This adds to what I need to know."

Sarah beamed. "Don't worry. I'll keep looking *for you, Graham.*"

Graham didn't look up. He kept staring at the papers, waiting for Sarah to leave. He didn't want to encourage her any further except to keep working on Jake's case. "Thank you," he finally mumbled without making eye contact. "I'll be back in touch." Sarah left.

Graham read through the entire file once again. Obviously, a significant number of screwballs had used a wide range of charities to amass an enormous amount of money to finance terrorism all over the country, but why would Pemrose be in possession of this information? A big chunk of the puzzle wasn't there.

CHAPTER 52

JACKIE HAD JUST SAT DOWN in the living room when George crawled up in her lap. "Daddy said those people from Matthew's university are meeting here tomorrow night." He sprawled across her lap like a lazy Golden Retriever.

"Yes, son. You'll enjoy meeting them." Jackie quickly glanced around the living room, sizing it up to make sure everyone could fit in their front room comfortably. "They're nice people. You'll like the students."

George looked thoughtfully at his mother. "And they can tell me about being a Christian?"

"That's what they do, George. They've helped me come to the same decision that your father told you about the other day. I believe it's extremely important that we trust God."

George nodded his head. "Yes and I want to be part of what's happening in our family."

"Wonderful." Jackie hugged her son. "That's the most important thing you could say."

"Jeff and I talked about this last night when we were lying in our beds. He doesn't understand it all, but Jeff said he wanted to be on Dad's side."

"Good." Jackie smiled. "That's also important to us."

"We're all in this together except for Mary." George frowned. "She gets really angry when you and Dad talk about God. She doesn't want me to bring up the subject."

Jackie's smile faded. She patted George on the head and fumbled for the right words. "Mary's been strongly influenced by her friends. We hope she'll change her mind soon."

"I don't think she ever will," George said. "Her friends are really, really important to her."

"Yes, Mary's at the age where she buckles under to the pressure at school."

"I can't talk about God in my school," George said. "I get in trouble if I do unless the teacher asks me about it."

"The teacher *asks you?*"

"Yeah, Mom. Once a week each one of us must go up to her desk and she demands that we tell her what is happening at home with our families. Do we attend Sunday Encounter groups. Things like that."

Jackie's heart leaped and she took a deep breath. "What have you been telling her?"

"Nothing! I don't want to get you and Daddy into trouble."

Jackie hugged him tightly. "Good. Very good, son.

Don't ever tell your teacher anything about what happens here in our home."

"Don't worry. I never answer her questions about religion." George crawled down and wandered off into the kitchen looking for a cookie. "I won't."

Jackie couldn't escape the conclusion that the school was checking up on them and every other family in the neighborhood. The realization left her nervous and upset. Graham needed to know about this frightening turn of events. At six o'clock when Graham returned from the office, Jackie was waiting for him at the front door.

"Oh dear, I'm so glad you came home on time!"

"Sure!" Graham kissed his wife. "I needed to get out of there as quick as I could, but the train station proved to be jammed. I didn't get on the train as quickly as I usually do."

"Sit down." Jackie pointed to a chair. "I had a talk with George today. Of course, he and Jeff are with us spiritually, but I'm concerned about what's happening at his school."

Graham sat down in a large living room chair across from Jackie on the couch. "At his school? What's going on?"

"I discovered the teachers question them on a weekly basis *about our religious activities*. Do you realize what this means?"

Graham's mouth dropped. "How long has this been going on?"

"Apparently for at least the last month!"

Graham. "Wow! That tosses another log on the fire."

"Something else happened today?"

"I've also found some disturbing evidence at the office

that Pemrose and company are in some way or another involved with terrorist activity. I haven't put all of this together yet, but with the increased electronic surveillance, this problem could be going anywhere."

Jackie inched nearer. "What do you suspect, Graham?"

"This afternoon I also discovered Bridges has Jack Stratton and Bill Marks included in this sweet little Inner Circle as Carson calls his hidden people. I'm not sure what their role is, nor exactly what Meacham does, but Jake Pemrose is in way over his head. He's become Mr. Big Time."

Jackie nervously rubbed her chin. "What are we going to do? We're extremely vulnerable."

"I've given that a great deal of thought. Do you have all of those emergency supplies that we discussed earlier?"

"Sure. The box is stashed away out in the garage."

Graham nodded his head. "Good. I don't have any exact plan in mind yet, but we need to keep everything ready. Anything could happen. I did transfer a significant amount of money into Mother's old account at the bank. We could use her bank card forever and go undetected. If we had to run, we've got money for a significant amount of time."

"I feel like we're caught in the jaws of a pair of pliers." Jackie wrung her hands. "Each day the squeeze gets tighter and tighter. On some of these days I'm afraid that the life is about to be squeezed out of me."

Graham reached out and took her hands. "Yeah," he said. "I know. I feel the same pinch."

"You're said time is running out on us. Well, I'm afraid the hands of the clock are reaching midnight."

Graham stood up slowly. "Yes," he said, "we are standing on the edge."

CHAPTER 53

THE NEXT DAY Graham came home unusually early to help Jackie make the final preparations for the New Seekers' meeting. He picked up bottles of soft drinks and potato chips since the group usually didn't have refreshments. By five o'clock all of the children were in the house. Graham put his coat in the front office and laid his cell phone on the desk. Mary wasn't particularly pleasant, but the boys had a great time helping their mother put up a few more Christmas decorations.

"Getting a little bold, aren't you?" Graham chided his wife and pointed at the scene on the table.

"Why not? I thought we needed a little more than those awful snowmen and holly branch decorations. I threw in that crèche scene your mother always had out at this time of the year. If we're going to get in trouble, we might as well do it right."

Graham laughed. "I'm sure none of the people who are coming tonight will have any problem with a nativity scene."

"Look in the morning room corner." Jackie took Graham's hand and let him through the kitchen. "How do you like my Christmas tree?"

"My gosh! I haven't ever seen a better one. Beautiful lights. Super."

"Dad," Jeff said, "I'm putting up candles in the windows."

"Good. You're doing a great job, Jeff. Let me help you."

During the next hour, the extra touches of color added an even more festive air to the house. Graham seemed to enjoy putting out the decorations more than anything he had done in years. Mary stayed in her room, avoiding even a hint of interest in the decorations. Periodically, she would peek out from a crack in her bedroom door to check on what was happening. Jackie chuckled when she spotted Mary's eye and the door immediately slammed shut.

Jackie had prepared a casserole earlier in the day to make supper fast and easy. After dinner, Mary got the job of putting the plates in the dishwasher. Once again she put on an insolent silence like heavy lipstick, and slammed the plates onto the trays without saying a word.

"Careful there," Jackie said, walking past with a watchful eye. "We don't want to break anything."

Mary scowled, but didn't speak.

"Seven o'clock!" Graham announced. "People should show up any second now."

"They come in staggered order," Jackie reminded him. "The kids feel it camouflages them better."

"Whatever makes them happy," Graham said. "I'm truly looking forward to the meeting tonight." The doorbell rang. "I'll get it." He walked into the living room.

Opening the door, Graham found Adah Honi and

Eldad Rafaeli standing in front of him. "*Shalom!*" Graham boomed.

"*Shalom aleichem,*" Adah answered.

"Come in." Graham ushered the Jewish couple into his living room. "You are the first to arrive."

Adah and Eldad walked into the living room, and they seemed unusually sober. "The others are behind us."

"Good. I trust everything is okay," Graham said. "Jackie is in the kitchen. She'll be here in a minute."

"We are concerned," Eldad said. "I have the distinct feeling that tonight we were followed."

The smile faded from Graham's face. "What did you see?" he asked Adah.

"I feel uncomfortable," Adah said. "I can't put my finger on it as certainly as Eldad has, but something isn't right."

Graham pulled on his chin. "Electronic surveillance has increased everywhere, but I haven't seen anything additional around this neighborhood. Of course, we've had many large groups meet here. No one would consider a gathering to be unusual."

"Still, coming to your house may not have been a wise decision," Eldad said. "I think we must be highly aware."

"Yes," Graham said slowly. "I know Matthew will bring some of his friends through the back way. That will help appearances." He glanced at his watch. "They ought to be coming soon."

Jackie came into the room. "I couldn't help but overhear your conversation. Don't worry. I know everything will work out all right."

"In Israel many times we have thought that," Eldad

said, "and then, as we thought, it didn't happen. We have learned to pay to every detail careful attention."

"Sure," Jackie said. "I understand."

The sound of students coming in the back door interrupted them.

"Hey! Mom and Dad! We're here!"

"That's Matt," Graham said. "I'm sure Jennifer came with him."

Matt walked in with three other young men. "Adah! Good to see you," he said, extending his hand. "Eldad, glad you're here."

"Where's Jennifer?" Graham asked.

"I don't know," Matt answered. "It's the strangest thing. She was supposed to meet me at the dorm, but she never came. We called her dorm room and her cell phone. I guess something unexpected turned up."

Adah looked into Graham's eyes. "I don't like it. Something has happened."

Graham rubbed his chin. "Are you concerned?" he asked Matt.

"Not really. Jennifer may have run into a lab assignment and simply couldn't get it done."

"Let's hope so," Adah said. "We must pray she is not in danger."

"I really don't think so," Matt assured her. "Hey, where are those potato chips?"

"In the morning room," Jackie said. "Go ahead and help yourselves."

"Let's go, guys." Matt motioned for the young men to follow him. "We can fill up before the others get here."

The doorbell rang and more students came in. Conversation immediately started and the tension eased. Graham tried to shake off his concern. Abruptly the telephone rang. He hurried into the office to answer it.

"Graham Peck here."

"Graham, this is Sarah Cates." The woman sounded breathless and as if she was whispering. "Thank God I got you. I can't talk long."

"Sarah, what's wrong?"

"They followed me from the office," Sarah panted. "I'm hiding out here in a telephone booth in the Metro train station near our building. I'm terrified!"

"Who followed you?"

"Pemrose and Meacham. They aren't far behind me."

"What happened?"

"Listen, Graham. I found out where the Muslim charity money went. I know who is behind the terrorism." She caught her breath and stopped for a moment. "I overheard Pemrose talking to Meacham in his office. The money went to Borden Camber Carson. He's the man behind all of these terrorist attacks on this country."

"*Carson?*" Graham was almost speechless. "*Borden Camber Carson?* You can't be serious."

"Yes," Sarah demanded. "Believe me. I heard Pemrose say that Carson is using fear about the attacks to obtain his objectives."

Graham couldn't speak. His knees nearly buckled and his mouth went dry. "Lord help us," he muttered. "Carson has been behind everything from the San Diego ship attack to the war in my children's school?"

"Exactly," Sarah said. "Listen, Graham. Pemrose and Meacham saw me running down the hall. Everything has gotten out of control. I don't know what these men have in mind, but I've got to get out of here before they catch me."

"Sarah, have you talked with anyone?"

"No, only you and I know what I've been doing in Pemrose's office."

"Okay," Graham said slowly, "listen carefully. Let me tell you what I think you can do. As soon as you hang up I'll . . ."

"They've seen me," Sarah blurted out. "Pemrose and Meacham are running this way!"

"Don't panic, Sarah. I can send some people to protect you. Just don't let them get you out of the booth."

"They're here! I can see Meacham's eyes. The man is horrifying."

"Listen, Sarah. Don't panic."

"I've got to get out of . . ." Two sharp popping noises cut her off; the sound of breaking glass filled the receiver. "A-a-a-h!" Sarah moaned.

"Sarah! Can you hear me?" Graham heard the sound of people scurrying, running. Women shouting. "Sarah, are you there?"

No one answered.

"SARAH!" Graham shouted. Somebody hung up the phone.

Jackie rushed to his side. "Graham! What in the world is going on?"

Speechless, Graham stared at the empty, buzzing sound coming out of his receiver. He slowly hung up the telephone.

"What's happened?" Jackie demanded.

"I—I think they just killed Sarah Cates."

CHAPTER 54

G RAHAM AND JACKIE struggled to walk from the kitchen into the living room. With Jackie clutching his arm, Graham stumbled into a large chair and bent over.

No one noticed the Pecks staggering in. The group gathering in the Pecks' highly decorated living room had shifted into high gear. Since no visitors had been invited, the regulars gabbed openly about their school experiences and what was happening in the news.

Adah Honi turned around and gasped. "Graham! Your face is white! What happened?" Silence settled over the room.

Graham opened his mouth, but nothing came out. Jackie huddled next to him like a frightened puppy.

"Something bad has happened!" Eldad Rafaeli nearly shouted. "What is it?"

Sweat had formed on Graham's forehead and he looked nauseous. He put his hand over his mouth. Sitting with his head hanging down, he tried to catch his breath, but it didn't come easy.

"Dad!" Matt broke away from his friends. "What in the world happened?"

Graham looked around the room, realizing that no one

was speaking. He motioned for everyone to sit down. "We are in significant trouble," he said slowly.

"Please." Adah dropped to her knees in front of Graham and Jackie. *"Tell us what has happened."*

Graham looked around again. Mary had come out of her bedroom and was standing at the edge of the living room door listening. He knew she needed to hear everything he had to say. "My secretary has just been killed, assassinated."

"What!" Mary darted into the living room. "Not Sarah Cates!"

"No!" Matt could barely gasp. "It can't be."

"Listen to me," Graham said. "I don't care what you do or do not believe. I am here to tell you the frightening truth. Those portraits you've seen all over the city reveal more than you would have ever thought possible. Borden Carson is not only the Anti-Christ; the man is a blatant murderer!"

All smart-alecky smugness left Mary's face and Matt's eyes expanded in consternation. The students looked dismayed and alarmed.

"Just before she was murdered, my secretary told me that she had discovered Carson was behind all of the terrorism breaking out in this country," Graham said. "He's using fear to achieve his purposes by terrorizing the people. I'm sure that I am now compromised in my own office."

"Look, Mr. Peck," one of the young men said. "We're prepared to stand with you. What do you need us to do?"

"Thank you," Graham replied. "At this moment, I'm not sure, but each of you must remember that electronic surveillance may be used to incriminate you. We are all in danger."

"This is what I suspected," Adah said. "One of the next steps in the Anti-Christ's plan is new believers to persecute. There are other people like us in this world who have now come to see that their hope is Yeshua, the Messiah. While we don't know where many of them are, groups like ours are springing up. They will be the target of Carson, or better, Hassan Rashid." She turned to Graham. "What will now you do?"

"I don't know," Graham said. "It is clear that Carson's people will not hesitate to kill. We must take them extremely seriously. Understand me?"

"*Ya!*" Eldad added. "We know how deadly they can be."

Graham heard a telephone ringing, but it wasn't the one in the kitchen. "Where is that?"

"Sounds like your cell phone," Jackie said.

Graham leaped up off the couch and darted into the office. His cell phone was still lying on the desk where he had placed it earlier. He stared, terrified to pick it up. After the fourth ring, Graham placed it on his ear.

"Hello," he said.

"Graham, this is Frank Bridges. I'm very disappointed in you. You've failed the test!"

"What test?

"The loyalty test," the mayor said. "For a number of weeks we've been examining you, expecting great things out of a man with your abilities, but unfortunately you haven't been up to the exercise."

"I don't know what you're talking about."

"I think you do. Our people monitored Sarah Cates's call to you earlier this evening. A few minutes ago Bill Marks played me a tape recording of what was discussed. I believe she said something like 'I'm hiding out in a phone booth in the Metro station.' Something of that order. Does that sound familiar?"

Graham froze, unsure of how to answer.

"Mr. Carson told us to check out each of the men in the Inner Circle down to their toenails. I've already done that with the other men. They passed and you were the last on the list. Actually, we've also had our people watching your son Matt extremely closely. Our specialists started checking his e-mail exchanges back around the first of November. We thought maybe he was acting without your knowledge."

Graham glanced up at Matthew. The entire New Seekers group had crowded into Graham's office and stood with their eyes glued on him. Graham quickly pulled the small extension wire from the back of the cell phone and pushed it into the side of the home telephone. He pressed the conference call button so everyone could hear.

"Our close surveillance of Matthew revealed you were aware of his affiliation with this subversive group meeting at your home tonight," the mayor continued. "Oh yes, Graham. We also know that everyone in your family has sidestepped the security clearance marking on your foreheads. Know a lot, don't we?"

Graham looked around the room. Everyone appeared as frightened as he felt. "What do you want?" he blurted out. "What's this all about?"

"We can't have you running around on the loose, Graham. I'm deeply sorry because I like the work you do, but the future is breaking in with new possibilities you haven't even yet considered. I regret the fact that you've become a problem for us . . . but you have."

Graham's mouth was dry, but he felt more than able to speak. "How do you know I'm no longer trustworthy?"

"Mr. Carson, or I might say Al-sayyid Rashid, first raised the question. He didn't like the look he saw in your eyes. As time has gone by, we've increased surveillance and used people like Al Meacham and Jack Stratton to study your movements. They've confirmed the suspicions raised by our leader, Al-sayyid Rashid."

The bottom fell out of Graham's stomach. He felt as if every wall in his house had fallen on him. "So what?" he suddenly snapped. "I'm not afraid of you, Frank. You're a hot air machine."

"Oh, far from it, Graham. Let me tell you how efficient I am. I don't believe you ever met one of the agents who works for me. You might even have liked Max, Max Andrews. Nice efficient man. Good with a gun. Know the name?" Bridges chuckled. "No, of course you don't. But I think you know his daughter. You don't have one of your members there tonight. Jennifer Andrews hasn't shown up. Right?"

Graham looked at the fear emanating from Matthew's eyes and didn't answer Bridges.

"Jennifer Andrews works for us. Let me tell you where she is, Graham. Jennifer is out in front with our men who have surrounded your house. She's been our main source of information on your son Matthew. Jennifer knows your family and the New Seekers group quite well."

Matt's mouth dropped. Several members of the group groaned and Adah slumped.

"What's that noise?" Bridges barked. "You got people listening in?"

"What if I've got the press here taking every word of your accusation down?" Graham pushed back. "For the record, I've got a reporter listening. You think you scare me?"

"I should, Peck," the mayor growled. "Don't try to bluff me. We're the people who sent that bum over to kill your mother to test your response. Then we took care of him. *You're next!*" Bridges hung up.

Graham nearly toppled out of his chair. Once again his rationality had been nearly kicked out the back door of his mind. "They killed my mother!" he screamed.

CHAPTER 55

ADAH PUT HER INDEX FINGER to her lips to silence everyone. She pushed the students out of the way and immediately flipped the room's light switch, killing all light in the office. Cautiously, she pulled the curtain back and peered out the window.

"They're outside," Adah said. "I can see across the street the shape of men."

Matt edged next to her. For several moments he watched silently. "Lord help us!" He pointed. "See to the left? That shape? It's a woman. It's Jennifer. She *is with them!*" He staggered back from the window.

"They killed my mother!" Graham growled. "And now we're surrounded," Graham said. "I'm not even sure what to do next, but they are not going to attack us and get away with it. This time we're going to take charge."

"They will particularly be looking for Eldad and me," Adah said. "I'm sure their henchmen will be after anyone who is Jewish. Rashid would order that approach."

"Listen to me," Jackie cut in. "I think the students should make a break for it out the back door before these thugs hit us. I've got an idea where we can hide our family and you two." She pointed at Adah and Eldad. "Matt will have to stay with us. He can't possibly return to the university."

"You're right, Mom," Matthew said. "They've been watching me, and Jennifer knows too much for me to return."

"Don't touch any of the lights," Graham said. "You students run for it. After you're gone Jackie will tell us what she has in mind. We've got few choices left."

"Stop!" Adah demanded. "I will pray first. Then you will run." Everyone froze in place. Graham nodded his head.

"Blessed art thou, O Lord God of the Universe. Put your hand of protection on these students. Keep them from harm and keep the evil ones from attacking us. In the name of Yeshua. Amen."

"Listen," Matt said. "Don't go out the back door. Leave through the garage. Crawl low along the hedges then cut straight through the neighbor's yard directly behind us. Once you get around their house, start running and don't stop until you reach the Metro train station. God bless you."

The students stealthily slipped into the kitchen and then through the garage. Jackie shut the door behind them and locked it. The family had gathered behind her in the morning room.

"Where do we go?" Eldad asked.

Jackie looked sheepish. "Graham, I never told you about this because, well, I just didn't, but there's an unexpected hiding place upstairs off the corner bathroom."

"The bathroom? But where?"

"When we had to repair the frozen water pipes upstairs last winter, the workmen made a hole through the back of the dirty clothes hamper that's built into the wall. They put down some boards behind it in the attic to make a sub-floor. Instead of sealing it back up, they placed a piece of plywood over the back. Once the plywood is pulled away, anyone could crawl on their hands and knees into the hamper and slide through the hole. Everything will look normal. The entry will allow us to hide in that space at the end of the roof line."

"You're kidding!" Graham blinked, trying to get the picture straight in his mind.

"No, it will be tight but we can all hide in there until these thugs leave."

"Look," Adah urged, "explain it later. Let's get up there and crawl through that hamper."

Graham looked at Mary. Her eyes were the size of quarters and she looked terrified. "We don't have any choice, Mary. Let's go!"

The family dashed up the steps to the second story without anyone turning on any lights and ran for the back bathroom. George and Jeff frantically clung to the hands of their father and mother. From somewhere behind their house, they heard the sound of gunshots exploding.

"Oh, Lord, save them," Adah prayed aloud as she followed the family.

CHAPTER 56

GUNSHOTS RANG through the cold, winter night, but the Pecks only hurried faster to get into the dark upstairs bathroom. Falling on her knees, Jackie started pulling dirty clothes out of the built-in hamper nailed to the wall. With the door wide open, she jerked out the piece of painted plywood at the back of the clothes catcher. Light pouring in through the window from the street lamp cast dim shadows and gave the family enough illumination to see what they were doing.

"Okay," Jackie said. "Adah and Eldad crawl in first. Be careful that you don't slip. We'll send the children in next, and Graham can bring up the rear."

Without saying a word, the two Israeli immigrants dropped to their knees and started inching through the narrow hole in the wall at the back of the hamper.

"It's tight," Eldad groaned.

"Don't stop!" Adah insisted. "Time is running out."

"You children must remember not to make a sound," Graham said sternly. "Our lives are at stake."

Jeff whimpered, but George nodded mechanically. The

distant, disjointed look had returned to his eyes. Mary shook, and Matt put his arm around her.

"We're going to be okay," Matthew reassured Mary. "Just don't make any noise, and watch your step. We don't want anyone falling through the ceiling and landing downstairs."

The little boys quickly crawled through the hole, and Mary had no problem, but it took Matthew longer. The slope of the roof hung just above their heads.

The sound of someone pounding on the front door echoed through the house. "Open up!" a man's voice demanded off in the distance. "We'll break in!"

"Hurry," Graham helped Jackie. "They're coming."

Jackie darted into the hole but her blouse caught on something. "I can't move forward!" she squealed. "I'm hooked on a nail or something sticking out of the door." She pushed and a ripping noise followed.

"Don't move!" Graham whispered. "Let me feel along the side."

The crashing sound of the front door breaking open shook the house. "Find 'em!" Jake Pemrose demanded far down below in the living room.

Graham felt a clamp where the door's hook fit and pulled Jackie's blouse loose. "Got it. Get in there!"

Gathering all the dirty clothing lying on the floor into the hamper, Graham started backing in. He could hear the footsteps of the men rushing through the house. At any moment, they would come up the stairs and start searching the bedrooms. After one last check that no clothing had fallen out on the floor, Graham pulled the hamper door shut, and started adjusting the plywood from the backside to make sure the hole in the wall was covered.

"They're not downstairs," a man shouted. "Check the bedrooms!" The sound of shoes pounding on the staircase became louder.

Graham fumbled with the plywood. It wasn't fitting back like it should. He could hear a man running toward the bathroom.

"The bedrooms are empty!" Al Meacham shouted. "I'll check the bathrooms."

Graham heard the click of a round being loaded into a gun's chamber. Meacham couldn't be ten feet away from the bathroom door. Suddenly the plywood settled into place. Graham held to the back of the board, making sure nothing slipped.

No one moved. Graham could not see the shapes of the family behind him, but he didn't stir. The sound of the hamper door suddenly opening chilled him, but then the door slammed again.

"Where'd they go?" Pemrose's voice penetrated through the wall.

"The family's got to be in here somewhere," Jennifer Andrews's voice drifted in. "People don't disappear."

"I don't know," Meacham said. "They don't seem to be anywhere around the house. Maybe they ran with those students."

"Any of them get away?" Pemrose asked.

"I don't know," Meacham answered. "No one expected them to take that route through the neighbors' property. We got a few shots at them. The Pecks could have been with the pack."

"Bridges won't be happy if they ran out the back door," Jennifer snapped.

"You looked under the beds?" Pemrose said.

Meacham cursed. "Of course not! No one's hiding under a bed."

"At least, look!" Pemrose ordered. "We've got to find Peck."

The sounds of men walking away faded. No one in the corner of the attic moved. The darkness was so pervasive that they could not see a wristwatch or anything more than the mere form of someone huddled next to them.

Graham kept his ear near the side of the wall and could hear men tearing up the house. Sounds of furniture being pushed back and forth drifted up the stairs. Beds were being shoved around. Men kept talking, but Graham couldn't discern what they said. After what seemed like an eternity, the house became silent again. Far off in the distance he heard several cars start, but the family didn't move.

CHAPTER 57

ONLY AFTER AN HOUR of total silence in the house did Graham speak. "I don't hear anything," he said.

"I think they're gone," Jackie answered.

"I'm going to crawl out, and then put the plywood back

in place," Graham whispered. "I think Mr. Big Time and his crew are gone. Don't anybody move until I come back." By now he could see heads shaking in the dark. "Understood?" No one spoke.

Without making a sound, Graham pushed the plywood forward and worked his way out of the hamper. Even in the dark, he could tell that Bridges's men had ransacked their house. Beds had been pushed aside and chests thrown away from the walls. The lights were still on downstairs and the damage was obvious. Graham inched down the stairs, watching carefully to make sure no one was waiting to grab him. The living room was in shambles, but the kitchen didn't look too bad. Tiptoeing, he slowly peered around the corners of each room, but the men were gone.

Because the Pecks' family cars were parked in the garage and blocked anyone pulling the stairs down out of the attic, Pemrose's men hadn't checked the attic, but they wouldn't have seen where the family was hiding in the distant corner if they had. Apparently, it hadn't occurred to the thugs that the students had sneaked in front of the cars and left through the side garage door. Once satisfied, Graham hurried back upstairs to get the family out of the attic.

"Looks like Pemrose's men assumed that we ran," Graham said. "No one's downstairs." He offered his hand to Adah as she crawled through the hamper.

Adah stood up and dusted herself off. "I thank God that you had such an unusual place. These men would have killed us."

"We don't have much time," Eldad said. "I'm sure they will be back in the morning further to look."

"We must run," Graham said, "and tonight is our only chance."

Jackie sat down on the side of the bathtub. "I've never been so frightened. I thought they had us for sure." She looked up at Graham. "But where can we go?"

Matt smiled. "You didn't like my idea earlier, but now it might be just what we need. I don't think anybody knows about our summer place up on Mohawksin Lake. We could drive up there."

Graham nodded. "I thought about this earlier when I asked your mom to gather up emergency supplies. It's on the rustic side, but we've got a complete home up there. Since it's equipped with a propane gas tank, no one would even know we were there for a considerable period of time. I think it's our only sure bet."

"What about money?" Mary abruptly said. "How will we eat?"

"I put money in your grandmother's old bank account and we can use her bank card. Several days ago I also set up a separate account under a different name," Graham explained. "We're covered."

Adah nodded. "Eldad and I can take a train back to Evanston and . . ."

"No, you can't," Jackie said. "They'd grab you in a minute. You must come with us."

"Oh, no. We couldn't," Adah said.

"You have to," Graham insisted. "Your safety is too important to us. We have room up there in the forest. Don't worry. The Bible calls this man the dragon. You must not be out there where he could breathe on you."

"Depending on the traffic and the condition of the roads, we can drive north in four to six hours," Matt said. "We've got three cars."

"That's right," Graham agreed. "I've got my small hydrogen coupe in addition to Jackie's car and my large auto. We'll need all of them."

Jackie looked at Mary, standing by herself next to the wall. "Mary, I'm sorry, but you don't have any choice. You must run with us."

Mary didn't say anything, but only stared at the floor.

"You children can only pack a small suitcase," Graham said. "Don't make a sound. Just get it done." The children raced out of the room.

Graham put his arm on his wife's shoulder. "We must run like scared rats."

"No, not like rats." Adah said. "We will leave like the children of Israel did when they left Egypt. Not afraid, but with confidence, going forward in faith!"

"Yes." Graham smiled. "Things have changed. We can leave now, trusting in our God!"

CHAPTER 58

GRAHAM HUDDLED the family and his Jewish friends close together in the kitchen. "Listen to me carefully," he whispered. "Remember, there's a curfew across the suburbs. We've got to be extremely careful."

Everyone nodded their agreement.

"In a moment we will get in the cars in the garage. Matt will drive the hydro-coupe by himself, and Adah and Eldad will be in Jackie's car. The rest of our family will stay together in my car. I'll raise the garage door and then we'll fly out of here." He looked around carefully at each one of them. "Okay?"

"What happens if someone chases us?" Matthew said.

"I don't know what we can do except split up and hope to get back together in Wisconsin," Graham said. "I think there's a McDonald's on the edge of Beloit. We could aim for that stop as a rendezvous point if we need to split up. I'm going to give Matt one of the phones in a wireless intercom set I've got out here in the garage. I'll stay in front and he can bring up the rear. If there's a problem we can communicate."

Adah nodded her head. "I will pray the whole time that the Holy One of Israel will protect us."

"Good," Graham said. "Remember. Don't stop your car until we get out of Arlington Heights. Surveillance could be anywhere." He thumbed over his shoulder. "I'm going to have Matt cover our car tags until we get to the edge of the town. If there's any camera surveillance set up around or outside of our house, they won't be able to trace our car numbers for a while."

Matt darted out into the garage.

"Any questions?" Graham said.

"Do you think we will ever come back?" Mary's eyes filled with tears.

"I don't know," Graham said. "I have no idea what's ahead." He shook his head. "No one can even guess what the future holds. We can only do what seems best for all of us."

Jackie put her arm around her daughter. "Don't worry, Mary. We're going to be all right."

Mary didn't say anything. For once she huddled protectively next to her mother.

"Okay, Dad," Matt said in a loud whisper. "I slipped hand towels over the tags. We're ready."

"Let's go!" Graham ordered, and everyone rushed into the garage.

In a matter of seconds, the cars filled with passengers and the electronic garage opener sent the large door up. The cars backed out quietly. Graham quickly looked up and down the street, but saw nothing except dark houses. At first, he drove slowly and then pushed the caravan faster. Within minutes they paused at the entry to Interstate 90 to uncover their license tags so they wouldn't attract the attention of the highway patrol. Within second, they sped on toward Rockford.

Traffic proved to be sparse at one o'clock in the morning and their motorcade moved easily down the broad highway. The crimson glow of the moon beamed down on them. Bypassing the town of Rockford, they drove on north toward Janesville like any other travelers in the night. No one seemed to be paying any attention to them.

Once they crossed the state line, the late hour took its toll and the children nodded off. The stars twinkled brightly in the cold winter night, while Jeff, George, and Mary slept in the backseat. Jackie dozed on the passenger side of the front seat. In the rearview mirror, Graham could see Adah and Eldad following him in Jackie's car with Matt bringing up the rear in the hydro-coupe. So far, so good.

Graham wondered if he would feel sleepy, but the possibility of danger kept him alert. By the time they had crossed the state line he relaxed, feeling they had broken away from any surveillance or curfews in Illinois. Their caravan sped through Madison without incident and went north on Highway 51 toward Wisconsin Rapids.

The dramatic events of the last several weeks surfaced again in Graham's mind. Discovering Jake Pemrose's hand in funding terrorism and Borden Carson's ultimate role in the attacks had left Graham in total turmoil, but Sarah Catcs's death utterly dismayed him. Sarah had her problems, but he could never accept her death. Clearly, circumstanccs had unfolded with a significance far beyond anything he could have dreamed possible, even in six lifetimcs.

CHAPTER 59

AFTER SEVERAL MINUTES, Graham thought about his mother again. Bridges's claim that he had sent the killer stung in a way that wrenched Graham back and forth between sorrow and horrific anger. Grief over Maria's death had not subsided, and the pain was still heavy.

Yet, Graham recognized that his feelings about death had changed. No longer was dying the staggering, terrifying monster that everyone in his office believed it was. Graham knew that his new relationship with God surprisingly changed the hooded specter into a comrade with a purpose he could trust.

Ringing deeply in his mind, he could still hear her familiar voice. She had been the source of so much wisdom throughout his life, often bringing insight and clarity that no one else could offer. He abruptly remembered playing checkers with her in the corner of their living room when he was only twelve years old.

Maria had pushed a checker forward, leaned back in her chair, and grinned at Graham. "Okay, Mr. Smarty, lets see what you do now."

Graham had stared at the checkerboard and been mystified by what piece to move. If he had moved to the left, his mother could jump him and pick up two checkers. However, going to the right might mean that she would end up taking even more pieces. He wasn't sure what to do. Graham had fumed.

"You know," Maria had said. "You are a funny little boy."

"What?" Graham had looked up in surprise.

Maria laughed. "You are a good boy. Yes, my son, you are a fine young man, and you are smart. You do exceptionally well in school."

"I try."

Maria nodded. "Yes, you are a good student and I am proud of your work, but you have one weakness, son. You tend to be naive."

"Naive? What do you mean?"

"Well," Maria spoke slowly, "you tend to think the best of everyone." Her voice became more earnest. "But you often fail to look behind their actions, and examine their motives. You don't think they are capable of the destructiveness that is natural for them."

"Are you serious?" Graham sounded mystified.

"It could get you in trouble someday," Maria said seriously. "I know that you won't remember that I told you this fact, *but assuming the best doesn't always work.*"

A car with bright headlights suddenly came up the other side of the hill. Graham hadn't seen another automobile approaching them for a number of miles and the lights interrupted his memories. The car flashed past and was gone.

In that moment Graham realized that his mother had been right, very right. In the past months, he had not even once thought about what Bridges, Pemrose, Meacham, any of them might actually be doing. Sarah Cates had been little more than a functionary until she drank too much and tried to seduce him. Each one of them had an agenda he had not even bothered to consider and it nearly cost Graham his life and the lives of his family. Being intelligent did not compensate for not paying careful attention.

The scene of playing checkers with his mother that afternoon returned to his mind again. They had continued playing that game for another five minutes when Maria suddenly put her hand in the middle of the checkerboard.

"What if I told you that we are no longer playing checkers," Maria had abruptly said.

Graham had jerked his head back. "What?"

"What if I told we are now playing the game of chess with the checkers?"

Graham had stared at his mother, not comprehending what she was saying. "You're not making any sense."

"Well," Maria had said with a sly twist in her voice, "what would you think if I said that the black checker over there in the corner is now a pawn and that white one is a king." She pointed around the board. "We could make the black checker on the end into a rook. Right?"

"I wouldn't know what to do," Graham said.

"It would slow you down a bit, wouldn't it?"

"Sure. How in the world would I know what was going on."

"Yes," Maria said. "Yes, you would be confused. Then, on the next turn I might tell you that the game we are now playing is actually called marbles and the goal is to get our players to the other side of the board first. Now, that would finish you off!"

"You bet," Graham said.

Maria nodded her head. "Son, we don't go to church much, but you know that I believe in God. I've learned something that could prove to be important to you. Just as I've been describing changing the rules in the middle of the game, the Lord often has purposes behind the scenes that we know nothing about. We think we're playing one game, and He actually has another one in mind."

Graham stared in confusion. "Another one?"

We think we're living our lives in one direction," Maria continued, "only to discover that God has taken us down a completely different path, and then later in our life we may find out that there was a third alternative behind the scenes that we didn't even consider. Only after a couple of decades might that last design become obvious." Maria patted him on the hand. "Life operates like that, you know. You might think your existence was like a checkerboard game; later you find it actually was a chess match, and much later it turns out to have been marbles all along."

Graham remembered staring at Maria, unsure of what to say, but feeling she had told him something of great significance. Suddenly, it was coming clear to him. He had thought the world was sailing straight ahead—a great home in the suburbs and an important job in Chicago politics. But in a matter of hours all the pieces on the table had been renamed. He was actually living in the middle of a battle to stop the forces of evil from destroying the world. He and his family were plunged into a conflict going on for centuries that they didn't even know existed. The game had turned inside out!

Rolling hills in front of Graham's car became filled with trees. Even though it was too dark to see them, Graham knew that tall pines were starting to appear. The town of Wausau wasn't far ahead . . . but what was *really ahead*? What was actually on the other side of the hills, waiting for all of them out there in the future? Graham knew more danger would be waiting than he had dreamed possible. His simple decision to trust God had plunged him into a battle where checkers *did* suddenly become chessmen.

He took Jackie's hand. She mumbled slightly and snuggled up next to him, warm and good. They could walk through this time together and endure. Mary was a problem, but the family could struggle and still stay together. He was thankful that Adah Honi and Eldad Rafaeli would be with them. The times would be hard, but in the midst of the battle Graham felt thankful, and that was a new kind of hope for him. Thankfulness. Yes, and that was a good feeling.

"Dad," Matt's voice echoed over the earpiece in Graham's ear. "I'm being followed!"

CHAPTER 60

OTHER THAN the headlights of the four cars, blackness surrounded the Pecks like a shroud. Flying down the highway at 80 miles an hour, Graham carefully studied his rearview mirror to understand what was happening behind him. Adah Honi was still following his bumper and he could see Matt driving at a safe distance from her, but another car was clearly on his son's taillights. Graham picked up the transmitter and spoke softly.

"Son, we're in Wisconsin. If it's not the highway patrol, no one from Illinois has any jurisdiction. They can't legally stop us."

"I don't care what's lawful," Matt barked. "I'm not sure where I picked this guy up, but he's clearly on my tail."

"Can you see who's in the car?"

"No, but he keeps talking into a cell phone. He's getting instructions from someone."

"Do you want me to pull over and stop?"

"Dad, I think stopping would play into his hands."

Graham thought for a minute. "Then let's try another angle. I'm going to slow down to fifty-five miles an hour. Let's see what he does." He took his foot off the gas pedal.

After fifteen seconds, Matt called back. "He's slowing down exactly like we are. No question but that this guy is following us."

"We need to know who he is," Graham concluded. "You got a flashlight. Right?"

"Yes."

"I want you to do this maneuver carefully, Matt. We don't need any wrecks. Set your rearview mirror so you'll get a clear facial view. Then turn on the flashlight and shine it over your shoulder. Find out if you've seen this creep before."

"Here goes nothing." The intercom went dead.

Graham hung on, hoping the light wouldn't cause an accident, but he didn't know any other way to fathom who was on Matt's bumper.

Suddenly, the earpiece buzzed. "Dad! I saw him. Jake Pemrose is following us! He's in the car by himself."

"Pemrose?" Graham gasped. "Lord help us! Okay, Matt. Hit the gas. I want you to pull around Adah and get in front of me. Let's see what Mr. Big Time does now."

Graham watched his son abruptly pull over into the opposite lane and fly up the road. The lightweight hydro-coupe had the capacity to jump thirty to forty miles per hour in seconds. Matt drove up parallel, gave his father a wave, and shot ahead. Graham watched carefully. For the moment Pemrose stayed behind Adah.

"What's happened?" Matt asked.

Graham kept speaking quietly. "He's still back there. We can drive this way for a while, but he's got to make a move sooner or later."

"Yeah," Matt said. "What's he trying to do?"

"I don't know."

But Graham did know. Bridges had threatened *him*, not the family or the Jews traveling with them. He had information that would hurt the mayor and Graham knew how to use it. While Pemrose might hurt someone in the family, the only person he would want to kill *was him*.

Graham looked around his car. He had never been much of a sportsman and didn't really like guns. Unfortunately, he hadn't taken any handguns, rifles, any weapons. He searched across the seat. No knives . . . no sharp-pointed objects . . . nothing. There wasn't one thing in the entire car he could use to protect himself. Nothing.

Headlights flashed behind him. Jake was starting to move out. All Pemrose needed to do was to draw parallel with Graham's car and the man could shoot a handgun from the shoulder. At the least, Graham would go crashing off the highway into the ditch at a speed that would produce a horrendous crash. At worst, Pemrose would kill him.

Graham looked in the side view mirror. Pemrose was clearly making his move. He was almost even with Adah Honi and would quickly pass her. Graham only had moments to do something. But what?

Graham looked frantically around the car a second time. Nothing.

Pemrose was picking up speed. In seconds he would be within easy shooting distance.

Graham felt his stomach churn with a nauseous sensation. The unnerving awareness that his life was about to end chewed on him. Death had always been a frightening specter and had grown worse since his mother's shooting. After he prayed with Matt in his dormitory, his own demise no longer seemed such a foreboding possibility, but he still wasn't ready to go. He didn't want to jeopardize the family. Yet, there wasn't anything he could do to save them.

Pemrose was moving up fast. The hood of his car remained only feet from Peck's bumper.

Nothing! Nothing in the car would save him. Graham gripped the wheel fiercely. Maybe he should wake up the family. On the other hand, maybe they would be better off asleep and unaware. Everyone had their seats belts tightened.

Pemrose was inching forward. The nose of his car was close to the back door of the Peck's car. Graham couldn't drive any faster because Matt was in front of him.

"What do you want me to do, Dad?" Matt's voice echoed in his ear. "Should I pull over in his lane?"

"He's not after you, son. It's me Pemrose wants. You need to stay out of his way. Speed up and I'll try to get away from him, but I'm sure his car can outrun us."

Matt's hydro-coupe jumped forward and Graham hit the gas pedal, pulling ahead slightly, but he knew Pemrose would only speed up. At that moment, he remembered the security protection piece Sarah Cates discovered in Pemrose's office and had given him. Graham crammed his hand in his pocket and pulled out the golden circular device. He stared at it. A red button and a green button stood out on the face of the strange instrument. But what difference did the buttons make anyway?

Pemrose's car was getting closer. Time was running out.

Graham glanced at the buttons without any idea of which one to push . . . or whether either one would do anything. His only conclusion was that red meant danger more often than green did. Red might be a better gamble. No matter which one he pushed, it was throwing the dice.

Pemrose's car steadily moved up. Obviously the man was about to attack. Graham glanced quickly and saw Jake with a gun in his hand. In a second he'd be in position to fire. He couldn't miss.

Graham pushed the red button.

Jake's car pulled alongside. Pemrose leered at Graham and mouthed words that were muted behind the glass. His lips seemed to say, "you're dead." The side window slowly began rolling down. Pemrose started to raise his gun. At that moment Jake hesitated. In the glow of Matthew's taillights, his face became completely visible. Pemrose's eyes abruptly widened in a strange stare.

Graham watched Pemrose's sarcastic grin turn into an unexpected shocked stare. The man's face twisted as if surprised by some unexpected pain. His lips opened slightly and he grimaced. Suddenly his mouth dropped and Jake gagged.

Graham gripped the wheel frantically, trying to stay in his lane, but the look on Jake's face was so strange he had to look again. Pemrose hadn't moved; he seemed frozen behind the wheel. A tiny trail of blood started running down his nose and over his lip. Red blotches broke out on his cheeks. Pemrose's eyes again widened in terror.

Graham clutched the strange security device and looked back once more while he kept frantically punching the red button. Jake slumped forward, his body covering the steering wheel. At that moment, Matt followed the curve in the road, turning slightly to the right. Pemrose's car went straight ahead, flying over the culvert and crashing into a field filled with trees. A brilliant orange explosion declared that Jake Pemrose had smashed into one of the large pines.

"Dad!" Matt shouted. "He's crashed!"

Graham took a deep breath. "He's gone, Matt. Mr. Big Time is dead."

"Thank God! We're safe!"

"Safe?" Graham smiled. "Yes, I think that's a good word. The world may be falling apart, but God is going to take us through. Keep rolling, son."

Jackie abruptly pulled on Graham's arm. "What was that noise? Sounded like an explosion." She rubbed her eyes. "Something's wrong?"

"No!" Graham relaxed for the first time. "*Nothing* at all. Just a slight interruption, Jackie. You can go back to sleep. We're going to be fine."